STARDUST

by

Alexandra Richland

Other Stories by Alexandra Richland

Starlight (Starlight Trilogy #1)

Starbright (Starlight Trilogy #2)

Frontline

Gilded Cage

Slip Away

Table of Contents

Dedication

For all the hopeless romantics and classic film fans who
accompanied me on this journey.

Act well your part; there all the honour lies.

— Alexander Pope, *An Essay on Man,* 1733-1734

Chapter One

Aidan Evans was a romantic hero. Yes, that Aidan. The surly Method actor who played juvenile delinquent Spike Rollins on the big screen. The notorious bad boy who refused to sign the standard Starlight Studios seven-year contract. The only person with the gall to confront ruthless studio boss, Luther Mertz. This was not a role in a motion picture. This was the man he'd become since Elizabeth Sutton entered his life.

Aidan made love to Beth last night. They didn't have sex. It wasn't a one-night stand or a selfish act of physical gratification to detract from his emotional void like his previous experiences with intimacy during his bleakest days when he lived in New York City. It was true lovemaking. Beth had let loose yet carried herself with elegance, taming his darkness while coaxing out his best self—everything he never realized he was capable of being.

Aidan toyed with the wisps of hair framing Beth's face. After she'd fallen asleep in his arms, he'd stared at her in the moonlight, and now, as sunlight tumbled into his bedroom from the open window. He absorbed everything he could, grappling with the fact that this was his reality—that this beautiful, delicate creature loved him and had given him her virginity in spite of all of his faults and past mistakes. There was no greater gift than Beth, no greater purpose than caring for her with all the good she inspired in him.

"Aidan?" Beth stirred and opened her eyes.

He brushed his lips to her forehead. "I'm here, little dove."

She shifted in the bed and winced.

Aidan frowned. "Are you sore?"

"Yes, but it's tolerable." She peered at him with big brown eyes. She looked so innocent, so trusting, so true.

He held her tighter. "I'll go to the local druggist and get you some pain medication."

"Please don't. It's a reminder of what we shared, so I'd rather bear it." Beth hooked her leg over his hip and snuggled closer. "I love you."

Aidan's erection pressed between her thighs. He smothered a curse. This was not the right time for his hormones to take over, but he couldn't help it. "I love you, too."

Her forefinger traveled his bare chest in a languid, circular pattern. "Would you mind if I took a shower?"

"Not at all." He pulled back the covers. "I'll set up everything for you. Wait here."

"Actually, I would like you to join me. If you want to, that is." Beth slipped out of bed and stepped over their Academy Awards. In the doorway, she stopped and held out her hand.

Aidan gaped at her, as if he was taking in her naked body for the first time. Her skin was flushed, well kissed. Her dark hair fell to just above her shoulders, sand-speckled from their visit to the beach yesterday. The swell of her breasts, the curve of her hips . . . everything about her was perfect.

If he wanted to?

Damn it. He wanted nothing more.

Aidan left the bed and embraced her. Her lip caught between her teeth. A daring spark lit her eyes. He pictured what she would look like soaking wet with the same expression on her face and promptly led her into the bathroom to bring his fantasy to fruition.

Under a pulsating spray from the showerhead, Beth wrapped her arms around his neck and pressed her body to his. Aidan kissed her, lapping up the water on her plump lips. Now there were no blankets to hide the physical effect she had on him.

Without delay, Beth took his erection in her hand.

He reached down and halted her first stroke. "No, baby. Not when I can't reciprocate."

Beth blinked up at him. "Then reciprocate." She broke free of his grasp and stroked him again.

A growl rumbled in Aidan's throat. His hand shot out to the wall to prevent him from falling. "I don't want to hurt you." He sounded hoarse, his mind and body overcome with arousal.

"You can let go, Aidan." Beth batted her eyelashes as she continued her sweet caress below. "Yes, I was a virgin up until last night, but I'm not as fragile as you think I am."

Aidan's desire skyrocketed. It was so tempting to give in.

Beth moved her hand faster, working him into a state so maddening it became more and more difficult to resist her.

"Your touch could never hurt me, Aidan." Her lips met his collarbone. She sucked hard.

Aidan closed his eyes and let out a hiss. She felt good. Too good. "Baby, it would be an honor to please you." He slid his hand down her breasts to her stomach, ending at the warmth between her legs. Gently, so gently, he touched her. "Tell me if it hurts and I'll stop."

Beth whimpered and writhed against him. "More."

She sounded so insistent, so certain.

Who was he to deny her?

Aidan dropped to his knees and spread her legs.

"Oh!" She gasped and latched onto his shoulders while he soothed her with his mouth, tasting everything her body created.

With all of his licking, flicking, circling, and rubbing, it didn't take long. His name blasted from her lips as her orgasm tore through her.

His name.

Fuck. It was enough to usher him toward his own release without a single stroke.

Aidan rose to his feet and kissed her. "Are you all right? I didn't hurt you, did I?"

She shook her head. "Not one bit. In fact, I'd say you cured me."

They shared a laugh.

"I'm glad." Aidan cupped her cheek and kissed her again.

Beth's hand reunited with his arousal. Aidan's muscles tightened and his moans deepened as she moved along his shaft. With the memory of pleasuring her so fresh in his mind and heavy on his tongue, he hurled toward his release far faster than he'd ever traveled before.

His orgasm slammed into him with such force he shook violently and cursed like he wasn't in the presence of the classiest, most beautiful woman he'd ever known. He emptied all over her hand and stomach in long, vigorous spurts.

Oh, man. There was nothing hotter than Beth all wide-eyed and smiling, dripping wet and coated in his essence.

He hugged her. "I love you so much."

"And I love you." Beth rested her head against his chest. They stood under the beating water for a few moments, bathing in each other and their mutual devotion.

After they washed up and emerged from the shower, Aidan secured a towel around his waist and stopped by his bedroom to grab a navy T-shirt for Beth, and a white T-shirt, a pair of black jeans, and black briefs for himself.

When he returned to the bathroom, Beth had vetoed her towel and waited for him gloriously naked. He crept toward her. His arousal hadn't waned even after his orgasm, but now . . . now it was out of control. The only thing keeping him from laying her on the bathroom floor and repeating what they did last night was his incessant self-reminder that she still hadn't recovered completely. He'd rather die than bring harm to her.

"I hope this is okay." He held up the navy T-shirt.

"I'm sure it will be." She smiled and took the garment from him. "Thank you."

All Aidan could manage was a nod. Beth dressed in the T-shirt, which covered her to her knees. Her taut nipples pushed against the dark fabric. Although she acted like she wasn't aware of the effect she had on him, her demure glances in his direction proved otherwise.

Well, two could play that game.

Aidan dropped his towel. Beth's breath hitched as she scanned his naked body unabashedly. He held back a smirk and put on his briefs and jeans. When he picked up his T-shirt, she tugged at his waistband, pulling him toward her.

"Can you leave your shirt off?" She caressed his bare chest like she couldn't get enough skin-to-skin contact.

Aidan flung his T-shirt aside. She traced one finger down his stomach toward his jeans, stopping just shy of his arousal. He groaned, lost in the memory of being inside her last night, moving in and out slowly . . . how tight she was . . . hearing her moans, feeling her clench around him when she met her release.

"There's so much more I want to share with you, Beth. Once you're feeling better, I'm gonna find new ways to pleasure you, to show you how much I love you."

"Promise?" She stood on her tiptoes and brought their lips together.

Aidan fastened his heated gaze on hers. "Baby, you can count on it."

Beth insisted on making them breakfast. She instructed Aidan to sit at the kitchen table and refused help as she prepared their food. After they ate, she wouldn't let him wash the dishes either, no matter how much he protested.

When everything was dried and put away, Aidan pulled her

into his lap. "What do you want to do now?"

She crossed her legs. The T-shirt he'd loaned her rode up, exposing her thighs. "How about we cuddle on the couch? If we go back to bed, the temptation will be too great to, you know . . ."

Aidan nuzzled her neck. "You think it makes a difference if we're in the bedroom or the living room? I would make love to you anywhere, baby."

Beth folded her arms across her chest. Her breasts swelled under the T-shirt. "That's not fair. You know we can't make love because I'm too sore, yet you're making it as hard as possible for me to resist you."

Aidan scanned her barely-covered body. "*I'm* making it hard for *you*?"

"Yes." Her lips twitched as her smile tried to escape.

Aidan chuckled. "Okay, little dove. Couch it is."

Beth stood. "Can you retrieve our Oscars first?"

"Sure." Aidan entered his bedroom and grabbed their awards off the floor and a blanket from the closet. He met Beth by the fireplace in the living room.

"What do you wanna do with these?" He tossed the blanket onto the couch and held up the Oscars.

Beth took the statuettes and placed them in the center of the mantel. "They look great here. Don't you agree?"

Aidan stared at them—the inscriptions, the shiny gold finishes. The elation one would typically feel in his position evaded him. "Yeah, I guess."

Beth's lips formed a pout. "I know awards don't mean much

to you, Aidan, but you should be proud of yourself. You deserve the Best Actor Oscar for playing Spike Rollins. You were phenomenal."

"I am proud. I just . . ." He frowned. "Winning Academy Awards means we'll be even more popular. The whole fame thing was overwhelming before, but now, well, more people will look up to you, Beth. More people will want to watch you, reach out to you, talk to you, and that's what I have trouble with most. I don't wanna share you. Not with your fans, the studio. Not with anyone."

Beth linked her hands behind his neck. "You have the real Beth. The public, our colleagues . . . they don't know me like you do. Not even our friends do. So please look on the bright side of all this. In a week, the final Los Angeles scenes for *Golden Gloves* will be finished, and then we'll be traveling to Chicago to complete the film. After that, our options are limitless. Our Oscar wins have opened new doors for us professionally. On a personal level, perhaps we'll be so popular we can announce our love to the world without Mr. Mertz's approval, and I'll incur zero punishment for it. Just think, we won't have to hide anymore."

Aidan sighed. He didn't like Beth under Mertz's thumb in any capacity, but she was right. The benefits could very well outweigh the cons. "I'm sorry. The last thing I want is for my pessimism to detract from your joy over your win. Your performance in *Sparkling Meadow* was phenomenal as well, and you deserve this recognition from the Academy, too."

"You haven't dampened my mood at all. There is no one I'd

rather share this moment with than you." Beth smiled—not just a happy smile, but a smile laced with seduction. It seemed his little dove had turned into quite the little vixen. "Now, just because we can't make love today doesn't mean you can't kiss me, Mister Best Actor."

"With pleasure, Miss Best Actress." Aidan captured her in his arms and closed the gap between their lips.

Beth returned his kiss with a passion that made him reconsider his outlook on everything. For now, they owned this town, and he had to admit he really did feel like a winner—but not because The Academy of Motion Picture Arts and Sciences said so. Awarded the privilege of caring for Beth and loving her like she deserved meant a whole lot more to him than any accolade from the entertainment industry. He felt like he had conquered the entire world, never mind Hollywood.

Chapter Two

Beth and Aidan arranged to have dinner with their friends two days after the Academy Awards. On the way, they stopped by Beth's house so she could change, and then they returned her loaned Oscar jewelry to Harry Winston.

During their drive, Beth smiled at her reflection in the side mirror. She always lit up in Aidan's presence, but since she'd lost her virginity to him, she beamed even brighter.

Intimacy did not refer to a woman allowing a man to touch her. Intimacy was sharing her dreams and fears with a trusted companion in the middle of the night. Intimacy was giving someone her undivided attention when hundreds of other people asked for it. Intimacy was having one person on her mind always, no matter how busy or distracted she was. The love she and Aidan shared was a true and rare gift. She was the luckiest woman in the world.

Aidan pulled up to the wrought-iron gates of Matthew McKenna's house and announced their arrival into the intercom. The gates opened. They traveled up the driveway and parked behind Nathan Taggart's Cadillac.

It was the first time Beth had been to Matthew's residence. The outside looked like an amalgamation of the White House and a Greek palace—indicative of his Hollywood status, but a contradiction to his humble personality. At least it had an inviting quality to it, unlike Nathan's mansion, which resembled a dank, medieval castle.

She shuddered. They had spent Christmas Day at Nathan's house. While the mood amongst them had been warm and gay, the setting was dark, cold, and drafty. She still had no idea how he lived there comfortably, or why he'd purchased it in the first place.

Aidan opened Beth's door. Tonight, he'd eschewed a suit jacket and tie in favor of a black sports shirt and dark gray dress pants, which complemented her cream satin evening gown with a black lace overlay nicely. She couldn't stop staring at him.

"You look very handsome, Aidan."

He helped her out of the Porsche. "And you look ravishing."

Her face flushed. "You've said that already. Twice, in fact."

"And I'll keep saying it, baby. Forever." Aidan drew her in for a kiss. Her heart beat so wildly she could have danced to the sound of it.

Hand in hand, they strolled up the front steps to the porch. As soon as Aidan used the brass knocker, an excited shriek erupted from inside the house. It was an Olivia Weston creation through and through.

The front door flew open. Beth's dear friend and roommate lunged at her, nothing but a flash of black hair and blue taffeta.

"I'm engaged! I'm engaged!" Olivia stuck out her left hand

so Beth could inspect the ring. "I wanted to call to break the news but decided it was best to share in person."

Beth smiled. "Congratulations."

Aidan nodded. "Yeah, it's great news."

"Wait a minute." Olivia placed her hand on her hip. "Beth, why don't you seem surprised?"

Nathan appeared in the foyer. He slipped his arm around Olivia's waist. Blond and tanned, he could've easily been an actor—the camera would love him, as would women all over the country—but instead, he chose to remain behind the scenes at Starlight Studios as a top executive.

"It's all right, Beth. You can tell her."

Olivia's eyes widened. "You knew he was going to propose?"

"Yes. Not when, but I was aware of his intention. He asked my permission a few weeks prior to the Academy Awards. He also showed me the ring."

Olivia folded her arms across her chest. "I can't believe you were able to keep it a secret."

"Not everyone has a big mouth like you, Liv." Constance Murphy entered the foyer, smiling. Matthew accompanied her.

Dressed in a sequined evening gown that hugged her voluptuous curves, with her platinum blonde hair curled and shiny, Connie looked a model in *Harper's Bazaar*. There was no question as to why she was the most popular pinup in all the movie magazines.

Matthew welcomed Beth and Aidan with a hug and handshake, respectively. As usual, the crooner was impeccably dressed in a tailored suit and groomed in the all-American way—the ideal look for a prime time variety show, like the family friendly musical showcases he'd hosted many times in the past, based on the popularity of his chart topping singles.

After an employee took Beth's fur stole and purse, the group was ushered into a lavish parlor adorned with marble sculptures and colorful frescos.

"Let's start the evening with a toast." Matthew uncorked a bottle of champagne, and the household staff distributed flutes. The group gathered in a circle. "We have two Oscar winners in our presence now, so a big congratulations is in order, even though they abandoned us by failing to show up at the post-show party."

Aidan and Beth laughed.

"Luther won't be too happy about that," Nathan said. "I'm just warning you so you can be prepared when you're back on the *Golden Gloves* set tomorrow."

Beth's gaiety plummeted. There was nothing more intimidating than a scolding from her boss.

Aidan shrugged. "I can handle Mertz. I've done it before."

"Congratulations is also in order to Nathan and Olivia, regarding their engagement." Matthew winked. "By the way, Nate, thanks for upstaging me on the ring. You're a real pal."

Nathan chuckled. "You're welcome."

Matthew's expression sobered. "And to my beautiful fiancée, Connie. There's no me without you. I love you."

Connie kissed his cheek. "I love you, too."

Matthew raised his flute. "Let us toast to long-lasting friendships, true love, and happily ever afters."

They brought their glasses together with a clink.

"Nate, Aidan, wait 'til you see what I had installed." Matthew emptied his flute in a few gulps and set it aside.

"Oh, brother. Here we go again." Connie rolled her eyes but smiled.

Matthew walked across the room, motioning for the men to follow him.

"What is it?" Olivia sipped her champagne.

"Matthew had a bar installed behind that Renoir painting over there." Connie jutted her chin in the painting's direction. "He got the idea from some European gangster film and likes to show it off at every opportunity."

Matthew displaced the painting as though he were opening a door, revealing a mini bar built into the wall. He removed a bottle of what looked like scotch from a lower shelf and proudly displayed it to Aidan and Nathan.

"Enough of that macho silliness." Connie turned her back on the men. "It's time to focus on more interesting matters. Olivia, tell us about Nathan's proposal."

Olivia beamed. "He surprised me with lunch in Malibu and then took me to our favorite spot overlooking the Pacific Ocean. He got down on one knee and, gosh, it was so romantic. I wasn't expecting it at all, though I always hoped we'd get married one day. I love him dearly." She sighed and admired her large square cut diamond set on a white gold band. "Isn't my ring gorgeous? And my fiancé is gorgeous, my wedding will be gorgeous, and our future children will be—"

"Gorgeous," Beth said, tossing Connie a smile.

"Okay, Beth. Now it's your turn. How was Oscar night?" Olivia waggled her eyebrows. "And I don't mean the ceremony."

Beth blushed. She still felt uncomfortable talking about intimacy on account of her conservative upbringing, although she had made great strides since she and Aidan had begun their courtship. "What do you mean?"

"Don't play coy. You and Aidan made love. It was obvious as soon as you two got here. You're always lovely dovey with each other, but this evening, my goodness."

Beth caught Aidan's gaze. A grin launched across his face, and there it was—the spark she loved so much, glistening in his eyes.

Her heart exploded in a million fireworks. Yesterday he'd declared his unwillingness to share her with anyone, but he wasn't the only one occupied by the need for possession. Would it always be like this? She couldn't imagine her attraction ever waning. He was just too good-looking, too charismatic . . . caring and brooding, sensitive and manly.

Connie giggled. "There's no use denying it, Beth."

She bit her lip. How could she put into words everything he made her feel? "Making love with Aidan was . . . it was perfect in every way."

Olivia hugged her. "I'm so happy for you."

Connie nodded. "Me, too."

"Thank you." Beth placed her hand to her angel pendant and fixed her beau with a flirty look.

Aidan's gaze acquired elements of fire, of longing. Even from a distance, she was unable to resist him. Months earlier, she never would have been so brazen, but he'd awakened a more liberal side of her. The thoughts that sprung to her mind—of what she wanted him to do to her body and what she wanted to do to his—were foreign and forbidden, but territory she couldn't wait to cross with him.

Matthew replaced the scotch and painting and strolled back to the women with Nathan and Aidan. "Did you see the papers covering the Oscars?"

Aidan brought his arm around Beth. Standing this close to him again made acting calm and composed an even greater struggle. "No, we haven't. We've been busy."

Their friends broke out into laughter. Beth's face flamed yet again.

"That's not what I meant." Aidan pitched her a grin. "Well, not entirely."

"Don't worry. I have copies of the *Times* for everyone." Matthew caught the attention of a member of his staff. "Randall, can you please bring in the newspapers from the kitchen—the Oscar editions?"

He bowed. "Yes, sir."

Randall returned with four issues of the *Los Angeles Times* from the day after the Academy Awards and distributed them to Matthew's guests.

The front page featured a photograph of Beth and Aidan posing together on the red carpet. Beth flipped to the entertainment section, locating articles on the ceremony and additional photographs, including the picture of them with Mr. Mertz.

She turned the page, choosing to focus on more positive aspects of the evening rather than their tense encounter with her boss. The main article contained details on their respective wins and also some inaccurate gossip, like Beth and her *Sparkling Meadow* costar, William Everett, had flirted with each other on the red carpet, and her *Venus Rising* costar, Jack Peters, glared at Will incessantly out of jealousy. The lies were harmless, but still. How did the press come up with such ridiculous stories?

Randall collected the newspapers and put them aside so the guests could retrieve them on the way out. The group then headed into a dining hall fit for a royalty and shared pleasant conversations throughout a dinner that lasted late into the evening.

Before Beth departed the house with Aidan, she visited the bathroom to insert her diaphragm. Olivia was spending the night with Nathan, so there would be no interruptions. As much as Beth enjoyed their shower session the day before, she was no longer sore and wanted nothing more than for Aidan to make love to her again and hold her for the remainder of the night.

In the foyer, Aidan greeted her with a kiss. "Are you ready to go, baby?"

She smiled as he assisted her with her stole. "Absolutely."

Chapter Three

Aidan followed Beth into her house. They barely made it beyond the front door before he took her in his arms. "Did you have a good time?"

"It was a wonderful evening." She gave a wistful smile. "Olivia was ecstatic, wasn't she?"

Aidan chuckled. "You'd think that diamond gave her superpowers or something."

"I know." Beth giggled. "I'm thrilled for her."

"So you were aware that Nathan was gonna propose?"

She nodded. "I'm sorry I didn't tell you. It's just that Nathan—"

"Hey, don't worry. There's no need to apologize." Aidan set their copies of the *Los Angeles Times* on the foyer table. His gaze landed on the stack of mail next to it. "Is that you?" He pointed to a photograph lying on top of the pile.

Beth removed her stole. "Yes, that's me at age six. My parents sent it to me. I opened it on the morning of the Academy Awards, but since it was such a hectic day, I forgot to put it away. They thought I'd get a good laugh out of it."

Aidan grinned. "I think your missing front teeth lend you a lot of character. It's nice to find out more about you, even if it's just a glimpse from a photograph."

"I'll ask my parents to send additional pictures with their next letter, then." Beth hung her stole in the closet and picked up the mail. "I'd be happy to show you more of my childhood."

They made their way to the kitchen. Beth turned on the light and placed the mail on the counter. They embraced again by the icebox.

"I bet you looked adorable when you were a boy." Beth brushed his hair back, admiring him with a devoted twinkle.

Aidan shook his head. "I was a short, chubby kid with a bowl haircut and buck teeth. Then, when I had a growth spurt in my early teenage years, I was extremely lanky. It was my most awkward phase."

"Well, you certainly grew out of that." She traced her fingers along his jaw. "I would love to see some of your childhood photographs."

Aidan frowned. "I don't have any in my possession. My pop has them all, unless he got rid of them after I left."

"Oh, Aidan. I'm sorry." Beth's gaze softened. "I know you don't speak to your father, but perhaps you could write him a letter, requesting a few photographs. I'm sure he'd send them to you."

Aidan's eyebrows furrowed. "To tell you the truth, there's not much about my childhood I want to remember. It's best if those memories stay buried."

"What about photographs of your mother? Surely you'd like

some of those."

Aidan shrugged and looked away.

Beth patted his cheek and smiled. "I've been thinking about buying a scrapbook so we can save our photographs and articles—like the *Los Angeles Times* article and the *Life* magazine article from your Santa Barbara race . . . our Central Park photograph . . ."

Aidan's grin returned. "A scrapbook. I like that idea."

Beth linked her hands behind his neck. "Aidan, do you think when we return to New York for the Heavyweight Boxing Championship in June, we can stroll through Central Park again? I loved it there."

Aidan brushed his lips to her ear. "Anything you want, baby."

"Anything? Well, what if I want to spend tonight in your arms . . . naked?" She trailed her hand down his chest.

Aidan groaned. "I'd love that."

Beth led him out of the kitchen. Once they reached her bedroom, their clothes were stripped off in record time, every item discarded onto the floor. Their lips met in a frenzy and their hands roamed, petted, and squeezed. Aidan was careful— he was always careful with her—but there was no denying it. This was primal, needy, and desperate from both sides.

Beth pried her lips from his. "Aidan, will you please make love to me? I'm not sore anymore."

"Baby, you never have to ask." He collected all of his strength and pulled away from her. "I'll wait here while you put in your diaphragm."

She batted her eyelashes. "I already did, in the bathroom at Matthew's house."

Aidan couldn't help the curse that escaped him. "Damn it, Beth. What are you trying to do to me?"

Within seconds, he had her spread out on the bed. She'd planned this, wanted him all evening, and he was more than willing to deliver.

Beth gasped as he showered her breasts with kisses and tugged at her nipples. Then her hand found his arousal and pumped him hard, and the need to take her instantly overcame him. He settled between her legs. Her warm, wet flesh caressed him, providing a sample of what could be his if he took her up on her offer. But he couldn't. Not like this.

He rolled onto the mattress and lay beside her. "Baby, the only way we can do this right now is if you're on top, so you can be in control. You just started feeling better. I don't want to do anything to hurt you."

Beth pouted. "But we've never done it that way. What if I fail to please you?"

Aidan took her hand and kissed it. "That's impossible."

"All right. But maybe we can switch positions later on."

Aidan nodded. "Only if you're not in pain."

"Deal." Beth crawled over him. A blush tinted her cheeks. "Can you help me?"

"Of course." He grasped himself and prepared for her descent.

Beth spread her legs wider and lowered onto him slowly. A grimace tensed her features and she halted abruptly.

Aidan throbbed for her, even though they had just gotten started. He'd missed this connection between them far too much. But he couldn't feel pleasure from it, not when she didn't feel it as well. "We should stop."

"No, please." She opened her eyes. "It doesn't hurt. I promise. It just feels a bit tight."

Slowly she sank, clenching his arousal like she could barely accommodate him. Aidan clamped his jaw shut.

Tight. Man, she wasn't kidding.

Beth lowered herself completely and let out an erotic gasp. Aidan's eyes rolled back as he finally allowed himself to succumb to her warmth, her wetness.

"Yes, yes, yes." Beth moved her hips, working his erection like she craved it.

As difficult as it was, Aidan didn't meet her thrusts.

Beth's lips dipped into a frown. "Does it not feel good?"

His eyes widened. "You feel incredible. I just don't wanna hurt you."

"I swear it doesn't hurt. Now, come on. Please." She lifted her hips and dropped back down so he was inside her fully again.

Aidan shut his eyes and grabbed at the sheets next to him, struggling not to lose control.

"Take me, Aidan. Whatever you want from me is yours." Again and again, Beth rocked into him, taunting him until his resolve disintegrated.

Releasing a growl, he flipped her onto her back.

"That's it, Aidan. More . . . *please*." Beth arched her back, urging him on.

"More is not something you want to say to me right now." Aidan grunted as she raised her hips, pushing him deeper inside her. "Trust me, baby. More is dangerous territory."

"Let go, Aidan. Show me what you want from me, what I inspire in you. And don't hold back." Her eyes locked on his. They harbored no hesitancy, no regret.

Aidan tried to convince himself it wasn't right. He shouldn't. But then . . .

"Ah, fuck it." He planted his hand on her hip and thrust forward, hard, his body and mind set to one purpose: her pleasure.

Beth whimpered and closed her eyes. Worry halted him before he attempted his next thrust. But her face still wore no fear, no pain, no disgust. Just pure desire.

Aidan tested her readiness again, thrusting with the same strength. The smile that drifted across her lips held a femme fatale twist. Dangerous territory, indeed. But damned if it didn't feel amazing to claim her this way.

Again he thrust. Her body tensed and she released his name on a moan. A green light.

More.

And more he gave. More thrusts, more caresses, more words of endearment, of lust, of ownership, of submission. More of his love, more of the honor she cultivated in him, more of the darkness stirring within him; the darkness he tried to repress whenever he was around her.

He liberated everything, plunging inside her over and over,

hurling himself deeper, filling her with his good, his bad, his vile, his beautiful. And she took it all greedily. Needed it. Gasped in protest whenever he pulled out—that instant before he drove into her again, sheathing her completely, seeking that special spot inside her, which he wanted to own right now above all else.

"Aidan . . . oh, Aidan . . ."

He pumped harder, faster.

"You're so beautiful." He sucked gently on her neck, worshipping her with his lips, his tongue, his erection, wishing he could touch every inch of her inside and out and all at once. "My beautiful little dove."

Beth's head flew back into the pillow and a wild cry escaped her throat. "Oh, yes!"

Her breasts bounced against his chest as her thighs gripped his hips and she clamped down on his arousal, rocking into him, pulsating, gasping, riding out her climax like she was possessed by him and all he made her feel.

Aidan screwed his eyes shut and pumped into her one last time. "Oh, fuck . . . Beth."

His orgasm seized him. He jerked and emptied inside her, holding on to her like the precious gift she was.

When they were finished, Aidan collapsed onto the bed, panting as if there wasn't enough oxygen to sustain him. Even the most rigorous boxing training didn't compete with this lovemaking session.

"My goodness." Beth shrieked with laughter and gave her legs a little kick. "That was magnificent!"

Aidan couldn't take his eyes off her. Her smile was so large there wasn't a doubt in his mind that he'd satisfied her. She was radiant, glowing. All on account of him.

He should've been smiling, too. He should've been proud of his ability to bring her such happiness. But instead, he was occupied by the overwhelming concern that he'd been too rough with her, used language that was too crude.

Aidan was always adamant to never expose Beth to his more reckless side, especially when they were intimate, no matter how much she begged for it or how much his actions were driven by his feelings for her and his desire to please her. It was his duty to protect her, and fueling her pleasure by tapping into his pain, his unpredictability, and his obsession wasn't healthy.

Yesterday he'd only used the gentlest of touches and was able to keep his passion in a safe zone, regardless of her encouragement to do the opposite.

Where had the romantic hero gone?

Aidan collected her in his arms and kissed her temple. From now on, he wouldn't take any risks. He wasn't a monster. He was a man—a good one, according to Beth—and he'd taken great strides to earn that title. The ease with which he'd transformed tonight, however, set a precarious precedent and made him question how emotionally stable he truly was.

Chapter Four

Charlie, the security guard, greeted Beth as she pulled up to the security hut at the entrance to Starlight Studios. "Good morning, Miss Sutton. Congratulations on your Academy Award."

She smiled. "Thanks. I still can't believe I won."

"Well, you deserve it." Charlie eyed her Cadillac. "My, what an impressive car."

"Oh, I forgot you haven't seen it yet. This is only my second time driving it to the studio. The first time was just after Valentine's Day. You were on vacation."

"What made you decide to buy this model? That's quite a lot of horsepower for such a young girl."

Beth giggled. "True. But its safety rating is also unmatched—or so I was told."

"I bet it is." The security arm lifted. "Have a wonderful day, Miss Sutton."

"You, too, Charlie." Beth rolled up her window and proceeded toward soundstage five.

This morning, she was filming with Clive Geary, the actor playing Joe Oliver's boxing trainer in *Golden Gloves*. Aidan wasn't needed on set until after lunch. Although he offered to take her to work, she insisted on driving herself so he could keep his appointment to have his Porsche tuned up at nine o'clock. Olivia had a day off—a rare occurrence—and chose to spend it at home preparing for dinner with their friends tonight. Beth and Aidan would join them after filming wrapped for the day.

Beth looked forward to the shoot but also dreaded the end of *Golden Gloves*. Working on a film with such depth and such a talented cast and crew had spoiled her. Aidan had control over the movies he acted in while she did not. What if Mr. Mertz assigned her to a motion picture filmed across the country—or worse, on another continent? And what if her next role lacked the complexity she found so creatively rewarding in her portrayal of Mary Oliver? It seemed that along with her budding fame came a slew of new worries.

This uncertainty made her cherish having Aidan as her costar even more, and she was determined to finish *Golden Gloves* on a positive note. Visiting Chicago was the source of much strife for Aidan because his father lived there, but she hoped filming a movie he loved and spending time with her in the city would make the experience enjoyable for him.

Inside the soundstage, the crew prepared for filming with so much energy it was impossible to tell it was six o'clock in the morning. With Beth's appearance, everyone stopped what they were doing and broke into applause, offering her congratulations on her Oscar win.

She thanked them and headed to her dressing room to get ready. Aside from the application of foundation and mascara, and the swap of her pedal pushers and blouse for a light cotton dress, she didn't look much different from when she arrived.

Back on set, Beth joined director Elia Kazan in the living room of Joe and Mary's apartment.

He greeted her with a kiss on the cheek. "I'm thrilled for you, Beth. No one deserved that Academy Award more than you."

Beth didn't think she could smile any brighter, but she was wrong. "Thank you. That means a lot to me coming from you."

"Since we're winding down the L.A. portion of our shoot, today will be an easy one." Kazan motioned to the living room couch. "Have a seat and we'll discuss the first scene."

Beth sat down and picked up her character's prop—two knitting needles and a half-finished scarf.

Kazan took a seat next to her to offer direction away from Clive and the crew. "Beth, as you know, in this scene, George convinces Mary to encourage Joe to return to boxing. George's visit is nice, but unexpected. This man is from Joe's past, a past that is painful for him but also the source of much of the joy in his early life. You're grateful to George for coming by, but apprehensive, so do some business that shows it."

"Some business, sir?"

He patted her shoulder. "Yeah. You'll figure out something."

Beth's eyes widened. She was honored he was so confident

in her. "Thank you, Mr. Kazan."

"You'll do great, kid." Kazan stood and exchanged a few words with Clive before claiming his place beside the camera. "Okay, lock it up."

"Lock it up!" yelled the first assistant director.

The red lights mounted over every exit illuminated. A buzzer sounded three times. All the talking died, and the clapperboard sounded off.

"Action."

Beth performed a basic stitch her mother taught her and settled into the scene. A knock signaled Clive's arrival.

Mary set her knitting project on the coffee table and rose from the couch. "Now, who could that be? I'm not expecting visitors this evening." She opened the door cautiously and smiled. "George! What a pleasant surprise."

"Hello, Mary." George removed his fedora. "I'm sorry for stopping by unannounced. May I come in?"

"Yes, of course." She stepped aside. "Joe isn't here. He's working a double shift at the factory today."

George took off his coat. "That's all right. I came to talk to you actually."

Mary's eyebrows drew together. While she considered George a dear friend, their association was solely on account of her husband's close relationship with him. What could they possibly discuss in Joe's absence?

She placed George's coat and hat in the closet and led him into the kitchen. "Would you like something to drink?"

"No, thank you. I'm afraid I cannot stay long." George sat at the table. "Mary, I've come to ask for your help. Joe needs to return to boxing and you're the only person who can convince him to do so."

Mary sank into her seat. Goodness. Joe, boxing again? Did she want her husband to return to the sport he loved? Absolutely. However, it wasn't that easy.

"Oh, George. It's a lovely idea, really. But what happened five years ago . . . it devastated him. I'm not sure he possesses the mental capabilities to fight again."

George nodded. "I get it. He feels guilty and afraid, but he belongs in the ring. He's a boxer. That's his identity, not some poorly paid factory worker."

Mary frowned. "It hurts me to see Joe so broken. The death of his opponent was a tragedy, but it also wasn't his fault. He won't accept that, though, no matter how many times I've told him."

"All the more reason for him to return to boxing—but not just fighting in general. I want to train him for the Middleweight Championship. It'll give him something positive to work toward, a purpose. It's the only way he'll overcome his past and reclaim his self-worth." George leaned forward and grasped her hands. "Every week, he visits me at the gym, Mary. He lights up when he watches the other guys train. Deep down, he wants to be them. I know it."

The memory of Aidan's recent breakdown on set yanked Beth out of the scene. Tears sprung to her eyes, her lower lip quivered. Just when she thought she couldn't go on, she channeled her real-life concern into her character and wept for her beau. She'd do anything to help Aidan achieve inner peace, just as Mary would do for Joe.

George offered his handkerchief. "I'm sorry. I didn't mean to upset you."

"I know you only want what's best for him. So do I." She dabbed her eyes. "I'll try my hardest to encourage his return, but you know how stubborn he can be."

"You can convince him." George stood. "I have faith in you."

Mary followed him to the door and returned all of his belongings, including the handkerchief.

George placed his fedora on his head. "Take care, Mary. Good night." He tipped his hat and left.

Mary shut the door and exhaled a deep breath. Could she do this? Could she convince her husband that George was right? A smile shot across her face. Yes. Yes, she could—if it meant Joe's happiness.

"I love you, Joe Oliver." She held her head high. "I'll make you see that the boxing ring is where you belong if it's the last thing I ever do!"

"And . . . cut."

Beth turned to her director. Clive walked around the fake wall of the apartment and joined her. The crew erupted into applause—a rare gesture from seasoned men who'd seen it all in the industry and then some.

"That was extraordinary." Kazan rushed the set. "My intention was to cut the scene when you two left the table, but your performances, especially yours, Beth—the dedication you conveyed, the love, the strength—incredible! I couldn't interrupt you. And those tears—Luther Mertz's people sure as hell didn't teach you such genius. That was Method acting completely."

Clive grinned. "I agree with Gadg, Beth. That was the best scene we've filmed together."

Beth didn't care if she looked childish. She hugged Kazan and then Clive, unable to contain her excitement. "Thank you both so much."

"We'll launch right into the next scene so we don't lose momentum." Kazan clapped once to get everyone's attention. "Let's set up for scene forty."

Beth claimed her assigned chair at the side of the set. While she waited for her call, a young messenger approached. Two men, one blond and one brown-haired, accompanied him—the same intimidating men who had disrupted the first day of filming.

Beth blanched. Thank goodness she was already sitting down.

"Miss Sutton, this is for you." The messenger handed her a telegram and departed without his companions.

She scanned the telegram.

Elizabeth Sutton,

Your attendance is required at Luther Mertz's office immediately.

— Ethel Ashby
Personal Secretary to Mr. Luther J. Mertz

Beth bristled. Normally she would comply with her boss's orders without question, but as a professional actress, filming *Golden Gloves* was her priority.

"I have a shooting schedule to adhere to, gentlemen. Please tell Mr. Mertz I will see him during my lunch hour."

The blond man stepped forward, his hands clasped in front of him. "Miss Sutton, the meeting cannot wait. You must come with us now."

Beth crossed her arms over her chest. "That's ridiculous. Why on earth—?"

She snapped her mouth shut. Of course. Aidan was scheduled to arrive at lunchtime.

The brown-haired man gestured across the soundstage. "Miss Sutton, we are not here to forcibly remove you from the set but merely escort you to your meeting."

"Escort me." Beth rolled her eyes. "I see. And if I refuse?"

The blond man cleared his throat. "Ma'am, please just come with us."

Kazan walked up to them. "What's going on here? I told you mopes not to bother us again."

"Miss Sutton is required to see Luther Mertz immediately." The blond man scowled. "The matter is not up for negotiation."

Kazan shook his head. "This is *my* goddamn set, *my* film. Not Luther's. He has no right."

The brown-haired man flashed a tight smile, as if his facial muscles had never formed the expression before. "According to Mr. Mertz, Miss Sutton will be back within the hour."

Kazan sighed. "Beth, I hate to say it, but it's best if you see

Luther now. The sooner you have this meeting, the sooner you're back. If we have to work an extra hour this evening, so be it, as long as it gets him off our backs."

"I suppose you're right." Beth narrowed her eyes at the two men. "Fine. Let's go."

A studio limousine waited outside. They made the trip to Mr. Mertz's office building in tense silence.

Ethel smiled from behind her desk as they exited the elevator on the top floor. "Mr. Mertz is expecting you, Miss Sutton. You can go right in."

Beth walked to the double doors guarding Mr. Mertz's office. Her *escorts* stayed behind. Perhaps she should've called Aidan to notify him of the meeting, but then he'd insist on accompanying her, which would be an admission of guilt. She wouldn't allow Mr. Mertz to bully her. She would defend her absence from the Oscars post-show party, which was surely what this nonsense was all about, and then be on her way.

Mr. Mertz's face darkened upon her entry. She sat across from him, barely able to look him in the eye, but doing so nonetheless.

"How dare you skip the Academy Awards post-show party. As you were told in advance, Miss Sutton, that is where you speak to the press on a more intimate level than on the red carpet and backstage at the ceremony. It is imperative for every nominated person to show up, but especially the winners. Now, I told you if you obeyed me, you could have your fling with Aidan Evans in secret, but this callous disregard of my orders has pushed me too far."

Beth wrung her hands but ensured her face didn't reveal her nervousness. "You see, sir, I wasn't feeling well and—"

"Don't play dumb with me, girl." Mr. Mertz's upper lip peeled back, like a serpent ready to strike. "I know you left the Pantages Theatre with Mr. Evans, probably on that motorcycle death trap of his, to go gallivanting around L.A. You're just lucky the press didn't catch you or else we would not even be having this discussion. I would've suspended you without pay indefinitely."

Nathan's prior advice on this very subject became Beth's only argument. "You won't suspend me. I've won an Academy Award and I'm one of the most popular actresses at your studio. Not to mention I'm currently starring in your next big motion picture, into which you've invested a lot of money. Delays in filming would only serve to expand the project's budget, which is something you go to great lengths to avoid."

Mr. Mertz seethed. "I have zero tolerance for threats, Miss Sutton. If you know what's best for you, you'll watch what you say to me from now on."

Beth shrugged, trying to act nonchalant, in spite of her overwhelming urge to cry. "Interpret it however you wish, sir."

Mr. Mertz leapt from his seat and rounded the desk. "Mr. Evans has implanted false ideas in your head. Make no mistake. You are nothing without me."

Beth cowered from him. "If you don't leave us alone, I'll tell the press all about your dictatorship at this studio and how you're trying to control my life."

Mr. Mertz swiped his hand across his desk, sending a

basket of pens to the floor. "Who do you think you are? You signed a contract. Even when you're not on official studio business, you are obligated to act as I see fit!"

Beth stood and moved so her chair was between them. "I don't understand. Wouldn't my relationship with Aidan be good publicity for *Golden Gloves*?"

"No, it will not!" Blood rose in Mr. Mertz's face. "Mr. Evans is reckless while your image is wholesome. We've been over this before, Miss Sutton. Until after the release of *Golden Gloves*, I have to assume that the public would be appalled if they found out about your relationship. I was able to downplay the Valentine's Day incident because you and Mr. Evans dined with friends, amongst many of my employees. This time, however, you were alone, proving you cannot be trusted to follow my orders."

Beth shook her head. "There's no evidence to support that I left the theater with Aidan."

Mr. Mertz scoffed. "You were the only two people absent from the post-show party. How dimwitted do you think I am?"

Beth gripped the back of the chair. "Why did you sanction our relationship in the first place, as long as we promised to remain discreet? I never questioned it previously, but now I realize there must've been a reason you were so agreeable."

Mr. Mertz waved his hand dismissively. "It doesn't matter. Now that you've pulled this stunt, I forbid you to see him off set. Then when *Golden Gloves* wraps, you won't have your costars excuse anymore. Do you hear me? It's over between you two."

Tears toppled down Beth's face. There was only one way

out. It was a difficult decision, but necessary. "Not if I quit."

Mr. Mertz's hands curled into fists. "You don't have the authority to quit. You're signed with my studio for another six years."

"I don't care. I'll seek legal counsel on the grounds of emotional abuse. If it means Aidan and I can stay together, I'll find a way. I'll sacrifice my career for our relationship."

"Sacrifice, huh?" Mr. Mertz crept toward her. His face flicked with an unreadable emotion.

Beth eased around the other side of his desk to ward off his advance. "Why won't you leave me alone?" She gasped for breath as though she were suffocating. "You haul me in here as if I'm some sort of criminal when I've always readily agreed to all of your orders, even when I felt uncomfortable."

Mr. Mertz drifted closer. "I'll leave you alone when you start obeying my rules completely, not picking and choosing which ones you will follow, according to what suits you."

Beth clutched the edge of the desk. "If I quit, your rules will mean nothing."

Mr. Mertz chuckled. "Oh, dear girl. Do you really think it's that easy?"

Beth sniffled. "What are you talking about? Of course it is. If I'm no longer your employee—"

"What will your beloved Aidan do?"

Beth brushed away her tears. "This has nothing to do with Aidan. He's not under contract."

Mr. Mertz smirked. "I have friends in high places, Miss Sutton. If you don't cooperate with me, I will drive Mr. Evans out of Hollywood and ensure he doesn't get any work in New York. You said you'd sacrifice your career for his, but if you break your contract, you'll be destroying him as well as yourself."

Beth's heart stopped. Acting was an important part of Aidan's salvation. It was his outlet for pain, his guilt. He needed it. She couldn't take that away from him.

"What do you mean by cooperate? What do you want me to do?"

Mr. Mertz stood next to her again, bearing down on her with beady eyes. She trembled. Oh, why did she think she could handle him on her own?

"Let's just say I have a way for you to keep your contract, continue to see Aidan in secret—with the option of revealing your relationship to the public if the test items I plant in the papers after *Golden Gloves'* release are received positively—and become an even bigger star than you are now."

Beth squared her shoulders in an effort to reestablish her assertiveness. "I don't want to be a bigger star." Her shaky voice betrayed her. "I'm interested in quality parts."

Mr. Mertz adjusted his tie. "Then you will find my proposition quite attractive. I have an epic film lined up for you after *Golden Gloves* is finished—an even grander affair than *Gone With The Wind*. Kenneth Locke will direct it. The starring role is perfect for you and the storyline is rich in substance, as you desire. What do you say? Do you think you and I can work something out?"

During Beth's screen test, Mr. Locke was rude and

uninspiring—the opposite of Kazan. However, if working with him meant Aidan's career would remain safe, she would do it.

But first . . .

"What's in it for you?"

Mr. Mertz grinned. Malice shadowed his features, warning her to remain on guard. "Much will be in it for me, Miss Sutton, if you agree to my specific terms."

Beth frowned. Something still didn't add up. "Under contract, I'm obligated to act in any film you assign to me, regardless of my opinion on it. Why would you agree to leave Aidan and me alone in exchange for my compliance with this particular project?"

Mr. Mertz tapped his fingers on the desk. "That's not the only stipulation if you want to save Aidan's career."

Beth gulped. "I love Aidan and I'll do whatever it takes to help him. I'll act in any film, conduct all the press interviews you want. Anything."

"Anything?" Mr. Mertz's grin widened, transforming him into a villain straight out of a horror picture. "Now that's what I want to hear, Miss Sutton. Kenneth will be glad to hear it, too. I've made a special arrangement for him since he is one of my top directors. He finds you very . . . delightful." He dragged his fingers down her arm.

Beth lurched away from him. How could she have been so stupid? "Is that why you agreed to allow me and Aidan to see each other in secret—so you could blackmail me?" Tears filled her eyes again. "Well, you're mistaken. I won't do something so immoral, so disgusting. I won't!"

Mr. Mertz grabbed her wrist and pinned her against the desk, blocking any chance of escape. "I need to let Kenneth know how cooperative you are firsthand before I sign you to the film officially."

Beth squeezed her eyes shut. "No! Don't touch me!" She struggled to break free, but he was too strong, too unrelenting in his quest.

His stale breath skimmed across her cheek. She gagged.

"Don't fight it, Miss Sutton. It's just one kiss . . ."

Beth's eyes popped open. Method acting was about drawing inspiration from one's true self to give an authentic performance, but there was also a symbiotic component to the relationship between performers and their characters. While Beth had channeled much of herself into Mary, Mary had taught her a lot, too—about strength, determination, and sticking up for the man she loved, even in the most harrowing circumstances.

"I said don't touch me!" Beth made a fist with her free hand and punched Mr. Mertz in the gut with all of her might, using the technique Aidan had taught her on the day she found out they would costar in *Golden Gloves*.

Mr. Mertz toppled forward, sputtering profanities, trapping her against the desk more forcefully.

She released an earsplitting scream. "Somebody help me!"

The double doors blasted open. Mr. Mertz jumped back, providing a suitable gap between them.

Nathan stood in the doorway, still and solemn.

Beth ran toward him, sobbing all the way, her hand

throbbing but intact. "Oh, thank goodness." She wrapped her arms around his neck. "Help me, please!"

"There's nothing to see here, boy." Mr. Mertz straightened his suit jacket, still huffing from her attack. "Miss Sutton was just on her way back to the set."

"You bastard." Nathan's voice cracked. "How could you?"

Beth pulled Nathan into the reception room. "Please, let's go."

"Don't do anything foolish, boy," Mr. Mertz called after them.

Nathan winced but didn't stop walking. They bypassed Ethel, who stood behind her desk, openmouthed and pale.

Nathan took the lead as they headed to the elevators. Beth wept on their walk to his Cadillac and throughout the drive to wherever he was taking her. She didn't care, as long as it was far, far away from Starlight Studios.

They ended up at her house. When Nathan parked in the driveway, Beth peered at him tentatively through her tears. Surely he would question her. Perhaps scold her.

Without a word, he helped her out of the car and ushered her inside.

Olivia met them in the foyer. Her welcoming smile vanished. "Oh, my gosh. What happened?"

"Mr. Mertz made a pass at me and said if I didn't give in to him, Aidan's career would be over." Beth covered her face and cried harder. "He wanted to hand me over to Kenneth Locke and . . . oh, it was awful! I tried to get away, but Mr. Mertz was too strong. I punched him. Then Nathan arrived and—" Her legs gave out.

Nathan picked her up and carried her into her bedroom. Olivia accompanied them.

After placing her on the bed, Nathan sat next to her. "Beth, has Luther done anything like this to you before?"

"I . . . I don't know." Her hand flew to her mouth. "Oh, no! You must tell Mr. Kazan where I am. He's expecting me back—"

"Forget about Kazan." Nathan's jaw clenched. "Come on, Beth. Think."

Beth brushed away her tears. It took her a moment to calm herself well enough to answer him. "During the last meeting I had with Mr. Mertz, he placed his hand on my knee. It made me uncomfortable, but I figured I read too much into it so I never mentioned it to anyone. I never thought he would—" Hysteria took hold again. "Oh, Nathan. Please don't tell Aidan. Please! He'll be on set at lunchtime. I must be there to greet him so he doesn't worry."

"You've had a difficult morning. You need your rest." Nathan's eyes clouded with . . . sorrow? Yes. But something else, too. Something far more tragic. "Everything will be fine. I'll handle it."

"But Aidan—"

"Just relax." He stroked her hair. "You're safe now."

Beth settled under the covers. She wanted to move, she really did. But her eyelids grew heavy and it wasn't long before hysteria and exhaustion dragged her into a deep sleep.

Chapter Five

Beth's eyelids fluttered open. There was a rumbling noise in the distance, growing louder and louder—a powerful, familiar roar—but she couldn't place it before it silenced abruptly. She blinked a few times against the sunlight that poured into her bedroom and caught the time displayed on the nightstand clock. Her eyebrows furrowed. Why was she at home at eleven thirty in the morning? She should've been at the studio—

"Oh, no." She clamped her hand over her mouth as her stomach churned. At the reminder of what happened with Mr. Mertz, she felt like crying, but her reserve of tears seemed to be depleted.

The studio. She needed to get back to the studio before lunch and act as if nothing happened.

"I can't believe you, Nathan. How could you?"

Beth's gaze locked on her closed bedroom door. She slipped out of bed and left her room to check what was going on.

Nathan and Olivia stood in the corridor, glaring at each other. When they noticed her, they froze, as though they'd been caught committing a heinous crime.

"What's going on? I—" Beth's eyes shot toward the front door. It flew open with such force the doorknob smashed through the drywall.

Aidan appeared in the foyer, a grim figure with ravaged hair and wild eyes. She blanched.

"I'm sorry, Beth." Nathan bowed his head. "I had to tell him."

Aidan stalked down the hallway. Hostility radiated from every muscle, every bone in his body. Nathan and Olivia tensed. Beth could only tremble, wide-eyed and numb.

Aidan stopped in front of her, towered over her. Instead of releasing the wrath that tightened his shoulders and gait, tears moistened his eyes, diluting his anger to sorrow. "Nate told me Mertz touched your knee during the meeting where he forced you to confess our relationship. Why didn't you tell me?"

Beth opened her mouth, but no reply followed. She preferred him to yell at her. This devastation and self-loathing of his she was witness to—it was worse than the most hateful words or tone. She was afraid of what it meant for his recovery.

"Damn it, Beth." Aidan curled his hands into fists at his sides, though his gaze remained soft. "Answer me."

Pain drilled into her chest, spilling the life out of her. Her trembling grew violent. "I'm . . . I'm sorry. I didn't think it meant anything. I had no idea it would lead to this. But don't worry, I hit Mr. Mertz before anything could happen today. Then Nathan arrived and got me out of there."

The tears that had eluded her when she first woke up now poured down her face. "Even if Nathan hadn't rescued me, I wouldn't have allowed it to go any further. I would never, ever do such vile things with Mr. Mertz. I would've kept hitting him, kicked him, screamed until my voice was gone—anything to get away!"

The sadness seeped out of Aidan's poise, renewing the volatile stance he held when he first entered the house. "What did Mertz blackmail you with? He must've threatened you with something if he thought he could get away with what he attempted today."

"He threatened your career, your lifeline!" Beth sputtered her reply through her sobs. "I said I would do anything to protect you, but when I realized exactly what he had in mind, I told him I wouldn't cooperate. He persisted. I swear I had no idea he would do something like this or I never would've—"

"This was all because of me?" Aidan's eyes bulged. "Whether Mertz's proposition was dirty or not, I wouldn't want you to make any sort of deal with him, especially on my account. That's a deal with the devil, baby. No good could ever come of that, no matter what."

"But if it had been something as simple as working on a film with a nasty director like Kenneth Locke, I would've done it." Beth gestured to him wildly. "I told you, Mr. Mertz threatened your lifeline!"

Aidan swayed, as though he was on the verge of collapse. "What are you talking about? Don't you know by now? You're my lifeline. You!"

Beth latched onto him, crying so hysterically she struggled to catch her breath. The tears, they wouldn't quit. They hindered her ease of speech, her stability, but she was determined to appeal to his tender side. "Please, Aidan. Let's get out of Hollywood. We'll leave everything behind and—"

"I destroy everyone I love." He gritted his teeth. And then the shaking started.

Dread knocked the air from Beth's lungs. She twisted his T-shirt in her hands, dug her nails into his shoulders, her love and desperation giving her a grip that was rougher than anything she'd ever used on him before. "No, that's not true! I made the mistake, not you. I trusted Mr. Mertz, even though you warned me not to. It's my fault. *Mine*."

"Mertz is gonna pay." Aidan pried her off him and inched backward, his chest heaving, his jaw on lockdown.

"No! Please let it go. We can run away together. Just you and me!" Beth's gaze roamed all over Aidan's face, searching for the gentle man who had carried her to bed, made love to her, and held her all night. It was in vain. His rage was too thick, impenetrable. He was a man consumed with the need for revenge, standing on the brink of eruption.

She stumbled forward and reached for him, but it was too late. He took off down the corridor so fast she didn't register he was gone until Olivia shrieked.

"Nathan, do something!"

Nathan stared ahead, reacting to nothing.

Olivia shook him. "Nathan, please!"

Still nothing.

Panic willed Beth to take action. She charged out of the house in her bare feet. By the time she reached the driveway, Aidan was already behind the wheel of his Porsche with the engine engaged. She launched herself against the driver's door, pawing frantically at the closed window separating them.

"Stay with me. Please don't go. Don't do this!"

Aidan changed gears. The car shot forward with a ghastly squeal of the tires and peeled off down the street. Beth scrambled after him, waving her arms in the air.

"Aidan! Aidan!" She yelled until her voice was hoarse, refusing to accept defeat as long as he could still see her in his rearview mirror. Last spring, she had run after him as he drove away from Romanoff's on his motorcycle, unaware of her pursuit. She was tethered to him so strongly then, and they didn't even know each other. Now she couldn't live without him.

"Aidan, please!" She gasped and dropped to her knees as he turned the corner.

Grief strangled her heart, making every breath, every cry nearly impossible. This was not how it was supposed to be. Somehow she had to reach him before something horrible happened. But her car was parked at the studio because Nathan had driven her home . . .

Nathan.

She sprung to her feet.

"Beth!" Olivia caught up with her. "Are you all right?"

"We need to get to the studio right away." Beth took Olivia's hand and dragged her back to the house.

Inside, Nathan stood in the exact same spot as before. Even his stoic expression remained unchanged. Beth gaped at him. She couldn't understand it. Why would Nathan allow Aidan to leave, knowing he was going after Mr. Mertz?

She tugged on his arm. "Come on. We must stop him!"

Nathan hung his head and didn't respond.

Beth yanked on his tie and pulled him close, forcing him to

look her in the eye. "Drive me or give me your keys. Either way, I'm using your Cadillac to get to the studio."

Nathan swallowed. "Fine. I'll drive you."

Instead of heading for the front door, he entered the living room.

Beth raced after him. "What are you doing?"

He picked up the telephone receiver and spoke to the operator.

"Nathan, we have to leave now. There's no time for this!"

Nathan fixed his gaze on hers. Beth shut her mouth; there was no way she'd dare say anything more. She'd always found comfort in his blue eyes. They reminded her of the ocean sprinkled by the rising sun, or the sky on the clearest summer morning. Now he looked as icy as—

She shuddered.

As icy as Mr. Mertz.

"Beth, if you want to stop Aidan, we're going to need help." He focused on his telephone call. "Matthew, it's Nathan. You need to get to Luther Mertz's office immediately. It's an emergency."

Chapter Six

Aidan pulled up to the studio's main gates and honked his horn repeatedly. He was going to destroy Mr. Mertz—destroy the savage who hurt his beautiful little dove, who made someone so innocent, so kind, and so precious feel such fear and pain.

"Starlight Studios security. How may I help you?"

Aidan leaned toward the speaker box. "Open up!"

"Who is this?"

"It's Aidan Evans. Now open the gates!" Aidan shifted gears as his demand was met. He slammed his foot on the gas pedal and gunned the engine, blasting through the security arm as the guard yelled after him.

Aidan took a shortcut to Mr. Mertz's office, using pathways forbidden to cars, honking and swearing at anyone who got in his way. He parked his Porsche at the back of the building and entered through the rear door. Lacking patience to wait for the elevator, he sneaked past security and headed straight for the stairs.

When he burst onto the sixth floor reception room, Ethel

and Caroline screamed and hid behind their desks. He shoved open the double doors to Mr. Mertz's office.

The studio boss sat at his desk with a smug grin plastered on his face. "So you were stupid enough to come here, after all."

Aidan broke into a run.

Mr. Mertz's eyes widened. "What are you doing?"

With a strangled cry, Aidan flew over the desk and latched onto him, sending both of them to the floor. When Aidan scrambled to his feet, he gripped Mr. Mertz's suit jacket and hauled him up, too.

"Unhand me, you animal!" Mr. Mertz writhed in his grasp. "Or I'll have you and your no-talent floozy run out of Hollywood!"

"You goddamn bastard!" Aidan shoved Mr. Mertz backward. He collided with the vast window overlooking the studio lot. "How dare you touch her!"

"Stay away from me!" Mr. Mertz gasped in between agonizing groans.

Aidan grabbed him again and dragged him away from the window, this time smashing him against a filing cabinet. "I'm not gonna leave until you get what you deserve." He waved his fist in the air.

"You can't hit me." Mr. Mertz's eyes narrowed. "As much as you may despise me, my influence in this town is unmatched. I'm invincible."

"Are you sure about that, old man?" Aidan clenched his fist tighter.

"You hit me and I'll charge you with assault—"

Aidan slammed his fist into Mr. Mertz's face. Mr. Mertz's eyes rolled back and his legs buckled. Aidan hit the studio boss again and again, utilizing all the boxing training he'd received while working on *Golden Gloves*.

"I always knew you were no good." Mr. Mertz had the audacity to smirk at him.

"Fuck you!" Aidan delivered more ruthless punches, but Mr. Mertz didn't fight back. "Come on, aren't you going to defend yourself, you sick bastard?"

"I'd never give you the satisfaction." Blood spilled from Mr. Mertz's nose and mouth. "You're not a man. You're a monster. And if you keep this up, murderer will be added to your resume."

Aidan staggered backward, as though Mr. Mertz had landed a punch. "No. No, you're wrong."

He surveyed his swollen, bloody hands—hands that had caressed Beth and were now used as weapons. The drifter who killed his mother . . . he'd had blood on his hands, too.

Aidan's stomach lurched. He closed his eyes.

Damn it. He was going to be sick.

Mr. Mertz chuckled. "You and your whore deserve each other."

Aidan's eyes snapped open. As his rage resurfaced, he hit Mr. Mertz as hard as he could. "Don't you ever talk about her that way, you fucking piece of shit . . . fucking bastard . . ." His fists flew fast and furiously, pounding into Mr. Mertz's pudgy face and gut over and over again.

"Monster . . . murderer." Mr. Mertz murmurs faded as he

slumped to the floor, spewing blood all over his fancy clothes.

Aidan reached for him again.

"Aidan, stop!"

He wheeled around. Beth entered the office with their four friends. She stopped short when their eyes met. Beth, so innocent, so kind, and so precious stared at him like he was a stranger. Shock dilated her pupils. Her mouth hung open—the mouth he'd claimed and cherished, tasted and savored.

His armor shattered . . . the tension eased from his body. A kiss. It used to be such an easy thing to obtain—a gift readily given to him by his beloved. Now it was a privilege he had lost, and rightly so. What a fool he'd been. He should've stayed away from her. Now she blamed herself for everything that had happened.

Disgust and regret curled his hands into fists again. That all-consuming rage returned. It was time for her to see what he was truly capable of, so there would never be any doubt in her mind that they shouldn't be together. He'd show her once and for all that she'd been wrong. He'd never achieve redemption, and he never was—nor would he ever be—worthy of her love.

Aidan turned away from her and yanked Mr. Mertz upright.

"No, Aidan. Don't!"

He drew his fist back and connected a punch to Mr. Mertz's face, unleashing a roar loud enough to drown out the haunting cries from across the room—a tragic melody of love and loss, sung by a broken little dove.

Chapter Seven

As Nathan turned into the studio's driveway, Matthew's Bentley approached from the opposite direction and fell in queue behind him. Nathan announced his name into the speaker box and the wrought-iron gates opened.

Beth's heart constricted. Up ahead, the security arm was cracked off and lying on the ground. Nathan cursed under his breath and tightened his grip on the steering wheel.

Charlie popped his head out of the security hut's open window. Terror deepened the wrinkles in his face. "Aidan Evans has gone on a rampage. I notified the rest of security of his arrival, but I have no idea where he is on the lot. Be careful. Be very careful!"

Nathan drove over the broken security arm and they continued on their way. Once they arrived at Mr. Mertz's office building, Beth didn't wait for him to park. She jumped out of the car and ran inside. By the time her friends joined her, she had already made it past the security guard in the lobby and pressed the button for the elevator.

Matthew tugged at his tie. "What the heck is going on?"

Nathan frowned. "Aidan is going after Luther."

"That's crazy! Why?"

"Luther made a sexual advance toward Beth and wanted to pass her off to Kenneth Locke, too. Thankfully, I got her out of there before things progressed."

"Oh, my gosh." The color emptied from Connie's face and she wobbled on her feet.

Matthew steadied her by curling his arm around her waist. "Wow, that's deplorable. Even for Luther."

Beth looked away. Although nothing had happened between her and Mr. Mertz, she was still ashamed she'd allowed herself to be put in that position in the first place.

The elevator arrived. They piled inside.

"Take us to the top floor. Make no stops along the way."

The elevator operator nodded. "Yes, Mr. Taggart."

"Did you take Aidan Evans for a ride recently?" Matthew asked on their ascent.

"The actor? No, sir."

Beth peered at Nathan. "Maybe he didn't come here, after all. I didn't see his Porsche out front."

Nathan shook his head. "Not a chance. He could've parked in the back and taken the stairs."

Even before the elevator doors opened on the sixth floor, Beth heard Ethel and Caroline's screams. The group raced into Mr. Mertz's office. Scattered papers, an overturned chair . . . the room was a mess.

Beth zeroed in on Aidan. He had Mr. Mertz cornered and was unrelenting with his punches and profanities.

"Aidan, stop!"

He turned around. Beth sucked in a breath. She couldn't believe his transformation. In spite of his predatory gaze and the grit of his teeth, the vulnerable, tortured boy within him was so evident. His anger was a reflection of a pain far greater than she'd ever recognized. How could she have been so naïve? How could she have thought she alone could save him?

Still, maybe she could stop him before this went any further. Maybe she could—

Beth saw the exact moment Aidan gave up on himself. His eyes darkened, his muscles engaged. Blood flooded his face, turning his complexion a deep red. He pulled Mr. Mertz off the floor.

"No, Aidan. Don't!"

Ignoring her plea, Aidan launched his fist in perfect form and collided with Mr. Mertz's jaw. Beth screamed along with Connie and Olivia. He said he'd die for her, do anything to defend her. She should've known he would kill for her, too.

"Stay back, ladies!"

Nathan and Matthew charged at Aidan like a pair of football players. It was two against one, but they still had difficulty forcing him off Mr. Mertz. When they finally succeeded, the studio boss fell to the floor, thrashing and moaning.

Matthew caged Aidan against the wall. "Stop it, man. What are you doing?"

Aidan lashed out over Matthew's shoulders, swinging his fists as if he thought he could reach Mr. Mertz from ten feet away. "Let me go, damn it. I'm not done with him!"

Nathan helped Matthew restrain him. "Aidan, you're going to kill him if you continue!"

Mr. Mertz used his desk as leverage to stand up. Once he was back on his feet, he gripped his stomach and coughed, fighting to catch his breath. His left eye was swollen shut and his lips bled. Small cuts lacerated his cheeks and jaw.

Amidst Aidan's curses and attempts to free himself, Connie approached Mr. Mertz. Beth couldn't decipher the emotion on her face. She blinked a few times and just stood there, staring at him. Beth and Olivia exchanged perplexed glances.

Mr. Mertz removed a handkerchief from his pocket and dabbed his forehead. "What the hell do you want?"

Connie's face distorted. She released a wail and lunged at him. "You bastard. You horrible bastard!" She pounded her fists against his chest. Tears streamed down her face. "I hate you. I hate you!"

Aidan froze. Matthew darted to his fiancée's side.

Mr. Mertz raised his hands to shield himself, but Connie's determination was inexorable.

Matthew dragged her away from Mr. Mertz. He hugged her tightly and whispered in her ear, but nothing sedated her. Tangled hair, red eyes, mascara streaked cheeks . . . the blonde bombshell with the world at her feet had fallen into a dark abyss.

"What's wrong?" Matthew framed Connie's face with his hands. "Tell me what's going on."

Connie only cried harder, but it was enough. Beth knew the

answer. The shame in her eyes was unmistakable. Familiar.

Mr. Mertz tucked his handkerchief back in his pocket. "Come now, Mr. McKenna. Surely your lover's escapades in her pre-stardom days are no secret to you. I'm surprised you would stoop to marry such a trollop."

Matthew withdrew his hands from Connie's tear-soaked face and stared at Mr. Mertz blankly, as if trying to decipher exactly what the inference meant.

"Luther, please don't," Nathan said from the far corner, where he still guarded Aidan.

"It's important he know the truth, boy." Mr. Mertz seemed steadier in his perch against the edge of his desk. "And don't you dare ever tell me what to do."

Mr. Mertz's attempt to regain his power ended there. Matthew flew at his flank and knocked him off his feet, pinning him against the wall and unleashing a fresh set of punches and venomous curses.

Nathan stood in stunned silence. The distraction allowed Aidan to wrestle free. He raced across the room and joined in the fight, leaving Nathan as referee.

The men gathered in a mob of flying fists and savage noises. All Beth could do was huddle with Olivia and Connie out of the path of destruction and scream for the fight to finish before someone ended up dead.

As Nathan held back Matthew and Aidan and tried to reason with them, Mr. Mertz seized the opportunity and crawled away. When he rose to his feet, he let out wheezy, labored breaths and stumbled against his desk.

"You're fired. All of you!" He pointed at Nathan. "Except you, boy."

Nathan paled. "You can't do this."

Mr. Mertz sneered. "I can do whatever I want. It's my studio."

"That's fine with me." Matthew walked to Connie and pulled her into his arms again. "I don't want my fiancée working here anymore, and I sure as hell don't want any part in the *Golden Gloves* theme song if your name is attached to the film."

Beth's eyes widened. *Golden Gloves.* She had destroyed Aidan and Kazan's dream project.

Her gaze landed on Aidan. He wiped his face, smearing it with blood. He'd won the physical fight, but emotionally he was more scarred than ever. His pain ran deep, creating a trench around his heart, which prevented anyone from reaching him and making him understand that he was a good man, regardless of his past.

Beth ran over to him and wrapped her arms around his neck. "Oh, Aidan! Are you all right?"

He went rigid and didn't return her embrace. "After today, you'll never see me again. There's nothing between us anymore. *I'm* nothing."

Beth recoiled. That word—nothing. It floated over them, suspended in the air like a dense storm cloud. She searched for a tangible sign in his face, in his body language—evidence that something was still there, that her hope that they could move on from this wasn't futile. That he still cared about her, loved her, in spite of everything.

There was nothing.

Nothing.

She tightened her hold on him, as if she was physically capable of preventing him from leaving. "You told me we would be together forever. You promised!"

Aidan squeezed his eyes shut. "Beth . . . Beth . . . Beth . . ." He repeated her name again and again, like he was devouring all the memories accompanying it. Then the dam protecting him from his self-loathing cracked. He fixed her with a granite gaze that shocked her into releasing him. "Consider my promise broken."

Without further regard for her or their friends, he left the office. Beth doubled over. She reached for her angel pendant, but she was still in costume, so it wasn't hanging from her neck. Somehow, that made everything worse.

"Aidan's got the right idea. Let's get out of here." Olivia linked her arm with Nathan's.

Beth hurried with them to the door. Maybe as a group they could convince Aidan to stay.

Four security guards arrived and crowded the exit, blocking their departure.

"Get out of our way!" Beth tried to push past them, but it was no use.

"Didn't you hear, Miss Sutton?" Mr. Mertz rounded his desk, straightening his tie. "The foul-mouthed hooligan wants nothing to do with you."

Hatred flashed in Nathan's eyes. "Let us out, Luther."

Mr. Mertz scowled. "Now, now, boy. Remember our

arrangement."

Nathan flinched.

Olivia gaped at him. "Nathan, what is he talking about?"

Mr. Mertz clutched his belly and expelled a chuckle. Unlike his usual modus operandi, his amusement exuded sincerity. "Miss Weston, you don't know Mr. Taggart as well as you think you do."

Nathan clenched his teeth. "Olivia, I want you to leave. And take your friends with you."

"My friends? You mean *our* friends!" Tears trailed down her cheeks. "You must come with us. We're your future, not Mr. Mertz!"

"I'm afraid you're mistaken." Mr. Mertz's bleeding lips stretched into a sinister grin. "He belongs to me."

"Are you kidding?" Matthew rushed over to Nathan. "You're choosing Mertz over us?"

Nathan's gaze chilled. "Yes. Now get out."

Mr. Mertz nodded at the security guards. They moved out of the way.

With a gut-wrenching sob, Olivia dashed out of the office. Beth, Matthew, and Connie followed. While her friends approached the elevator, Beth made a beeline for the stairs.

She ran all the way down to the main floor and burst through the back door. Twice she scoured the perimeter of the building, but she was too late. Aidan was gone.

Chapter Eight

After Aidan left, Beth gravitated to the only place she belonged. As she lay curled up in his bed, wearing his T-shirt, time slipped by uneventfully. Neither morning nor night held significance anymore. Even the day seemed smothered in blackness.

She had no idea how long she had been at his house but was thankful he'd given her a key on Valentine's Day. All she wanted to do was shut herself off from the world and mourn his loss without distractions.

Even in his absence, Aidan was still with her, dominating her universe. She couldn't shed him, nor did she want to. She didn't want to forget the details of his face, how she felt when he touched her, the way her heart swelled whenever he said he loved her. It was all she had left now.

Although she wished to remember only the good times between them, she was tortured by the fact that she hadn't fought hard enough for their relationship. Aidan had been right in front of her, and foolishly she had let him go. She should've held him tighter or argued with the security guards blocking the exit so she could've run after him right away. Something—anything—other than what she'd done.

Her appetite was gone. Every movement fatigued her. Her head ached and a muddy haze hampered her thoughts. In an effort to cope, she hummed the tune Aidan wrote for her or immersed in the scent of his clothing and bed sheets, but it only made her miss him more. Sleep brought no relief. She dreamed of them together, kissing, laughing, and so in love—only to wake up screaming, shaking, and sweaty, forced to come to terms with her new, lonely, pointless existence all over again.

She hoped Aidan would stop by his house before leaving town. He didn't specify a departure, but there was no way he'd remain in L.A. New York City was the most logical destination, and he'd want to bring his belongings with him, right? Well, when he did show up, she'd be waiting. And this time, she would not allow him to leave without her.

A noise echoed through the house. Beth shot up in bed, straining to hear more. A thump followed, then a creaking door.

"Aidan!" She jumped out of bed and shot down the hallway. When she reached the front foyer, she collapsed into a sobbing heap on the floor. "Aidan! Aidan!"

"Beth!" Connie kneeled next to her. "Are you all right?"

"All right?" Beth screeched the words through her parched throat. "Of course I'm not all right. You're not him. He's gone. He's gone!"

"Come on, get up." Connie held her arm and coaxed her to stand.

Beth jerked away and dropped back to the floor. "Leave me

alone."

"I'm not leaving unless you're coming with me."

Beth pulled her knees to her chest and rocked back and forth. "I can't. I need to be here when he returns."

"And what if he doesn't return?"

Beth hiccupped. "He must. All of his clothes are here. His Triumph. He . . . he loves that motorcycle."

Connie sighed. "Oh, Beth. What's happened to you?"

"I can't go on." Beth cried so hard she could barely talk. "Not if he's not with me. I . . . I can't . . ."

"Take some slow, deep breaths. You've worked yourself up into such a state." Connie rubbed her back. "How about we move from the hallway? We won't leave the house, I promise. The floor just isn't very comfortable."

Beth nodded and allowed Connie to escort her back to Aidan's bedroom. Connie turned on the table lamp while Beth crawled under the covers. Even in the dim light, her eyes stung. She was so used to darkness.

Connie sat at the edge of the bed and folded her hands in her lap. "Beth, it's not beneficial for you to stay here. You won't heal this way."

"I don't want to heal. Don't you understand?" Beth let out a whimper. "I won't feel whole again until I'm reunited with Aidan."

Connie rolled her eyes. "That's ludicrous. I knew you before you officially began dating Aidan. You weren't helpless then. In fact, you were doing well on your own."

"I don't want to live if he's not with me."

Connie scowled. "You know, I never said anything before because you're my friend and I didn't want to be rude, but your relationship with Aidan was never healthy."

Beth's anger rose up over her anguish. "Excuse me?"

"Your dynamic with him is what got you into this mess in the first place. You always put his needs before your own instead of considering what's best for you as well, and he did the same. You were both self-sacrificing to a fault and depended on each other way too much."

Beth scrambled to the opposite side of the bed, as far away from Connie as possible without ending up on the floor. "You have some nerve to tell me our relationship was no good. Aidan made me a better person. As for depending on someone, that's called true love. I'm sorry you have the misfortunate of lacking a relationship as strong as ours." She thrust her finger toward the door. "Leave. You're not welcome here."

"No. Not until you hear me out."

Beth scoffed. "You've said quite enough already, thank you."

Connie crossed her arms over her chest. "You and Aidan existed in a bubble for so long, where the sun rose and set solely for the two of you. Did you ever consider that you weren't the only people affected by what occurred in Luther Mertz's office?"

Beth frowned. "What do you mean?"

Connie's mouth dropped open. "What do I mean? How about Olivia, for starters. She lost Nathan just like you lost Aidan. He hasn't returned home. He hasn't contacted her, nor can she reach him. Now you've abandoned her, too, to mope around here like everyone else ceases to exist."

Connie shook her head. "You think your pain is the only pain that matters and no one else can relate or come close to feeling as bad as you do. Well, you're wrong. I'm upset, too, you know. Yet I've still made it a priority to check in on Olivia. Why can't you make the same effort? She's always been there for you. And this is how you show your gratitude?"

Beth clutched the covers. "I didn't mean to abandon her. Being here just feels right. I don't know how else to deal with everything that happened."

"You fight. And I don't mean in the physical sense. I mean mentally and emotionally collecting yourself enough to move forward and take back control of your life." A tear rolled down Connie's cheek. "I went through hell during my first year in L.A. and bottled up my feelings for a long time, trying to forget what happened to me. When Aidan went after Luther, something inside me snapped. I dreamed about revenge for years, but confronting him didn't cure me like I hoped it would. And I guarantee Aidan came to the same conclusion. I don't know why he's so disturbed, but it's obvious his contention with Luther is not the culprit. It's simply an outlet for his pain."

Beth bowed her head. She'd never forget Connie's attack on Mr. Mertz—the torment on her face, her tragic, desperate attempt to hurt him like he'd hurt her. Perhaps if she had put as much effort into learning about her friends as she did with Aidan, she would have noticed that Connie was troubled—Nathan, too. While she'd made it her mission to help Aidan find peace, her friends deserved the same consideration. She'd failed them.

Beth scooted back across the bed and finally took a good look at Connie, past the perfect teeth, perfect complexion, perfect figure. Her eyes were bloodshot, her hair hung in unkempt curls with dark roots. For the first time, she didn't wear makeup. Connie was a natural beauty, yes, but so sad. Why hadn't she seen it before?

"What exactly happened with Mr. Mertz?"

The passion that encouraged Connie to stand her ground moments ago drained from her eyes. "When I arrived in Hollywood, I was a naïve, seventeen-year-old named Mildred Johnson. Luther was like the Wizard of Oz to me, with the ability to grant me anything and everything I wanted. Insisting I had star quality, he put me through the studio's beautification process and legally changed my name to Constance Murphy. He also arranged a meeting between me and a famous director—" She closed her eyes on a shudder.

Beth grasped Connie's hand, granting the support she should've provided long ago.

Connie exhaled deeply and opened her eyes. "I lost my virginity to that director in a bungalow at the Chateau Marmont. He was much older than me and married with two children. I didn't like him, let alone love him. In fact, there was no romance at all, just pain and tears. But I agreed to have sex with him because he promised he'd ensure that Luther gave me the lead in his next film if I did. Afterward, he told his driver to take me home and I never heard from him again. I've seen him around the studio and at social events, but I can't look him in the eye. It's too upsetting. I'm too ashamed."

Beth's heart shattered. Aidan had been so sweet and gentle when they made love. She couldn't image sharing intimacy with someone she didn't care about, or someone who didn't care about her.

"But you were young, Connie. It's not your fault."

Connie glared at her. "That's not an excuse. My parents raised me to respect my mind and my body. I never should've allowed my acting ambitions to negatively influence my behavior. But I was so desperate to make it in Hollywood. My parents . . . they weren't thrilled with my career choice, but they didn't forbid me from becoming an actress. Instead, we came to a compromise. If I didn't get signed to Starlight Studios within a year and have a promising future in the film industry, then I had to return to New Jersey.

"I sacrificed everything about myself I was proud of in order to get to where I am today, all because I didn't want to go back home a failure. My parents would've welcomed me with open arms, regardless. But still, I wanted to show them I could make it on my own, you know?"

Tears trickled down Connie's face. She wiped them away with the sleeve of her blouse. "Needless to say, after that night with the director, I was invited to many *business meetings*, all arranged by Luther. I was passed around like a prostitute, constantly reminded that I wasn't a talented actress, but if I shut up and did as I was told, then one day I'd become a big star. So I went along with it.

"Finally, I received top billing in *Closure*, the role that launched my career, and they left me alone—moving on to the next new girl on the lot, I'm sure. But I didn't care at that point. I'd made it, and all I wanted to do was forget everything bad I'd done to earn my success. My rationale was that I couldn't change what happened, but I could make sure no one took advantage of me again.

"Then I met Matthew." Her lips lifted a little. "We fell in love and all of my former indiscretions became nothing but distant memories—until I saw Aidan attack Luther. I thought after Matthew learned the truth, he'd call off our engagement, but he didn't. He's sticking by me and even assisting me in arranging another wedding now that our June one is canceled on account of Luther's involvement. He tells me he loves me unconditionally and understands why I withheld everything from him. He also wants to help me address my past and move on in the right away."

Beth squeezed her hand. "I'm truly glad you two are still a couple."

"That doesn't mean I click my heels together and everything is perfect. In films, love conquers all and the good guys win. Real life isn't so black and white. It'll take a lot of hard work to deal with everything that happened to me. It's daunting, and I'm scared to revisit it all, but I'm not giving up. And that's my advice to you, Beth. Although it took me years to get to this point, I'm making positive changes nonetheless, and that's the important thing."

Beth moved over to provide space for Connie to sit on the bed properly. "I'm sorry I've been so selfish with everyone besides Aidan. What I'm going through pales in comparison to your journey. It was insensitive of me to treat you poorly when you showed up here. Thanks for not giving up on me. You're a true friend."

Connie kicked off her shoes and settled her back against the headboard. She stretched her legs in front of her. "Do you know why I was cold toward Aidan right from the beginning?"

Beth considered the question for a moment. "I always assumed it was because of the whole studio-trained actors versus Method-trained actors rivalry in the film industry."

Connie shook her head. "It's because Aidan secured a prestigious leading role in Hollywood in an honest way, whereas the higher-ups convinced me I had to sleep my way to the top. I was jealous that it was so easy for Aidan to stand his ground, make demands, and get everything he wanted."

She frowned. "Beth, I know Nathan arrived and drove you home before anything happened between you and Luther. However, when I heard the news, I felt ill. Maybe if I'd spoken up early on, I could've stopped him from going after you—and other actresses, too. I will always regret putting myself first."

Beth patted her shoulder. "You're not alone. I felt uncomfortable when Mr. Mertz touched my knee during a meeting that happened weeks ago, but I didn't say anything to anyone. Imagine how many other women have done the same."

"There was a time when I considered going to the police, but I never went through with it." Connie's expression crumbled with the arrival of more tears. "What was I supposed to tell them? Sure, what Luther and his cronies did was immoral, and using bribery to obtain my consent was despicable, but I had, in fact, consented. There were no grounds for charges to be laid."

"Oh, Connie." Beth pulled her in for a hug.

Connie cried into her ear. "I'm so sorry. My comments about your relationship with Aidan weren't meant to be hurtful. I came here today to help you, and to see you so distraught because he's gone . . . it breaks my heart. Aidan may enrich your life, but without him you're still worthy. If it's meant to be, you'll reconnect. Until then, you shouldn't lock yourself in his house and fade away."

Beth sniffled. "You're right, but how can I move forward? *Golden Gloves* is terminated. My film career is over."

Connie grasped her hands. "Listen to me. My career isn't finished, your career isn't finished, and neither is Olivia's. We're strong women, and we don't need to depend on Starlight Studios anymore."

Beth tossed her a dubious look. "Even Aidan, who wasn't signed under contract, was forced to make films for the studio. That's where the money comes from. It's impossible to green light a project without Mr. Mertz's involvement and approval."

Enthusiasm sprung to Connie's eyes again. "I know it's a long shot, but I have the courage to try to assert my professional independence now. It can start with you, Olivia, and me. Things may not change overnight, but if we rally—"

"Putting the broken pieces of my personal life back together is hard enough, Connie. I don't know if I can salvage my career, too, and be independent in the industry." Beth retracted her hands. "You know how it is in this town. The three of us—three women, no less—cannot change a studio system that's been in place for decades."

"If you're not going to act anymore, what will you do?"

Beth shrugged. "Before signing my studio contract, I wanted to be a teacher. Maybe I'll go back to school. I have more than enough money saved to tide me over until I graduate and find a job."

"And what about your fans?"

"They won't miss me. I've haven't even been at the studio for a year. Another actress will catch their fancy and they'll forget all about me. That's how the business works, isn't it? I'm sure Mr. Mertz is plotting my replacement as we speak."

Connie pursed her lips. "Do me a favor and don't give up on acting just yet. Allow yourself some time to digest everything that's happened and we'll revisit this later. You may see things differently."

Beth nodded. "In the meantime, you're right. I need to return home to Olivia."

Connie's face brightened. "She'll be glad to see you."

Beth's heart pounded as she looked around Aidan's room. She was afraid to leave, but her priority was to not abandon her friends, especially when they needed her most.

"What time is it?"

Connie checked her wristwatch. "Almost three o'clock." She smiled. "And that's afternoon, not morning."

Beth couldn't help but smile, too. "Do you mind if we stay a little longer? I promise we'll be gone before dinner."

"Sure, I don't mind."

Beth and Connie lay down on the bed, facing each other and sharing a pillow. They linked hands and closed their eyes.

"Connie, please tell me all about Mildred Johnson and growing up in New Jersey."

For the first time in days, Beth heard laughter—carefree, glorious laughter.

"Well, I was raised in Westfield. It's a middle class town about a half an hour drive from Newark and an hour from Manhattan. I'm the eldest of two children. My sister Eleanor is two years younger than me and so smart. She's studying economics at the University of Pennsylvania. Isn't that amazing? I was always horrible at math. I'm so proud of her. My mother, Alice, is a homemaker. She has a great sense of humor and plays tennis every day. It's her favorite pastime, but she isn't exactly an Olympic contender." Another laugh. "Then there's my father . . ."

Beth smiled and giggled as she listened to Connie's childhood stories with an appreciation she'd lacked for a while regarding her own upbringing, her own origins.

By the time they left Aidan's house later that evening, the next road on her journey was paved: It was time for a trip back to Clarkson.

Chapter Nine

Aidan never set out for Chicago. He just kind of ended up there. Initially, his plan was to head straight to New York. He still had his Upper West Side apartment, and the whole point was to get as far away from California as possible. His Midwestern detour wasn't a surprise, though. His father was one of the main reasons behind his failure to lead a normal life. A face-to-face confrontation was inevitable someday.

Aidan parked in front of his father's house in the posh suburb of Wilmette just after midnight. The two-story brick residence looked exactly as it did when he left over five years ago, aside from the addition of a white picket fence in the front yard. A familiar Oldsmobile was parked in the driveway, confirming his father still resided at this address. On the outside, it seemed like an ideal place to raise a family. Inside? Well, that was another story.

Aidan trembled as he emerged from his Porsche and shut the door. He could stand up against anyone except the man with whom he was supposed to feel most comfortable. Before he went any further, he needed to relax. Confidence was vital to his success.

He placed his keys in the pocket of Spike Rollins' red windbreaker and lit a cigarette. On a roadside stop somewhere in Nevada, he had cleaned the blood from his hands and face and bought a white T-shirt to replace his soiled one. He'd also purchased several packages of Winstons. With *Golden Gloves* terminated and Beth no longer in his life, there was no motivation to stay healthy anymore.

Aidan strolled down the driveway and stopped at the side of the road to take a drag. It had rained recently and looked as though it would again soon. A dense fog hovered in the air, mixing with the smoke billowing from his cigarette. How long had it been since he left L.A.? Four days? A week? He couldn't be certain. Exhaustion clouded his mind. Time held no meaning. Missing Beth was the only thing that reminded him he was still alive. No dead man could hurt this intensely . . . feel this debilitated, this hopeless.

Grief, sorrow, and guilt—the combination created a fatal foe. For years they lurked inside him, feeding his anger, his fear, his unpredictability, waiting for the opportunity to consume his soul and show him he was never in control; prove to him that even when he kept his nightmares and daytime visions at bay, he was the puppet, not the master. All the progress he'd made in the last few months was nothing but an illusion. He was no stronger than the ten-year-old boy who had wept over his dying mother and did nothing to save her.

Aidan had lost crucial memories of his mother over the years: the sound of her laughter, the flowery freshness of her scent, the radiance of her smile. Sure, he remembered pieces here and there, but the fine details eluded him. But it wasn't like he was worthy to remember her anyway. All that was good in him had vanished when he left Beth, the only woman who had ever penetrated his battered armor. The only woman he'd ever made love to. The only woman he'd ever loved and would ever love in the romantic sense.

He would lose Beth's memory, too. Not the impact she had on his life, nor the depth of his feelings for her. But over time, the little things—her laughter, her scent, her smile—would fade, regardless of how hard he fought to keep them.

Aidan bent over as nausea seized his stomach, his head, his heart. He retched and retched but emptied nothing. The grief, the sadness, the guilt—they couldn't be purged, no matter how violent his cries, how desperate his pleas, how steadfast his resolve.

He expelled a rough scream toward the heavens, taunting the lightning that blasted from the sky to strike him down, open up the ground he stood upon, and let him plummet straight to Hell. He was the worst kind of man. No, not a man. A monster.

He had ripped all the feathers off his fragile little dove.

"Beth, I'm sorry. I love you so much and I'm so fucking sorry." His cigarette tumbled to the asphalt. He gripped his hair with both hands and keeled over again, this time releasing a strangled sob into the night.

On the evening Aidan had left Chicago for New York, he had only his meager savings of his allowance and no concrete plans aside from establishing his independence from his father.

After his acceptance into the Actors Studio and his critical success on Broadway, he'd often thought, *Man, if only my pop could see me now. I'd show him!*

With a curse, Aidan stomped on his cigarette, dimming the ashes against the damp pavement. Back then, why did he have the need to show off his accomplishments and prove his father wrong? Most disturbingly, did his visit here tonight—after he'd sworn he would never return—indicate he still, somewhere deep down, desired his father's approval?

As he recalled his eighteen-year-old self hitting the road that would lead him to great professional achievement, the discovery of the love of his life, and ultimately heartbreak, he determined the answer was no. He didn't desire paternal approval anymore because in the last several years he had realized his father had never been worthy to hold such power over him in the first place.

Then why could he not continue to New York without seeing the man first?

Aidan walked back to the house, fighting the urge to have another smoke. Procrastination wasn't going to get him to the East Coast in a timely manner. He had defeated Mr. Mertz. He could handle his father, too. Besides, with the erratic way his nerves fired, he'd run out of cigarettes long before his courage trumped his anxiety.

With confidence as shaky as his legs, he ascended the first several steps to the porch. White light scorched his eyes.

"Fuck! Not now. *Please.*"

Aidan dropped into a sitting position and placed his head

between his knees, yanking at his hair as if he could extract the memories of his mother's attack along with his roots. Flashes of her broken, bleeding body and echoes of her screams launched from his subconscious, hijacking his muscles, his bones, his blood, until he was nothing but a sweaty, spastic mess.

When the vision ceased, he wiped his face with the sleeve of his jacket. Releasing a deep breath, he looked to the starless sky. It was fitting there was nothing for him to wish upon tonight. His luck had run out ages ago—if he ever had any luck in the first place.

The completion of his climb to the porch was made with steadier steps than the initial journey. He raised his curled hand to the front door but lacked the gusto to execute a knock.

When he exited the freeway, he'd gone through several scenarios in his head on how he would confront his father— jumping out of his Porsche immediately upon his arrival, hurling rocks at the windows along with profanities, and kicking down the front door were all attractive options—but now that he was here, the part of him still tormented by his mother's murder and the neglect and blame his father subjected him to made him want to run away.

A stealthy entrance seemed like a more practical approach. Aidan walked the length of the porch and lifted the potted plant in the corner. The spare house key was still hidden under the pot as it was before he left for New York. This time, he didn't pause before fitting the key into the lock and opening the door.

Darkness greeted him inside, accompanied by a tomblike silence, which made him question whether his father was even home. Lightning flickered through the house as he made his way down the corridor as quietly as possible, soiling the hardwood floor with his muddy boots.

When he opened the door to his father's office and turned on the light, he found the wood paneled room in pretty much the same condition as it had been five years ago.

Neatly stacked papers embossed with Dr. Evans' signet sat on his antique oak desk next to black-framed reading glasses. High back leather chair? Check. Fleischer stethoscope? Check. Remington DeLuxe Model Five typewriter? Check. All the accessories of a well-to-do physician.

Several new plaques were mounted on the walls. Their inscriptions confirmed they were presented to Dr. Evans in the last five years. They praised his skill, his genius, and his compassion, as if he was a patron saint of the medical community. He even had a photograph taken with the mayor, which had graced the front page of the *Chicago Tribune* last month, according to the date on the newspaper clipping. The sole photograph perched on the desk—a framed picture of his second wife Betty—established what Aidan had figured all along but hoped to disprove: It was as though he and his mother had never existed.

Aidan flicked off the light and left the office before he tore the place apart. The kitchen at the back of the house was equipped with new cupboards and appliances, a far cry from their dingy kitchen in Fairfield. His mother had loved to cook, but of course, his father had never provided her with such nice accommodations.

Aidan passed through the archway connecting to the living room. His steps faltered. His mother's piano . . . it was still there. Old and scuffed, it didn't fit amongst its fancy surroundings, but to him, it was the most beautiful item in the house.

The cover lifted with a creak of its hinges. Aidan grazed his scabbed, bruised fingers across the keys—the same keys his mother had touched years ago. Rehearsing with her had brought him so much joy. Now the reminder plagued him with such agony he didn't know how he'd play a single note ever again.

Grief. Sorrow. Guilt. Beth. He squeezed his eyes shut. Fuck. He needed to travel across oceans, not just the country, if he ever expected to extract himself from her life for good.

With his hand over his heart, Aidan walked to the patio doors leading to the backyard. Pulling back the drapes revealed an empty swimming pool and a manicured lawn—everything the same as before. Lightning struck again, followed by the roar of distant thunder, and then the sky opened up, unleashing the storm. Raindrops pelted against the glass like bullets fired from a machine gun.

"Back away from the window, mister. I'm warning you, I'm armed. So don't try any funny business!"

Aidan turned around slowly. Lightning flickered like camera flashes on the red carpet, illuminating his surroundings briefly. His father stood across the room, dressed in flannel bedclothes, holding a baseball bat poised to strike.

Now that Dr. Evans was no longer a grainy image on a

black and white newspaper clipping, Aidan identified his physical changes since their last encounter. His brown hair had grayed at his temples, and the lines in his forehead and around his eyes burrowed deeper, promoting the experience and wisdom befitting of a respected member of the medical profession. His hostile gaze and the scowl tightening his features disclosed the man behind the prominent title—the man Aidan knew all too well.

"Put your hands where I can see them." Dr. Evans waved the bat as if he was Babe Ruth. When Aidan was growing up, his father never played sports or even listened to them on the radio. In fact, he was surprised his father owned a bat in the first place.

Aidan took a step forward.

Dr. Evans drew back the bat. "Halt, I say!"

Lightning flashed again, igniting the living room with a fluorescent glow.

His father's eyes widened. The bat fell to the floor with a clatter. "Aidan? Good Lord, son. Is that you?"

A frown tugged at Aidan's lips. The man had some nerve to call him son. "Yeah, it's me."

Dr. Evans turned on a table lamp. "I thought you were an intruder!"

With his eyes downcast, Aidan muttered, "Aren't I?"

"I heard footsteps, creaking noises." Dr. Evans shook his head. "Darn it, son, you frightened me! If you wanted to come for a visit—"

"I didn't plan on coming here, Pop. Or hell, maybe I did."

Aidan raked his hands through his hair and returned to the piano. His fingers fell to the keys corresponding to the first notes of Beth's song.

"What was that tune you and your mother always used to play?" His father approached the instrument cautiously, confirming that blood ties were not strong enough to mend the bonds of broken trust. "It was not overly sprightly, but it had an uplifting chorus."

Aidan retracted his hands as if the keys had electrocuted him. "How would you know? When you weren't at work, you locked yourself in your home office. Ma and I barely saw you."

His father tossed a wistful look toward the backyard. "I may have spent a lot of time in my study, but I still used to listen to you two laugh and play every evening after dinner. That particular song always bought a smile to my face."

Aidan's eyes narrowed. There was a rare vulnerability in his father's gaze that he didn't quite know how to interpret. "It was a Tchaikovsky piece. Opus 39, No. 4. *Mamma*."

"You played beautifully, son, and at such a young age, too." The vulnerability vanished with the next strike of lightning, replaced by a more familiar expression of wariness and contempt. "Why are you here, Aidan? You're a long way from Hollywood or New York—wherever you're living these days."

"I'm here because . . ." Aidan screwed his eyes shut as misery, horror, and loneliness hit him with the determination of a boxer fighting for the championship title. Beth's screams during his attack on Mr. Mertz, her pleas for him to stay . . . Nathan and Matthew's despair, Connie and Olivia's tears . . .

Kazan, the closest person he had to a father, abandoned without an explanation. In one afternoon, he had destroyed his relationships with all the people who mattered most to him, and for some reason, gravitated to the man he couldn't care less about. Why, indeed.

Aidan opened his eyes and ground his teeth to conceal his quivering lips. "Why did you keep the piano?"

His father's eyebrows furrowed. "I bought it for your mother as a wedding present. Why wouldn't I keep it?"

Aidan shrugged. "You moved on pretty fast after her death, marrying Betty within the year. The only reason you didn't get rid of it then was because you knew I wouldn't allow it. I'm surprised it didn't end up in the junkyard five minutes after I left for New York. It's not like you were concerned with preserving her memory, so you wouldn't have kept it for sentimental reasons."

His father glared at him. "How do you know how I felt after she died?"

"You're right. I don't." Hatred escorted the words from Aidan's mouth. "You distanced yourself from me even more after her murder. You barely acknowledged me unless you were harping on me about something stupid. The only thing I knew for sure was you blamed me for what happened to her."

Dr. Evans rubbed the back of his neck. "Your mother died a long time ago. I don't see how all this is relevant anymore."

Aidan rolled his eyes. "Only you would think what happened to her is no longer important."

"I refuse to be interrogated in my own home." Dr. Evans

thrust his forefinger toward the hallway. "Go back to your new life and keep out of mine."

Aidan curled his hands into fists, fighting the urge to clock his father in the jaw. "No way. I'm done running."

Dr. Evans' features coiled with bewilderment. "Running from what?"

Aidan dragged his hands through his hair. "Damn it, Pop! You have no idea how messed up I've been all these years. You never bothered to talk to me, to listen to me. You never cared about me!"

"I kept the piano because I loved your mother very much—"

"This isn't about the goddamn piano!" Aidan threw his hands in the air.

Dr. Evans sighed. "Then what is it about?"

Aidan gestured to him wildly. "Don't you see?"

His father's eyes sharpened like daggers, spearing him with the truth.

"No, of course you don't. You never did, did you?" Aidan lifted a framed portrait of his father and Betty off the coffee table and pointed to their smiling faces behind the glass. "Who the fuck is this man, Pop? This carefree, happy man. Tell me, because I sure as hell never met him growing up."

His father's lips formed a tight line. "Are you intoxicated? Your hands are covered with lesions and contusions like you've been in a fight. And this crazy talk you're spewing? It makes me question your mental stability."

Aidan's anger unleashed, rivaling the raging storm outside. He smashed the framed photograph to the floor, shattering the glass. With wide eyes, his father stumbled backward, reaching for the bat on the floor.

"The fourteenth anniversary of her death was a month ago. Do you even miss her? Do you even care?" Broken glass crunched under Aidan's boots as he marched toward his father. "I think about her every day. Her loss has haunted me every goddamn second since she died."

"If you don't leave right now, I will call the police and have you arrested for trespassing." Dr. Evans grabbed the bat and raised it in the air.

Aidan eyed the weapon with calmness solidified by acceptance. He had no doubt his father would hit him. For his mother's sake, he wished it hadn't come to this.

"Graham? What's going on? I heard a crash." Betty entered the living room, clad in a pink housecoat, with curlers secured in her brown hair. When her eyes landed on their visitor, a smile sprung to her face. "Aidan, dear!" She rushed toward him. "How lovely it is you came home."

Home. If not for the graveness of the situation, Aidan would've laughed. This house was never his home, and the man standing before him was never his father.

Dr. Evans extended his free arm, preventing his wife from advancing further. "Betty, stay back. There's broken glass on the floor."

Betty looked at her husband and gasped. "Graham, what are you doing with the bat? This is your son!"

"Go back to bed." Dr. Evans trained his eyes on Aidan. Even without the weapon, his threat was clear.

Aidan sneered. "Yeah, Pop. You better send her away. You wouldn't want your perfect present life to conflict with your horrid past, right?"

Betty took another step forward.

Dr. Evans moved to the side, blocking her way. "Betty, do as I say."

She dropped her gaze and retreated into the hallway without further protest.

Lightning lit up the house like fireworks. In the wake of distant thunder, Dr. Evans hurled the bat across the room, knocking the lamp off the table and immersing the space in darkness. He stalked toward Aidan, a menacing shadow in red and blue flannel.

"You want to talk? Fine, we'll talk. Man to man."

Aidan corrected his posture. "It's about damn time."

"Now, I don't know where you got the ridiculous idea that I was never there for you." Dr. Evans shoved his finger at Aidan's chest. "I worked hard to provide you with a roof over your head and food on the table. You wanted for nothing."

"Materialistic stuff, sure. But I'm not talking about that, Pop. When my mother died, so did all the love in our house." Aidan smacked his hand away. "Your blame infected me to the point where I can't sustain a healthy relationship with anyone. It destroyed me, made me toxic to everyone around me."

Dr. Evans laughed, but it lacked humor. "You think you've had a tough time since your mother died? It's me who has suffered—"

"You didn't see what I did. You never heard her screams,

wrenched the knife from her chest, or held her while she bled!" Aidan winced as his voice cracked. Damn it. He couldn't break down now. With his jaw clamped shut, he released a fortifying breath. "I have fucking nightmares, Pop, and visions that attack me when I'm awake."

"Nightmares?" Dr. Evans scoffed. "That's what bothers you? Like some kid afraid of the dark or a monster hiding under the bed?"

Aidan curled his hands into fists but kept them at his sides. He shook too violently to connect a successful punch anyway. "You have no idea what true guilt feels like—what it does to your self-esteem, your soul."

Dr. Evans' face glowed red. A vein in his forehead bulged. "If anyone is a victim in this room, it's me."

Aidan gaped at him. "There's no way you've suffered half as much as I have!"

"You're wrong!"

"You're fucking delusional!"

"I was not at work the evening your mother was murdered!"

"Huh?" Aidan crept backward, like he'd stumbled upon a bloodthirsty predator and preferred not to be its next meal. "What do you mean? You had an overnight shift at the hospital."

The shake of his father's head was more excruciating than if the man had gone for his jugular. "I was with Betty. We'd been seeing each other for two years at that point."

"You—you *what*?" Aidan sucked in a strangled sob, introducing a load of air into his lungs that still couldn't relieve the sensation that he was drowning. His heart pounded, as if hoping an insurgence of blood and oxygen could eliminate the ache brought on by deceit and betrayal. And the room . . . oh, man . . . the room spun so fast he felt he was about to vomit.

Aidan staggered to the couch and wrapped his arms around his midsection, staring at the shards of glass on the carpet to try to settle his stomach, like a cruise ship passenger focusing on the horizon to ease seasickness. All this time he had blamed himself for his mother's murder, but his father had played an even bigger role. The drifter had targeted her because her husband was away and she was vulnerable. And it was all on account of an illicit affair.

Aidan launched across the room. His gait was unsteady, but his determination to confront his father was anything but. "You self-centered bastard! You cheated on my mother, the most honest, warmhearted person in the world. The woman who loved you more than you're worth. She put up with your bullshit job, which kept you away from us, and remained a dutiful wife without complaint. And this is how you repaid her? By abandoning her and leaving her open to an attack?"

Dr. Evans' nostrils flared. "You can play the part of a teenage gang member successfully, but it seems you've forgotten how to act like a man. This behavior of yours is an embarrassment."

"Is that why you never cried after she died?" Aidan choked back a sob. "Did you even care that she was gone? Or were you happy she was out of the picture for good so you could be with your mistress?"

Dr. Evans recoiled as though Aidan had clocked him. "I

loved your mother dearly."

"You're a liar and a cheat." Aidan raised his fist, blinking back his tears. "I thought I hated you before, but man, that's nothing compared to how I feel toward you right now."

Dr. Evans lifted his chin. "I have longed for punishment for over fourteen years. Go ahead, son. Hit me."

Aidan drew back his hand but didn't follow through on the punch. His hesitation didn't make any sense. This had to be why he was here, right? To inflict physical pain on his father as payback for the emotional anguish he had suffered since he was a boy?

Why, then, could he not take action?

"What are you waiting for?" His father's eyes darkened. "Hit me."

Thunder roared, fragmenting the tense silence. Aidan uncurled his fist. Violence had caused his mother's death. Violence had ended his relationship with Beth. No good would come of him beating his father to a bloody pulp.

"Pop, your punishment isn't going to be by my hand. I'm tired of throwing punches. I'm tired of beating myself up and hating who I am." He squeezed his eyes shut. "I'm just so fucking tired."

"Son." Dr. Evans placed a hand on his shoulder.

Aidan jerked away from him. "Don't ever call me that again. You don't deserve a son, and you certainly never deserved my mother." He motioned to the piano. "I'll be arranging for a moving company to collect that. You better not get in my way, or so help me." He headed for the front door.

"Wait, Aidan! Why don't you stay the night? Perhaps in the morning we can figure out a way to mend our relationship."

Aidan paused under the archway. "You don't care about fixing our relationship. All you want is an outlet for your guilt. Well, you know what? I refuse to be your scapegoat anymore. I've been a victim for far too long already. I'm going back to the only person in this world who ever truly cared for me, aside from my mother. I sure as hell might not be decent, but I'm gonna try my best to be for her from now on. No more fisticuffs, no more bloodshed. I'm focusing on love, not pain."

Dr. Evans took an imploring step toward him. "But I have prayed for redemption!"

Aidan hung his head, not out of intimidation, but exasperation. "You know something, Pop? I ran away from people I cared about because I thought I wasn't worthy of their love and friendship. Tonight, I've learned a valuable lesson. What I've done can be righted if I try hard enough, but the shit you've pulled? Hell, there ain't no redemption for that. You're gonna have to live with your sins for the rest of your life while hopefully I'll get another chance to start fresh."

Dr. Evans folded his arms over his chest. "Is it an apology you're after? Fine. I'm sorry."

Aidan shook his head. "That's not good enough."

"What is it you need from me, then?"

Aidan sighed. His father would never comprehend how much he had suffered since his mother's murder, no matter how hard he tried to explain. "We needed you the night she was attacked, in her hospital room in the days following, and I needed you when I cried myself to sleep every night for years after her death. It's too late, Pop. You failed us both."

"I did the best I could!" Dr. Evans stomped his foot. Now who was the one acting like a child? "If I had known what would happen to your mother, I never would've met up with Betty that evening."

"That evening? So you don't regret the affair, only seeing Betty that one fucking evening?" Aidan vibrated, as if every single molecule in his body had a personal vendetta against his father. "You're despicable. I never should've come here. It's a fucking waste of time trying to reason with you."

Aidan punched the wall on his departure from the room. His father and Betty. He couldn't wrap his head around it. Sure, he didn't think highly of his father, but he never would've pegged the man as an adulterer.

Had his mother?

Aidan collapsed against the wall in the front foyer. The hyperventilating resumed . . . the vertigo. He closed his eyes as tight as he could. Did his mother go to her grave knowing her husband had been unfaithful to her?

That goddamn bastard.

Aidan's rage resurged, poisoning his residual patience and decency to the point of extinction. His muscles tightened, his heart thumped, his temples throbbed. Just the thought of his father was enough to launch his blood pressure into an unhealthy zone. Was this the person he wanted to be for the rest of his life—angry, contemptuous, and on the verge of violence all the time?

Beth had always said he was a good man. He never agreed but had often hoped the potential was there. But how could he rid himself of years of self-hatred and resentment toward his father? After all, his father was responsible for ruining his life. It was his father's fault that he—

Aidan's eyes shot open. So that's why he was here tonight. It wasn't to blame his father to ease his own guilt like his father had done to him for years, or to complain about how much his father had destroyed his self-worth. It was for a far greater and more complex reason—something he had never considered before, something that would finally allow him to move forward.

Forgiveness.

Aidan didn't love his father and never would, but if he forgave the man, he could forgive himself for not being able to help his mother and come to terms with the fact that he wasn't as bad as he thought he was all these years.

With the surest steps since his arrival, Aidan returned to the living room. His father stood by the piano. The baseball bat rested at his feet.

"Pop?"

Dr. Evans startled. When his gaze landed on his son, a scowl overtook his lips. "What?"

"I forgive you."

He huffed. "*You* forgive *me*? Is this some kind of joke?"

"It's either revenge or forgiveness, and I'm done with negativity. After everything that happened to our family, I need to release my hostility to move on. I owe it to myself, my mother, and the girl I left behind." Conviction strengthened

Aidan's delivery, lending him the tone of a man far beyond his years. "I forgive you because if there's ever a chance of me starting over, I can't harbor any more pain, and your confession tonight has been the most painful of all."

Dr. Evans' expression morphed from surprised to furious. His lips peeled back, revealing clenched teeth. "How dare you act as if this is solely my fault. I didn't tell you about Betty to give you a crutch to deflect the blame from yourself. I'm not a monster!"

"Well, neither am I." Aidan squared his shoulders. It felt good to say that and truly mean it.

With his purpose fulfilled, he headed for the door again.

"You still could have done something, you coward!" Dr. Evans spewed his remarks from the living room. His menacing voice followed Aidan down the corridor. "You hear me? I'm not the only one responsible for her death!"

Aidan exited the house, muffling his father's shouting with the closing of the front door. The fog had lifted, revealing a full moon and a twinkling sky. The walk to his Porsche was completed with a grin on his face that rivaled the radiance of the stars. The grief and sorrow he still had to contend with, but finally he was free from the guilt that had imprisoned him since childhood.

After checking the gas gauge, Aidan secured his seatbelt and shot off down the street. The rain hit the windshield so hard even the fastest speed of his wiper blades couldn't clear it properly. Familiar with the car's handling, he eased his foot down on the gas pedal without worry. His father had called him a coward for not saving his mother, but his only cowardly act was abandoning Beth. He was thousands of miles from L.A. but vowed not to rest until she was in his arms again.

Although Aidan regretted leaving her, he didn't regret coming to Chicago. The knowledge and self-discovery he had gained on his trip were what had been missing in their relationship previously. Now he could love her the right way and set them on a healthier path. He just hoped it wasn't too late to earn her forgiveness.

Chapter Ten

Nathan Taggart's footsteps echoed along Hollywood Boulevard as though he walked on a vacant soundstage at Starlight Studios, where he'd been imprisoned for the last six years. On the outside, he seemed to have it all, but he was no more authentic than the fantasies played out in the motion pictures created by his employer. He was the studio's main "fixer", with the power to cover up scandal, obtain anything for anyone, and make dreams come true. Yet he was forced to compromise his own ideals, his own dreams, on account of bribery. The most devastating consequence was the loss of Olivia, whose love he accepted eagerly, selfishly, even though he didn't deserve her.

Nathan missed Olivia's laughter, her enthusiasm, her optimism. Foolishly, he believed that her goodness and faith in him that he, too, was good was enough to counteract the aspects of his life of which he was not proud. Instead, his deceit chipped away at their union and overrode his positive traits until all of his faults were revealed and she was faced with the truth about the man she thought she knew.

Nathan was convinced he would pay for his actions

eventually, but he'd always thought the cross would be his to bear alone. Unfortunately, not only did he destroy his relationship with Olivia, but he also ruined his friendships.

When Nathan found Beth trapped in Mr. Mertz's office, he was disgusted with himself. He had carried out deplorable orders for Mr. Mertz in the past, but nothing on that scale. Indecency toward women was something he would never tolerate. If he were aware, he never would've allowed it to happen. Somehow, he would've put a stop to it.

Ignorance was no excuse, however. He should have suspected that Mr. Mertz's depravity would extend to such horrible acts. Even though he was not directly involved in this aspect of his boss's business, his silence regarding other matters made him just as guilty.

Seven days had passed since everything fell apart. Nathan had yet to return to the Bel Air or Malibu houses he'd lived in since joining Starlight Studios. Instead, he checked into the Roosevelt Hotel—charging his stay to the studio—and reported for work every morning as usual. He was devastated to the point of numbness, which enabled him to avoid tipping off Mr. Mertz and his colleagues that something was wrong. Meanwhile, he secretly devised a plan to never return. He couldn't be a silent player for much longer.

Rumors circulated around the studio that an incident had occurred with Mr. Mertz, but details were scarce. Mr. Mertz kept a low profile and chose not to have Aidan and Matthew arrested. He valued his pride too much to reveal their attacks on him. He even paid off the security guards who showed up in the aftermath, and Charlie, who manned the front gate.

For the first time in years, a studio cover-up happened without Nathan's assistance. On behalf of Mr. Mertz, he had hushed various scandals involving many of the studio's top stars. Adultery, homosexuality, and alcohol and drug abuse were some of the common themes—anything that would damage an individual's career or the studio's reputation. But this he would have no part in.

Nathan wasn't sure if Ethel, Mr. Mertz's longtime secretary, knew what was going on behind her boss's office doors, but following the incident with Aidan, she had to be aware now. Since then, however, she had been stationed at her desk, carrying on with her job as though nothing vile had happened. Caroline also continued to play the role of dutiful secretary. What had they been bribed with? What lies had they been fed to get them to stay and keep quiet? Sure, Nathan's continued presence on the lot suggested that Mr. Mertz still had hooks in him, too, but at least he was trying to break free. If Ethel and Caroline were smart, they'd get out sooner rather than later.

The official word from the studio was that *Golden Gloves* was terminated permanently. Elia Kazan demanded a meeting with Mr. Mertz when the news broke, but he was ignored.

Nathan had heard that Beth returned to her hometown of Clarkson. He wouldn't blame her if she never came back to L.A. As for Olivia—well, he didn't know her location. His search into where she'd fled turned up nothing. Aidan's whereabouts were a mystery, too.

Aidan was obviously troubled long before he came to

Hollywood, but Nathan never investigated his past. For once, he refused to use the skills Mr. Mertz had taught him to pry into someone else's private life. Shamefully, that didn't stop him from exploiting Aidan's weaknesses to execute his revenge against Mr. Mertz.

When Nathan informed Aidan of what he'd witnessed between Beth and Mr. Mertz, he thought he did it because they were friends and Aidan needed to know the truth and defend his girl. But the relief he felt when Aidan went after his boss confirmed his real motive: Mr. Mertz would finally get what he deserved.

Nathan regretted that he didn't stand up for himself and the people he cared about. While Matthew and Aidan defended the women they loved, he let Olivia walk out of his life without a fight and lost everything. Mr. Mertz's hold on him was too strong to have done anything else at the time, but it had now come to the point where regardless of the consequences, he, too, had to take drastic action.

Near Hollywood Boulevard and Highland Avenue, Nathan stopped in front of a small movie theater in such need of refurbishing it looked abandoned. This weekend, the featured film was one of his favorites. But he'd known that when he started his walk tonight, hadn't he?

He stared at the marquee for a few minutes before he assembled the courage to approach the box office. "One for the nine o'clock showing, please."

The ticket agent grinned. "It's been quiet 'round here for a while. A young man like you interested in the classics gives me hope for the new generations of moviegoers. These days, everyone would rather go see the talkies with their big budgets and fancy Technicolor. I just don't get it." He shrugged. "Anyway, that'll be ten cents, mister."

Nathan paid and entered the building. In recent years, the only time he went to movie theaters was on official business. He was able to screen films at the studio whenever he liked, so there was never the need to see them the old fashioned way. He had grown detached from many things since he began working for Mr. Mertz. It felt good to reclaim some normalcy again.

Nathan sat in the back row and placed his fedora on the chair beside him. Only two other people were here—a couple holding hands and whispering in the dark.

A frown graced his lips. There was a time when the theater would've been packed with patrons. Yes, the great technological advancements over the last twenty-five years had churned out many incredible films, but where was the appreciation for the origins of motion pictures? Recognition of the people who pioneered the film industry and influenced the movies made today?

The low hum of the projector filtered in from the back room and the film's credits appeared onscreen. Jubilant theme music followed. With the commencement of the opening scene, a mix of pride and sorrow broke through Nathan's numbness.

A beautiful blond woman strolled down a crowded city street with impeccable poise, dressed in a stylish hat, blazer, and complementary skirt. The camera zoomed in on her smiling face, capturing her at the height of her popularity at Starlight

Studios, when she looked the way he always wanted to remember her, before her mental illness took hold and dried up the life within her vibrant blue eyes.

Nathan gripped the armrests and breathed deeply, keeping his eyes on the screen. No matter how painful it was, he couldn't leave. He needed a reminder of why he'd agreed to do Mr. Mertz's bidding in the first place; a reminder that amongst his many sins was a purpose that was honorable and pure.

Six years ago, on a crisp spring afternoon in New York City, was where it all started. He was a naïve young man then, just shy of his eighteenth birthday . . .

Nathan exited the elevator and stepped onto the ward. White walls, tilted flooring, and silence surrounded him. It seemed like he was the only one here. According to the wire he received this morning, his mother was admitted three days ago. No information was provided on the extent of her condition. He had no idea how they found him. For years, she'd only gone by her professional moniker.

Marion Taggart, known publicly as Marion Whitney, had worked at Starlight Studios for over twenty years. She was the most popular silent film actress until talking pictures arrived and her attempt to transition to sound failed. She continued to make movies but never reclaimed her status. When her star faded completely, Nathan only heard from her through letters. He received the last one six months ago.

Marion had lived in Los Angeles during her time with the studio but insisted it was not the proper place to raise a child, so she sent Nathan to live with his father on the family ranch in Salinas, California while she worked in Hollywood.

For years, Nathan cut out pictures and articles from entertainment magazines to gather information on his mother, and whenever her films played at the local theater, he'd steal a nickel from his father's change jar in the kitchen and ride his bicycle into town to watch her.

Nathan's fondest memories were his mother's visits to Salinas during his summer and winter breaks from school. She wore extravagant clothes and her hair and makeup were always flawless, like she'd stepped off a film set, not a country bound train. His bleak life on the ranch always brightened in her presence. She never stayed long, though, explaining that she needed to return to Hollywood to make money so she could give him everything he wanted.

All he wanted was her.

His father, Lloyd Taggart, was a proud rancher who loved horses almost as much as he loved the bottle. In the evenings, Nathan often found him passed out in his favorite wicker chair on the front porch, surrounded by the acres of property paid for by his wife's monthly checks.

In their household, it was assumed Nathan would help his father run the ranch full time after high school. But Nathan wasn't interested in that life. He planned to tell his father in his senior year but never got the chance. Lloyd was killed when one of his stallions kicked him in the head, rendering him unconscious, and he choked on his own liquor-saturated vomit. Nathan discovered his bloody body the next morning.

Nathan never returned to high school after that. Nor did he become a full time rancher.

Following his father's death, Nathan couldn't reach his mother—calls to her West Hollywood, Malibu, and New York homes yielded no response—so the bank seized the property. He didn't particularly want to keep the ranch, but it was still tragic to lose it under such circumstances.

When his mother finally contacted him, from a foreign address in Manhattan she referred to as her new main residence, he wrote her back with news of her husband's death as well as the foreclosure. He never received a reply.

Six months later, Nathan relocated to New York with barely a nickel to his name. Fast-paced urban life was very different from what he was used to. The streets were crowded, the housing options he could afford were dismal at best, and the air was thicker, infused with a chemical smell that burned his nostrils. Nevertheless, the energy of the city and the seemingly endless professional opportunities inspired him. There were many esteemed national newspapers based out of New York. He hoped to get a job at one of them and work his way up the ranks to become a columnist eventually.

Living in New York also meant he was closer to his mother. Nathan had visited the address accompanying her last correspondence, but the doorman said she'd moved out years ago, which meant she wasn't living there when she sent him the letter. Questions clouded Nathan's mind. Today, he wanted answers.

"May I help you, sir?"

Nathan stopped in front of a workstation occupied by a nurse. "Hello, my name is Nathan Taggart. I'm here to visit my mother, Marion Taggart."

"There's no one here by that—" The appearance of her smile eroded the tension in her face. She looked young, perhaps only a few years older than him, but the clinical coolness in her eyes suggested she'd experienced far more than he ever would by that age. "Oh, you mean Marion Whitney. I apologize. It's easy to forget that Taggart is her real surname, given, well, who she was."

Was.

Nathan cleared his throat. "I received a telegram requesting my presence here immediately." He withdrew the cable from his pocket and held it up. "I'm not sure who sent it. It's unsigned. I just know it came from this institution."

"Ah, yes." The nurse pursed her lips. "Mr. Taggart, why don't you sit on one of the chairs behind you and I will let Doctor Littman know you're here. He is the head psychiatric practitioner at Bellevue."

Nathan sat down and placed his fedora in his lap. He rifled through a back issue of National Geographic Magazine until the doctor's arrival.

"Hello, Mr. Taggart." The physician extended his hand. "I'm Doctor Peter Littman."

Dressed in a tweed suit jacket and slacks, the man didn't look like a physician, but the confident way he spoke and carried himself held a scholarly significance that somehow confirmed he couldn't be anything else.

Nathan stood to shake the doctor's hand. "Good morning."

"Please accompany me to my office and I will explain the reason for the telegram. It's best if we speak in private."

Nathan picked up his hat and followed the physician. At the end of the hallway, Dr. Littman unlocked a door decorated with his nameplate, and they entered a wood paneled room that smelled of smoke and freshly brewed coffee. Nathan sat in the seat offered to him.

Dr. Littman claimed the chair on the other side of the desk and lit a cigarette. "Son, there is no easy way for me to say this, so please excuse my bluntness. Your mother was found walking the streets, speaking incoherently, and lashing out physically at those around her. Fortunately, a concerned citizen was able to subdue her and bring her here. She had her driver's license and Screen Actors Guild membership card in her pocket, which is how we identified her and consolidated her two surnames, Taggart and Whitney. I conducted an assessment upon her admission and concluded that she's had a complete psychotic break and needs continuous observation. Presently, she is under self-harm monitoring."

Shock lanced through Nathan, carving up his hope that he had been called to the hospital for something not too serious.

"Self-harm?" His lips trembled, but he refused to cry in front of the physician.

Smoke billowed from Dr. Littman's nose with his deep, tight-lipped exhale. "I'll cut right to the chase, Mr. Taggart. Your mother was once a rich and famous actress, but I'm afraid her funds have run out."

Nathan gaped at him. "That's impossible. She owns properties in Los Angeles and—"

"All of her homes have been foreclosed. And since this is a private hospital and her condition is so unique—in the general health care sense, that is—insurance does not cover her stay."

Unique . . . as in taboo . . . as in no insurance company would support a mentally ill person since it was not considered a real affliction.

Nathan frowned. "What does this mean?"

Dr. Littman leaned forward, his cigarette grasped between two fingers. "If you cannot come up with the money for her treatment, we will have to release her. And if that happens, well, based on my professional medical opinion, the results will be catastrophic. You see, her mental illness has already progressed to the later stages. Proper psychiatric interventions are crucial to her survival."

"So this came on suddenly?"

The physician took a long drag on his cigarette. "No, there must have been warning signs. Do you remember frequent crying bouts? Emotional withdrawal?"

"No. I . . . I haven't seen her a while. Although . . ." Nathan's gaze landed on a brass locomotive paperweight on the desk. Four Christmases ago, when his mother came home for the holidays, she was jittery, not sleeping, and seemed despondent.

He placed his head in his hands. How had it come to this?

"So if I don't come up with the money for her stay, she will be put out on the street." Nathan raised his head in *preparation for the physician's reply.*

Dr. Littman nodded. "I'm sorry."

Shame brought color to Nathan's cheeks. "I don't have any money."

"That's what I figured." Dr. Littman sighed. "You're just a boy, but by law we had to try."

Nathan leapt from his chair, clutching his fedora. "I'm not a boy. I'm a man. I turn eighteen next week. As for the money, I'll get it. I'll beg, steal. I don't care. I'll do whatever it takes. Just tell me how much I'm looking at here."

Dr. Littman shook his head. "We're talking two, perhaps three thousand dollars, depending on her course of treatment. I won't know the full extent of her needs until she's been here at least another month under my observation."

The weight of the physician's disclosure forced Nathan to sit back down. Two to three thousand dollars? He couldn't come up with that.

"And that's per year." Dr. Littman stubbed out his cigarette, though he'd smoked only half of it. "We kept her these last few days free of charge solely because we needed time to contact her next of kin. I'm sorry about your father, Mr. Taggart."

Nathan slumped in his chair. Tears obscured his vision, despite his efforts. If the doctor was correct about his mother's condition, he now had his answer as to why her contact with him had become so sporadic and finally nonexistent.

"May I see her?"

"She received her last dose of medication two hours ago, so

it should be safe."

Nathan's eyebrows furrowed. "You're mistaken, sir. My mother would never hurt me."

Dr. Littman folded his hands on the desktop. "Mr. Taggart, she is not the woman you once knew."

Nathan set his jaw. "I need to see her."

Dr. Littman's gaze traveled all over Nathan's face, as if he were assessing maturity, readiness. Psychiatric stability, most likely. It was his specialty, after all. Finally, he stood. "Come with me."

Nathan exited the office with the physician. In a quiet voice, Dr. Littman conversed with the nurse Nathan had spoken to earlier. Lucille was her name. She would escort him to his mother.

Dr. Littman patted Nathan's back, bidding him a somber farewell. Nathan refused to make it a permanent one.

"How long does she have before you let her go?"

Dr. Littman's expression softened enough to convey pity. It made Nathan even more determined to help his mother. "If you don't have the funds to cover at least six months of her stay in advance by tomorrow, she will be discharged before rounds on Monday morning."

Nathan nodded. "I will see you again soon, Dr. Littman."

He provided the physician with a firm handshake and followed the nurse.

Lucille unlocked a door at the end of the corridor, which led to another hallway, and then another. All of them were decorated the same—white walls, tiled floors. All of them were silent. The anticipation, the fear, was enough to drive Nathan toward madness.

"It's so nice that Marion has another visitor. I'm sure she'll be glad to see you."

Nathan peered at the nurse curiously. "Another visitor?"

Lucille closed and secured the door from which they had just emerged. "Why, yes. An older gentleman has come in to see her every day since she was admitted. He says he's known her for a long time. He's here now, so you can say hello."

Nathan hung his head. He didn't know enough about his mother's personal life to recognize the man the nurse described. How pitiful.

A sign that read Authorized Personnel Only guarded the next door Lucille unlocked. On the other side, a security officer manned a small desk.

"You'll have to leave all of your personal possessions here, Mr. Taggart." Lucille shared her instruction casually. She'd obviously said the same thing many times previously. "Empty your pockets and please remove your tie. Your shoes do not have laces, so you can leave them be."

Nathan left the items with the security guard and followed Lucille down the corridor. Muffled screams radiated from the locked rooms they passed. There were no windows in this hallway, just steel doors, a concrete floor, and the same white walls. The family ranch came to Nathan's mind. Perhaps his mother would fare better in the countryside. Perhaps taking her out of here would be the cure she needed.

"This is the gentleman I was talking about." Lucille's

bright voice pulled Nathan from his thoughts. "Mister . . . I'm sorry, sir. I didn't catch your name."

Nathan locked eyes with a heavy-set man with thinning gray hair and a beady gaze. A shudder tore through him. He glanced at his surroundings. There had to be a draft coming from somewhere. Poor insulation, maybe.

"I'm an old friend of Marion's," was the man's reply.

Although he looked familiar, Nathan couldn't place him. "Hello, sir."

"Mr. Taggart, let's see your mother, shall we?" Lucille gestured to the steel door across from them.

The man nodded, as though providing Nathan permission. "I'll wait here. After you've concluded your visit, we'll speak further."

The nurse disengaged the lock and opened the door. "Marion, you have another visitor!"

Grasping his fedora, Nathan entered the room after Lucille. The door slammed shut behind them, trapping them in a concrete, windowless space with only one buzzing, flickering light bulb to guide them.

"Mama." Nathan's eyes widened. He couldn't take another step. His mother rested on her back on a rickety-looking bed, dressed in a hospital garment that looked many sizes too big for her frail form.

He swallowed hard and studied her from his spot by the door. She stared at the ceiling. Blank. Unseeing. Her usual blond hair had grown out several inches, revealing gray roots that matched her complexion. But the worst part? The buckled leather restraints shackling her wrists and ankles to the bedframe.

"What have they done to you?" he whispered.

Lucille brushed his mother's matted hair back from her forehead. "You look very pretty today, Marion."

His mother responded to nothing. Not to Lucille's voice, not to her touch.

"Why don't you come over and say hello, Mr. Taggart?" The nurse addressed him in a voice suitable when speaking to a toddler, but he was too stunned to be offended.

Nathan willed his feet to move. His mother needed to see a familiar face, hear a familiar voice. That was the problem.

A rank odor assaulted his lungs and churned his stomach as he grew near. He refrained from pinching his nostrils.

Dear God. When was the last time his mother had bathed?

Up close, her appearance was even more startling. Her eyebrows were not drawn in. Deep wrinkles creased her face, making her look older than her true age. Her pupils were dilated. She still hadn't blinked since his arrival.

"Mother." He cleared his throat in a bid to eliminate the hoarseness in his voice. "It's Nathan, your son."

No response.

Lucille smiled down at her. "You were giving us some trouble earlier, but you're relaxed now that you've had your medication. Aren't you, Marion?"

Nathan shifted his gaze away from his mother's face. He sucked in a breath. Her arms were bruised over prominent veins. The hospital was administering her medication by injection. What medication? And how frequently? Given her current state, he was afraid to ask.

"Is she like this all the time?"

Lucille linked her hands in front of her. "Considering the degree of difficulty she presents when she's completely lucid, we find it best to keep her sedated. Comfortable, I mean."

His mother blinked.

Hope sprung to Nathan's heart. It was brief, like the flickering light above the bed, but something was better than nothing.

"Mother? It's Nathan. Your son." He bent over her. "I'm here."

She blinked again.

Nathan placed his hand to her cheek and almost withdrew it instantly. She felt ice-cold. A tear rolled down his face. "I'm going to take care of you. I promise."

Her lips parted.

"Are you trying to say something, Marion?" Lucille asked her question loudly, as though his mother was hearing impaired.

Nathan took his mother's hand. "Mama? What is it? Talk to me, please."

His mother's eyes, no longer the ocean blue color from his childhood, fixated on his. The scream that blasted from her throat launched Nathan across the room. Convulsions racked her body, her hands and feet confined by the restraints.

Nathan's fedora fell to the floor as he smashed his palms against his ears, trying to block out her cries. He didn't realize he was still retreating until he collided with the far wall. Lucille called for assistance while his mother wailed and flapped on the bed as if possessed by a devilish creature.

Two nurses burst into the room. One held a needle and a brown vile. Nathan watched in horror as they yanked up his mother's gown, turned her on her side as much as the restraints would allow, and injected her right buttock with a clear liquid. The nurses remained calm throughout the process. Just another day at the office, wasn't it?

His mother's convulsions grew more sporadic, less intense, until she was merely twitching. Her screams calmed to whimpers. Then, finally, silence overtook the room and she stilled.

Nathan lowered his hands from his ears. Trembling, his heart hammering against his ribcage, he could only stare, though his vision was blurred. He touched his cheeks. They were wet from tears. He wiped his face quickly.

"I'm sorry you had to see that, Mr. Taggart," Lucille said gently. "But now you understand the severity of the situation."

Nathan gulped. He definitely did. While he hated to see his mother tranquilized, the alternative was much worse. He'd been foolish to think a country escape would save her. No, that would be up to Dr. Littman and the rest of the staff at Bellevue. But most importantly, himself.

Nathan grabbed his fedora off the floor and walked to the door. "Let me out."

As promised, his mother's "old friend" waited for him in the hallway. The man's expression was apathetic. How any friend of his mother's could not be deeply affected by her condition was a mystery to him.

"You two may speak privately." Lucille departed with the other nurses, leaving Nathan and the man at one end of the hallway and the security guard at the other.

"That was difficult for you, wasn't it?" It was more of a statement than a question. The condescension that sharpened the man's gaze compelled Nathan to answer anyway.

"I'm fine, sir. It's her I'm concerned about."

The man nodded. In approval? Or maybe understanding. It was hard to tell. "You're a strong boy."

Nathan straightened his posture to match the man's calm and confident exterior. "I am not a boy."

"Ah, yes. Your eighteenth birthday is on Wednesday."

Nathan froze. "How do you know that? Who are you?"

"My name is Luther Jensen Mertz."

Nathan's jaw dropped. "Mertz. As in the founder of Starlight Studios?"

Mr. Mertz's eyes narrowed, as if he was insulted that Nathan would think he was anyone else but the owner of the largest movie studio in the world. "That's correct."

"I've seen photographs of you before. I just couldn't place you until now."

Mr. Mertz adjusted his tie. "Of course you have. I am a prominent and influential man."

Nathan dipped his gaze. Though he stood a few inches taller than Mr. Mertz, he had never felt so small and inconsequential than he did in that moment.

Mr. Mertz smirked. He seemed to feed off Nathan's discomfort. "I was notified that the wire I had Dr. Littman send you was delivered this morning, so I came to Bellevue to await your arrival."

"You sent the wire?" Nathan's eyebrows furrowed. "How did you know where to find me? How did you know my mother was even here?"

"Because I was the one who had her admitted."

Nathan shook his head. He couldn't have heard the man properly. "Excuse me?"

"I had a cohort of mine follow her. She'd been living in various shelters and wandering the streets during the day. When I was told how greatly her condition had deteriorated, I sent him to collect her. Marion was a dear employee for many years, and Bellevue is an excellent hospital, better than the facilities out west. Her mental illness requires top-notch intervention. Thus, here we are. As for how I found you, I have many resources at my disposal. It wasn't challenging."

"While I'm grateful for your concern, sir, my mother cannot afford her treatment."

"Yes, I know. Bad investments destroyed her fortune."

Nathan recoiled. "Then why did you put her in here?"

Mr. Mertz's smirk widened into a haughty grin. "I've heard that you're a bright boy, a hard worker. I've also heard that you're trying to make a name for yourself in the newspaper industry."

"How did you—?"

"You will learn quickly not to question me, boy." Mr.

Mertz's eyes dimmed. "The bottom line is this—I will pay for all of your mother's hospital expenses."

Nathan clutched his fedora to his chest. "Thank you, sir."

Mr. Mertz held up his hand. "But I need something from you in return."

"Anything."

"I want you to work for me in Los Angeles."

Nathan's joy transformed to wariness. "Why? I know nothing about the entertainment business."

"I need someone I can trust, someone to do whatever I say, a young lad I can meld into the perfect right-hand man. There will be jobs I request of you that you wouldn't concede to under ordinary circumstances. Depending on me to pay for your mother's medical bills gives you the motivation to keep your mouth shut and obey me without question."

Nathan swallowed hard. "What kind of jobs?"

Mr. Mertz's glare intensified. "Does it matter? Your mother needs help, and I am the only person she knows in a position to do something about it. Plus, I can ensure her illness remains a secret. You wouldn't want her condition to be leaked to the press, would you? Her good name will be scorned publicly and permanently. Everything she worked for professionally will be destroyed."

Nathan blanched. Blackmail. This was blackmail through and through.

"Your present interests may lie in journalism, Mr. Taggart, but I think you'll find the motion picture industry much more fascinating, especially since you'll start at the top as my personal executive assistant, instead of slaving away for years without a guarantee of ever earning a prominent title, as would be the case with the newspaper business.

"No one will ever know that your job is related to your mother. I won't reveal our arrangement to anyone, and nor will you. There are conditions to my offer, of course. I will teach you everything you need to know in order to fulfill your duties to my studio and to me. You will be respected by industry professionals, connected to everyone who's anyone in town, and you will achieve all the acclaim you desire. I will provide you with a house, a car, living expenses, and travel expenses, anything else you need. However, you will not earn a salary, as you will be indebted to me. Understand?"

Nathan searched Mr. Mertz's face for any signs of sympathy, remorse. "So you want someone to work for you who will remain discreet and ask no questions. And you would actually let my mother be put out on the street if I declined."

Mr. Mertz glanced at the door guarding her room. He gritted his teeth. A muscle in his jaw twitched. "Yes. Now give me an answer or I leave immediately and you'll never hear from me again."

Nathan exhaled a shaky breath. If he agreed to Mr. Mertz's proposition, he would live on the other side of the country, so he couldn't visit his mother often. Also, he'd be working in the industry she'd tried to shield him from his entire life. On the other hand, if he refused, she wouldn't receive the care and treatment she so desperately needed. And it would be selfish to request a transfer to a Los Angeles facility if Bellevue *hospital was one of the best mental health institutions in the country.*

He stuck out his hand. "You have a deal."

Mr. Mertz's lips curled into a smile that seemed more sinister than celebratory. He made no effort to accept the handshake. "Go home and pack your belongings. A studio car will pick you up from that abysmal apartment of yours at seven thirty to take you to the airport. Your flight is booked for nine o'clock tonight."

Nathan lowered his hand. "My flight is booked already? But how did you know—?"

"Enough!" Mr. Mertz's scowled. "You are not allowed to question me from now on, boy."

Nathan bowed his head. His mother . . . he was doing this for his mother. "Yes, sir."

Nathan had only seen his mother a few times since that visit six years ago, most recently in October when she had one of her worst psychotic episodes to date. For months, he thought his mother's condition might have improved, but since she was so strongly sedated, no one could tell. To test his theory, he requested that the hospital decrease the dose of her medications. Two days later, she grabbed a metal fork during dinner and drove it into her arm. Nathan flew to New York City as soon as he received the news, lying to Olivia and his friends about the purpose for his trip.

Dr. Littman continued to press for a lobotomy. However, Nathan had conducted his own research and found that the procedure often did more harm than good. Despite his mother's horrifying incident, he stuck to his decision, because doing the right thing was important to him. In so many aspects of his life—except loving Olivia—he had done a lot of wrong.

Onscreen, his mother danced with her leading man at a lavish party, smiling and laughing, so bright and lively. The film ended with a close-up and a fadeout. As the score swelled to a triumphant conclusion, Nathan blinked back tears.

The houselights came on and the couple walked up the aisle.

"Wasn't Marion Whitney the greatest?" the young man said.

His female companion beamed. "She sure was. I wish she was still acting today."

"Hey, mister." The young man directed his attention at Nathan. "Don't you think Marion Whitney is one of the most talented actresses in movie history?"

For the first time in a long time, a genuine smile spread across Nathan's face. "Yes, she most certainly is."

After the couple left, Nathan stared at the blank screen. His mother had loved acting. She belonged in motion pictures and shone in every role. At least he'd managed to preserve her legacy. However, he still had one last job to do—one he could no longer put off.

Within an hour, Nathan stood at the front gates guarding the home of Luther Mertz. He had never been there before— never been invited in the entire time he'd worked for the man— but he rang the buzzer without hesitation.

"Mertz residence," came the response from the intercom.

"This is Nathan Taggart. I want to speak to Luther immediately."

"I'm sorry, but it's late and—" There was a pause. "One moment, Mr. Taggart."

The gates opened. Nathan approached the house. Stonework and gothic sculptures lent the property a dark ambiance so out of place amongst the palm trees and colorful gardens of the surrounding area. He was shocked it had been built in the neighborhood in the first place.

No wonder he hated the homes Mr. Mertz had bought him. No wonder he never felt comfortable there. The styles were too similar to his boss's.

Nathan climbed the front stairs two at a time. The door opened. His steps faltered.

Mr. Mertz appeared in the entryway, dressed in a dark red silk robe over navy silk pajamas. Beneath the faded bruises and cuts on his face, he scowled. "What are you doing here?"

Nathan pushed past him and entered the house. "Is your wife home?"

"Answer me, boy. Why are you here?"

Nathan pointed at Mr. Mertz. "No, you answer me. Is your wife home?"

"No, she's not. She's gone to Palm Springs for the weekend with her sister." Mr. Mertz slammed the front door shut. "Now explain why you're at my home so late at night, without an invitation. And what does your visit have to do with my wife?"

Nathan looked around and broke into a sweat. While the

style of the house's exterior was merely familiar to his own, the interior décor was practically an exact replica—a carpeted grand staircase leading to a long corridor overlooking the entrance hall, marble floors, dark red walls, bleak frescos. Mr. Mertz's stamp was on every aspect of his life.

"I don't want your wife to hear what I have to say, that's why. She's much too decent to know the truth and still be married to you. I'm not going to be the one to reveal to her how dreadful you really are. Not tonight, at least."

Mr. Mertz yawned and shuffled to the staircase. "Go home, Nathan. Whatever you have to tell me can wait until Monday."

Nathan exhaled an unsteady breath. "Don't walk away from me. You'll want to hear what I have to say right now."

Mr. Mertz halted. "And what's that?"

"You need to step down from your position at Starlight Studios."

Mr. Mertz laughed. "You're insane. I built the studio from the ground up. Why would I ever leave?"

"Because I've written about your sordid affairs. The final draft is complete. If you don't retire, I'll send it to every major newspaper in town, leveraging all of my connections. They may have agreed to hush up studio scandals in the past, but I doubt they'd ignore a story about a highly respected, married studio mogul sexually preying on young, innocent, up-and-coming actresses."

Mr. Mertz pegged him with a glare. "How dare you? After all I've done for you. I involved you in the financial workings of my studio, in decisions regarding employee contracts, film deals, and other professional negotiations. I also gave a job to that wardrobe girl you like so much. Sure, her portfolio was impressive, but so are many other portfolios. I never would've hired her if not for your encouragement."

An icy spike drove up Nathan's spine, supporting a defensive stance. "You will not mention Olivia again. Do you understand?"

Mr. Mertz rolled his eyes. "The girl is trivial in this matter. Without me, you wouldn't be the success you are today. You owe me your gratitude and your loyalty."

Nathan's eyes narrowed. "I owe you nothing. You made me handle all of your dirty work. That's not success. That's the lowliest position of all."

"Someone had to do it, and I chose to put my trust in you. Now look how you've repaid me." Mr. Mertz shook his head. "I have so much dirt on you and the jobs you've carried out for me, I could bury you. Make no mistake. If I'm going down, I'm taking you with me."

Nathan lifted his chin. It was time to call Mr. Mertz's bluff. "If the press receive my letter, your good name will be scorned. Everything you worked for will be destroyed. Your ego is too large to allow it to get that far."

Mr. Mertz laughed again, but this time it sounded hollow. "You're forgetting an important detail. If you follow through on this threat, no matter the outcome, I'll stop financing your mother's care."

"Good. I don't want you associated with her in any capacity."

Mr. Mertz scoffed. "Her expenses have skyrocketed in the last six years—far higher than you realize. You'll never be able to pay for everything on your own."

"I've built two kinds of reputations at your studio, Luther." Nathan ticked off the list on his fingers. "One—a stern right-hand man with the power to make the worst scandals disappear. And two, an honest, loyal, hardworking businessman who held down a prominent executive position at one of the largest companies in the world. I'll be more than able to find a job elsewhere and fund her medical bills. It might take time, but I'll do it. In the end, we'll be better off without your support."

Mr. Mertz's lips pressed into a hard line. "You can't keep me away from Marion."

Nathan sneered. "Why do you care?"

Mr. Mertz squared his shoulders. "Because I love her."

Nathan stumbled backward. His fedora fell to the floor as he grabbed at his hair. His mother and Mr. Mertz? Impossible.

"Did you prey on my mother like you did with Elizabeth Sutton?"

"Never." Mr. Mertz tightened the belt on his robe. "She loves me, too. Or I should say she *did* love me, before her disease advanced and she forgot who I was. But know this—my love for her will never die, regardless of her condition."

Revulsion swerved through Nathan's veins. He locked his knees so he wouldn't collapse and fastened his eyes on Mr. Mertz. He had to assess the man's expression as well as hear him. Only then could he tell fact from fiction.

"You're lying. No one could ever love you."

Mr. Mertz's gaze glowed with conviction. "It's the truth. We were together for almost ten years."

Nathan paced the foyer, but no amount of exercise could relieve the stress brought on by Mr. Mertz's revelation. "Is that the real reason my mother stayed in Hollywood and kept my father and me in Salinas—because of you?"

"Goodness, no." Mr. Mertz waved him off. "She kept you in Salinas because she loved you and wanted better for you than the Hollywood way of life."

Nathan stopped pacing. "How do you know that?"

"Dear boy, she talked about you all the time! When I told her I would leave my wife and weather any scandal to prove my commitment, she refused to divorce your father solely on account of you."

Nathan walked the room again—back and forth, back and forth—trying to make sense of everything. He had so many questions—questions he was afraid to ask. But he knew he'd regret it if he didn't. "What about my father? Did she love him?"

Disapproval darkened Mr. Mertz's features, as if it infuriated him to associate Nathan's mother with another man. "Your father was a difficult person to get along with. You must understand, they married very young. When Marion was offered a studio contract, your father forbid her from becoming an actress. He demanded she remain up north and be a housewife, confined to the ranch. But that was not the life she wanted for herself. She went against his wishes and signed anyway. Your father lasted only a few months in Los Angeles before he returned to Salinas without her.

"When you were born, Marion was adamant that you not be raised in Hollywood. She enjoyed acting but felt L.A. was not the proper environment to raise a family. That's how you came to live on the ranch with your father. As she became more and more popular and her salary increased, your father had a hard time handling it all. He was no longer the breadwinner. For any man, that's a source of humiliation. When he grew more attached to his whiskey than his family, however, he no longer cared. From what Marion told me, your father loved her very much—but the girl she was at sixteen, not the woman she had become."

"You mean the woman you made her become in order to fit in at your studio and fall for your tricks." Nathan's hands curled into fists. "You separated my parents."

Mr. Mertz smirked. "Nonsense. Before your mother and I began our affair, I wanted you and your father move to Hollywood and did all I could to encourage it. After all, women her age were expected to be married and have a happy home. But your father couldn't be persuaded.

"In order to erase suspicions, I planted stories in the papers that he was a successful oilman who had business ties in the north, which kept him away from his wife. Where Marion drew the line was with you. She refused to have you photographed. She made every effort to keep you out of the spotlight. She hated being separated from you but strongly believed it was for your own good. Her dressing rooms were always decorated with your photographs, you know. You were the love of her life."

Mr. Mertz's eyes flickered with tenderness, but his steely

gaze remained in place. Nathan perused his features, studied them. It was a mask—all along it had been a mask—concealing the truth: love for his mother.

"Marion began distancing herself from me after I told her I would divorce my wife. Our meetings became fewer and farther between, even though she said she still loved me. Then, one day, she abruptly ended our relationship. I was distraught, Nathan. My world crumbled."

Nathan sat on the staircase and placed his head in his hands. Numb. He was numb to it all. "You love her, yet you blackmailed her only son?"

Heavy footsteps headed in his direction. "Over the years, Marion changed. She was often depressed and suffered from violent mood swings. Concerned, I offered to set her up with the best doctor in the country, but she refused to acknowledge her condition. In the months following your father's accident, she became extremely ill and I eventually had her admitted to Bellevue. It was the most upsetting time of my life. Marion was physically present, but mentally I'd lost her forever. You have no idea what that did to me."

Mr. Mertz's conceit drew Nathan from his detachment. He raised his head. "You're speaking as if she's dead."

"She might as well be!" Mr. Mertz charged over to the staircase. "You've seen her. What kind of life is that? All I can do is pay her medical bills and make her existence as painless for her as possible. Meanwhile, I suffer daily."

Nathan bristled. "It's always about you, isn't it? Even someone else's misfortune."

"I was looking out for you as well. I didn't want you to see your mother out on the street." Mr. Mertz motioned to him. "My wife is unable to bear children. Don't you see? You should've been mine. *My* son."

Nathan leapt to his feet. Mr. Mertz crept backward, exposing alarm beneath his confident façade for the first time. "You disgust me. You wanted to reclaim the part of my mother that was lost to her illness and at the same time get me to do your immoral bidding. That's not love. That's not honoring her."

"I was in a bind, Nathan! The sins of my employees extend beyond my control. I need to keep indiscretions out of the papers and uphold a decent image for my studio. Simultaneously, I struggled with the cognitive loss of your mother and wanted to hang on to whatever part of her I could. By convincing you to work for me, I got both of my wishes. And I've treated you well, despite what you might think. I've even grown to love you."

Nathan balked. "I was never your son and I never will be. As for loving me, you don't know how to love. It only serves to prove how delusional you are if you think you do."

"I would do anything for Marion. Anything." The mask slipped away. Mr. Mertz's eyes were wide, pleading.

Anything.

Nathan blanched. "My God. You would've paid for my mother's medical bills whether I agreed to work for you or not."

Mr. Mertz didn't hesitate. "Yes."

Nathan choked back his shock. The past six years—all of his mistakes, his moral compromises—had been for nothing.

"When I heard about your mother's poor investments, I tried to give her money, but she never accepted my help. Only when her illness progressed was I was finally able to support her. Hiring you was merely a bonus."

Mr. Mertz's confession stoked Nathan's anger, yet he was determined to stick to his original plan. Even after Aidan and Matthew's attack, Mr. Mertz was still the powerful studio mogul with the influence to continue as he always had been without consequence. If Nathan had any chance of putting a stop to everything, it wouldn't come from spilling more blood or adding cuts and bruises to his appearance. It would come from applying the tactics Mr. Mertz taught him over the years: manipulation and assertion of control.

"I didn't do anything untoward with your mother. I want you to know that. Our desire for each other was mutual." Mr. Mertz's gaze softened, displaying a vulnerability Nathan had no choice but to believe. The man was many things. An actor wasn't one of them. "I began seeking company from actresses after Marion was institutionalized, in an effort to fill the emotional void she'd left behind. For all of my attempts, however, I realize she is irreplaceable. So from now on, I'll stop. You have my word."

Nathan recoiled. "How dare you place the blame on my mother to try to justify your actions. This has nothing to do with her. And your word means nothing. For all I know, you were cheating on my mother back then, just like you cheated on your wife."

With a vicious curse, Mr. Mertz lunged at him. Pain

hijacked Nathan's skull as the back of his head collided with the floor. Mr. Mertz came down on top of him, their faces so close their noses touched.

"Don't you ever—" Mr. Mertz gasped for breath, expelling strained wheezes. "Don't you ever question my love for your mother again." With hacking coughs, he rolled off Nathan and staggered to his feet.

Nathan stayed on the floor, staring at the glistening chandelier above him. The house was empty—filled with many beautiful and expensive things, yet completely empty. Calmness enveloped him. Despite his current position, he had the upper hand.

"Loving her doesn't make what you did right. It all needs to stop now, Luther, and the only way I can assure that happens is if you announce your retirement."

Mr. Mertz drew himself up to full height. Sweat glistened on his brow. His breathing remained labored. "Are you vying for my job? Is that what this is all about?"

Nathan stood and brushed off his suit jacket. "I never want to set foot on studio grounds another day. I wouldn't associate my wife with Starlight Studios, nor our children."

"Wife?" Amusement sparked in Mr. Mertz's eyes. "Your fiancée left you. Or have you forgotten already? There will be no children in your future, boy. You have no one except me."

"You're wrong. I still have my mother."

The comment earned him another laugh. "She's incapacitated. She doesn't love you anymore. She doesn't even know who you are."

Nathan placed his fedora on his head. "Oh, she knows. Maybe not in her mind, but in her heart."

Mr. Mertz's lips twitched, hinting at the worry broiling under his pretense. "You don't have to leave. As I said, I'll stop everything. We can still be a team."

Nathan strode to the front door. "And as I said, I don't trust you. And for the record, we were never a team. You instilled fear in me and forced my hand."

"Nathan, don't do this." Mr. Mertz clasped his hands as though in prayer. "I'll do anything you ask. Please don't keep me from Marion."

The corners of Nathan's mouth lifted. One week ago, Mr. Mertz's submission would have stunned him. Now he felt nothing but pride.

He cocked his fedora to the side and ran his thumb and forefinger along the brim. "I just did."

Without an ounce of hesitation or remorse, he opened the door and left.

Mr. Mertz's confession about his mother had devastated him. However, the passion Mr. Mertz exuded when he'd declared his love offered Nathan a new perspective. While he would never accept their relationship, he hoped that when Mr. Mertz and his mother were romantically involved, the studio mogul was not the dreadful man he knew today. He had to believe that if he expected to make it through this difficult time.

On foot, Nathan returned to the Bel Air house Mr. Mertz had purchased for him. He wanted to gather a few belongings before he skipped town. New York seemed like the best move.

He'd be closer to his mother and as far across the country from L.A. as possible. With any luck, he'd find a job out there and a decent place to live soon.

As he entered the drafty front foyer, he frowned. Olivia had dreamed of buying a smaller house after the wedding, one she could decorate herself, a loving home to raise a family. That had been his dream, too. If only they could have shared it together.

Nathan didn't have many possessions that weren't bought by Mr. Mertz, so a single suitcase was sizeable enough to store everything he desired to bring with him to New York: the mementos from his relationship with Olivia and memorabilia he'd collected on his mother since childhood. There was no need for him to stop by his Malibu beach house. None of the items in that place meant anything to him.

After setting the suitcase by the front door, he sat on a sofa in the reception room, resting his head—which was still tender from his collision with Mr. Mertz's floor—on a throw pillow. Tomorrow he'd finance his departure from L.A. through Starlight Studios. Unfortunately his allowance over the last six years hadn't amounted to much, given his lavish lifestyle. After that, however, he'd finally be free from the studio.

With his plans in place, Nathan closed his eyes and felt himself drifting off . . . until the shrill ring of the telephone blasted through the room. He cracked open his eyelids but didn't budge. Mr. Mertz was probably calling. Then again, what if it was Olivia?

He sprung from the couch and lifted the receiver. "Hello?"

"Hello, this is the Western Union operator. I would like to

speak with Mr. Nathan Taggart."

"This is he."

"I have a party from Chicago looking to make a long distance connection with you. Will you accept the charges?"

Nathan's brow creased. Chicago? Who would be calling him from there? "Sure. I'll accept the charges."

"One moment, please."

"Hello? Mr. Taggart?"

Nathan frowned. The caller was male, and his voice was unfamiliar. "This is Nathan Taggart. Who is this?"

"Mr. Taggart, I'm Doctor Patrick Billings, a staff physician at Chicago Memorial Hospital. Do you know Mr. Aidan Evans?"

Nathan grabbed his chest. His heart tightened and beat so fast he thought it would blast through his ribcage. He fumbled with his tie, desperate to loosen it from his collar. What was happening to him? He couldn't breathe all of a sudden.

"Yes. He's my . . ." *Brother.* "He's my friend. Why?"

"We found your business card in Mr. Evans' wallet. On the back was your home number. Given the late hour, I tried it first instead of calling your office. I apologize for disturbing you, but you're the closest to next of kin we can locate."

Nathan swiped his sleeve across his forehead. Panic descended upon him like a violent wave he couldn't surface from.

"I . . . I don't understand." *Breathe. Just breathe.* "What is this about?"

"Mr. Taggart, you must get to Chicago as soon as possible." An ominous pause filled the line. "There's been an accident."

Chapter Eleven

Olivia had been waiting in the foyer of their house when Beth unlocked the front door and stepped inside. They hugged each other and Olivia welcomed her home. Beth was ashamed of how she'd treated her friend and was determined to make amends, but Olivia insisted all was forgiven. They vowed to reconstruct their friendship around their broken hearts and to soldier on together. Beth was truly grateful to have Olivia in her corner.

When Beth told Olivia that she wanted to spend time with her parents in Clarkson, Olivia decided to return to Portland to visit her family. They booked first-class flights, quite the change from the coach-class train trips they made separately when they first moved to Hollywood, and then bid farewell to Connie and Matthew.

Beth left her music box and the photograph of her and Aidan standing alongside Central Park at home, but she wore her angel pendant. She often reached for the necklace in moments of need, but sometimes the reminder of all she had lost annihilated any comfort it brought her. Did Aidan still wear his ring? If so, did it provide him solace or only heartache? Regardless of what had happened between them, she hoped he hadn't thrown it away.

As the airplane lifted off the tarmac, en route to Oregon, Beth shed fresh tears, even though she'd been certain she was all cried out. Her experience with Mr. Mertz had shattered her Hollywood dreams. However, her journey in becoming Elizabeth Sutton was not to blame for her sorrows. She cherished her new life, every friend she had made, the love she had found, and no longer considered Marie Bates and her movie star identity two separate entities. While she looked forward to returning to Clarkson, leaving L.A. disconnected her from a large part of who she was. She feared she'd never be able to reclaim what was lost.

Upon their arrival in Portland, Beth and Olivia exchanged telephone numbers and promised to speak in a few days. Initially, it was difficult to locate a driver who would make the one-hour trip to Clarkson, but when Beth offered an outrageous sum of money—the first half delivered upfront and the rest when they reached her destination—her predicament was solved. She didn't mind paying more than the usual fare. The money she earned from Starlight Studios seemed tainted anyway.

On the drive, the bustling cityscapes transitioned into rural country roads and quaint communities. Beth's sunglasses and headscarf provided the perfect disguise and also hid her disheveled appearance. She wore no makeup, and her eyes were puffy from the crying bouts that hit her when she least expected them. Even after her determination to remain strong, her instability would not pass. All it took was a recollection of Aidan's soft kisses or the song he composed for her and she fell apart.

The taxi driver tried to engage her in small talk, but she wasn't interested. Questions like what she did for a living and where she flew in from were not easy to answer. Eventually, he stopped making the effort.

Prior to her departure, Beth wrote a letter to Mr. Kazan, addressed to his temporary office at Starlight Studios, even though he might not receive it due to *Golden Gloves'* termination. The cable contained one phrase: *I'm sorry.* She owed him a personal visit, or at the very least a telephone call, but she couldn't go through with it. She had let him down and could only imagine how poorly he thought of her.

When they reached Clarkson's town limits and drove by memorable landmarks from her childhood, Beth reached into her purse for another tissue and tidied her appearance as best as she could in preparation for seeing her mother and father. Spring thaw had arrived, and plants and trees prepared to bloom. Oh, how she'd missed the change of seasons.

Many familiar faces strolled through downtown, enjoying all that small town life offered. Everything looked the same as she remembered—her old church, the schoolhouse, the market. There were no chauffeured cars. Children played under the supervision of their parents, not nannies, and no one was concerned about wearing the latest designer clothes, carrying expensive purses, or smearing on layers of cosmetics. Clarkson was charming, family-oriented, and blasé, representing everything she wanted to recover in her life. Perhaps leaving Elizabeth Sutton behind was best, after all.

"Please make a right on Rural Route Seventy-Nine," she said to her driver as they crept up to an intersection on the main drag.

"Yes, miss." He stepped on the brakes, allowing a family of four to cross, and then made the turn.

When Beth's childhood home came into view, nostalgia fused with relief pushed to the forefront of her emotions. She steeled herself enough to supply the final directions to the driver.

"It's the white house on the left. Number three." She cringed at her hoarse and unsteady voice. It seemed her acting abilities had vanished when she left L.A. If she couldn't keep calm now, what hope did she have in convincing her parents—or herself, for that matter—that everything would be all right?

They passed her family's mailbox, simply labeled *Bates,* and parked behind her father's Chevrolet station wagon. The two-story house and separate garage, which served as her father's shoe repair shop, had changed minimally. The window shutters had a fresh coat of dark green paint on them, no longer the rotting wood they were before she left. There was a new screen door in front of the old oak one and fresh soil in the garden. Beth was pleased that her mother had used some of the money she'd sent them to decorate. If any good came from her studio salary, it was that she was able to provide her parents with the small luxuries they were unable to afford previously.

The driver exited the taxicab and opened the back door. Beth stepped onto the driveway, her heels crushing the gravel beneath her. She breathed deeply and revealed the closest thing she could to a smile. The air smelled crisp, refreshing.

The driver retrieved her suitcase from the trunk.

She handed him the remainder of his fare. "Thank you, sir."

He placed her suitcase on the ground so he could pocket the money. "It was my pleasure." He tipped his hat and reached for her bag again.

Beth picked it up instead. "It's all right. I can carry it."

"Miss, it's no trouble."

"Please, I prefer it this way."

He shrugged. "If you say so. It was nice meeting you, and I hope you enjoy your visit."

Beth's eyebrows furrowed. Why did he assume she didn't live here?

She tightened her grip on her suitcase and walked up the driveway. Wind chimes dangled beside the entryway and a welcome mat carpeted the front door. Since her arrival was unexpected, it felt wrong to walk right in, so she utilized the doorbell. While she waited for an answer, she removed her sunglasses and wiped her eyes, squinting at her surroundings, even though the sun had yet to make an appearance. She could do this. She could smile and pretend everything was fine.

The oak door opened. Beth's mother, dressed in a flower-print cotton dress and white apron appeared on the other side. Mrs. Bates' expression shifted from inquisitive to joyous. Then horror struck.

She opened the screen door and enveloped Beth in hug. "My darling girl. What's wrong? Oh, my poor baby!"

Beth's mask of indifference shattered. Acting was centered on truth, not lies. How foolish she was to think she could hide her feelings from her loved ones.

Returning the embrace, she sobbed into her mother's shoulder, incapable of thought or speech, only sadness. It was great to be home, but their reunion did nothing to mend her broken heart.

"Barbara, what's going on?" Mr. Bates' footsteps drew near.

Beth looked beyond her mother. Distress and fury burned in her father's eyes, topped by creases buried so deeply in his forehead they looked like they'd been carved there permanently.

"What happened? Did that boy hurt you?" Mr. Bates marched onto the front porch. "So help me, Marie. If he laid a hand on you—"

"No, Aidan would never—" Beth released a wail and cried harder.

"Come inside, sweetie, and I'll make you something to eat." Her mother patted her back. "You must be famished from your travels."

"But Barbara—"

Mrs. Bates served her husband a look that warned him not to tread further. He frowned and didn't press the matter. Based on his mumblings as he gathered Beth's suitcase and followed her into the house, however, he wouldn't remain cooperative for long.

The aroma of freshly baked bread greeted Beth as she

entered the kitchen and set down her purse, sunglasses, and scarf. She took a seat at the table while her mother opened the icebox. Her father hovered close by, assessing her in intimidating silence. Although she appreciated her parents' attention, it was not her intention to encourage pity or have them wait on her. She was merely too exhausted to object to their hospitality presently.

"What would you like to eat, dear?" Her mother scanned the available food. "We have ham and cheese. I could make you a sandwich."

Beth's chin quivered. "Actually, if you don't mind, I'd like to rest now."

Her mother shut the icebox and presented a small smile. "Of course."

Her father shook his head. "Before she goes upstairs, I want to know what's going on and whether the authorities in Los Angeles need to be notified of any wrongdoing."

Mrs. Bates hushed him. "Not now, John."

"No daughter of mine is going to be treated poorly. Marie, look at me."

Using all of her might, Beth met her father's stern gaze.

"I know you're upset, but you need to tell me what happened immediately. You're frail. Unkempt. This is not the young woman I saw at Christmas." The lines in his forehead tunneled deeper, aging him beyond his years. "I never should've let you move to Los Angeles. I should've made you stay here where I could've kept an eye on you."

Beth exhaled a shaky breath. Just when she thought she

could manage an explanation, her grief won out. "Please let me lie down. I promise we'll resume this discussion later."

Her father exchanged worried glances with her mother. "All right. I'll fetch your luggage and bring it to your room."

Beth nodded, thankful for the reprieve, and made her way to the staircase. The floorboards creaked as she walked down the second floor corridor to her old bedroom, bypassing her parents' bedroom and the sole bathroom in the house.

The door to her room was open. Everything looked untouched since the day she departed. The quilt her mother had made for her was draped at the foot of her bed how she always liked it, and the tattered stuffed teddy bear from her youth was perched atop her pillow.

Beth sat on the bed and looked at her father tentatively. He stood in the doorway with her suitcase at his feet.

"Your mother and I . . ." Fondness softened his features, displaying warmth and welcome. "We're glad you're home."

Beth clutched her teddy bear. "I'm glad to be here. I love you both very much."

Her father nodded and left, pulling the door closed.

Beth settled underneath the covers, enveloped by their freshly laundered scent. Sparrows chirped outside her window amongst budding trees and a gentle breeze. She placed the teddy bear aside and closed her eyes, listening to their merry tune.

My, how far she'd come in such a short amount of time, and at such a young age. In Hollywood, she was thrust into a world where she had to grow up quickly, but in fact, she was still only nineteen years old. It was ironic, wasn't it? She had left Clarkson to find herself and her journey led her back here.

Before she moved to L.A., Beth envied those with the ability to take flight and travel to new and exciting places whenever they pleased. Granted the opportunity to spread her own wings, she'd learned that reaching even the greatest heights left something to be desired. The allure of descending back to Earth was as enchanting as soaring up to the sky.

Chapter Twelve

Beth awoke to sunlight streaming in through her window—a rarity in Clarkson, but welcome after living in shadow since Aidan left. According to her bedside clock, she had slept for over twelve hours. No wonder she felt so well rested.

She stood from the bed and winced. Her reflection in the vanity mirror contradicted how she felt. Her wrinkled dress hung from a body that was thinner than normal. Tangled, matted hair framed bloodshot eyes. Aidan had sported a similar look on Halloween. If he could see her now, he wouldn't have abandoned her. She was certain.

Tears stung her eyes, but she wouldn't give in to her sorrow. She bathed, dressed, and by the time she joined her parents in the kitchen, she felt much more confident in explaining what happened while keeping her composure.

"Good morning, Mama. Good morning, Papa."

Her father looked up from his newspaper and studied her with an inquisitive concern that made her regret leaving him to stew overnight about what might be wrong. The sense of security she was accustomed to in her youth enveloped her, infiltrating the holes in her heart. She was loved here. For the first time since her return, she felt whole.

"Good morning, Marie."

"Hello, sweetie." Mrs. Bates set her teacup on the table. Always the most patient and altruistic member of their family, she smiled with carefree ease and provided no insight into the concern that had surely kept her up most of the night. She was an active member of the Clarkson Women's Social Club and often volunteered in the community, especially helping those in need, but nothing took precedent over protecting the well-being of her husband and child. "What would you like for breakfast?"

Although Beth's appetite was still diminished, her parents' expectant expressions made it impossible for her to admit it. "Do we have oatmeal?"

Her mother stood. "Absolutely. Have a seat and I'll make some for you."

Beth sat across from her father. He folded his newspaper and put it away, offering his undivided attention. There was no point in delaying the inevitable.

"Papa, I want you and Mama to know I'm all right." Beth phrased her next words carefully. If she shared too many details, her father would never allow her to leave the house, never mind Clarkson. "There was an issue at work. Nothing you need to worry about, just a disagreement with Mr. Mertz. *Golden Gloves* was shut down and my studio contract was terminated."

"Was Aidan the cause of this disagreement with your boss?" Her father's nostrils flared. "And where is he now that you have no job, no way of supporting yourself?"

"Aidan isn't to blame. Mr. Mertz and I . . . we didn't see eye to eye on something. Aidan tried to rectify the situation, and this resulted in the termination of our film and my employment at the studio. As for Aidan's whereabouts—well, he's giving me some space."

Her father leaned back in his chair, though his shoulders never lost their tension. "During my visit to Los Angeles, I spoke to Aidan about his lack of respect toward authority. I knew his attitude would get him in trouble one day. I just didn't think he would bring you down, too, given how strongly he said he felt toward you. Are you certain he didn't tell you to argue with Mr. Mertz? You don't need to protect him, Marie. I'm your father. I deserve to know the truth."

"No, Papa. Aidan tried to help me after the fact. If anything, he taught me to stand up for myself. The whole experience has been harrowing, but I'm a stronger woman because of it. My fragile appearance may project otherwise, but that's only because everything happened recently. I will get through it. I know I will."

"Are you moving back to Oregon? It's not too late to attend Teachers College in Portland."

Beth sighed. Abandoning acting was a painful but likely choice. "Right now, I'm not sure what I'll do. I need time to process everything before I make a decision."

Her mother placed a glass of apple juice and a bowl of oatmeal drizzled in honey on the table. "Here you are, dear. Enjoy."

Beth smiled. "Thank you."

Mrs. Bates reclaimed her chair. "I'm going to the market this morning. You're more than welcome to accompany me."

"I'd love to." Beth picked up her spoon and dug into her oatmeal.

Thankfully, her father seemed satisfied with her answers—for now. He resumed reading the newspaper while her mother drank a fresh cup of tea.

After Beth finished her breakfast, she returned to her bedroom to prepare for shopping. She met her mother in the foyer and they walked to the station wagon together.

"Mama, how have you been?"

Her mother backed out of the driveway. "I've been well, but I'm a lot better now that you're home."

"I appreciate you telling me that." Beth looked to her lap. "I didn't want to be a burden."

"You could never be a burden. You're our daughter. We love you, and you always have a home with us." Unspoken inquiries lingered between them. It wasn't until they turned onto the main road in the direction of downtown that her mother lifted the veil. "Marie, what really happened between you and Aidan? I know it's not customary for a daughter to speak with her father about such things, but you can speak to me."

"Aidan broke up with me." Beth's shoulders sagged. "Not because he wanted to, though. I think he blames himself for what happened at the studio, even though it wasn't his fault. So after he confronted Mr. Mertz on my behalf, he left, believing it was best for me. I haven't heard from him since."

"I'm so sorry, Marie." Her mother parked at their destination and pulled her in for a hug.

Beth closed her eyes and breathed deeply, easing the ache in her chest. There was nothing like her mother's scent: Prell, wildflowers, a hint of vanilla. It was the scent of her childhood, of afterschool baking, weekend adventures in the park, and cozy bedtime stories.

"Don't give up on your relationship, sweetie. From what I gathered during my trip to Los Angeles, Aidan is very taken with you. With a love as strong as yours, the bonds don't sever easily. Perhaps after some time apart, some reflection, you two will reunite."

"I want that more than anything. I suppose I'll just have to be patient." Beth exited the station wagon and joined her mother in front of the market.

The sky had clouded over. It was a typical Sunday morning in Clarkson. Women socialized and shopped while men smoked and shared casual conversations on the sidewalks.

Beth blinked back tears and held her head high. A leisurely day occupied by quality time with her mother was exactly what she needed to get her mind off Aidan's absence. In particular, she couldn't sulk and give the townspeople a reason to question the motive behind her return.

"Barbara!" Mrs. Foster waved at Mrs. Bates on her scuttle across the road. In her late seventies, the baker's wife had a few more wrinkles than Beth remembered and a plumper figure that nearly filled in the loose skin she used to have hanging from her jowls.

"Lorraine." Mrs. Bates added a nod to her greeting. "It's lovely to see you. How are you?"

"I'm fine, thank you." Mrs. Foster gestured to the garment bag draped over her arm. "I'm dropping off a dress for dry-cleaning and then popping in to see Mrs. Marthery. We started a knitting group this winter, you know. Presently, we're making sweaters to donate to the church's Easter clothing drive. You should help us if you have time. We could use the extra hands. Anyhow, what brings you to town this morning?"

"My daughter and I are going to the market."

Mrs. Foster's gaze landed on Beth for the first time since her approach. "Marie, it's been so long since I've seen you. I didn't recognize you." Her lips curled, distorting her welcoming grin into a grimace. "You've been living in Los Angeles, correct?"

Beth's polite smile masked her wariness. Mrs. Foster was Clarkson's own Hilda Hooper. It was best to be on guard around her. "Yes, ma'am."

Mrs. Foster's grimace deepened to a scowl. "I saw your film, *Sparkling Meadow*, under encouragement of some fellow Clarkson residents—you know, to support our local talent. The kiss in the barn between your character and that young man—two unwed individuals—really pushed my moral limits. Why on earth would you participate in such debauchery, and for the entire world to see?"

Beth gulped, though she should've expected Mrs. Foster's criticism, given the woman's staunch Christian beliefs. "Well, I—"

"Hollywood is a wicked, wicked place." Mrs. Foster wagged her finger in Beth's face. "It was only a matter of time before those movie folks forced you into compromising your good character. I'm just glad you changed your name professionally, so there's a chance you haven't ruined Clarkson's impeccable reputation."

"I was only acting." Beth's retort remained civil. However, her frown revealed her irritation. "And the kiss was filmed tastefully."

Mrs. Foster huffed. "Just the fact you agreed to display affection onscreen appalls me. Many young girls watched that film, including my great granddaughter. I hate to think they now believe it's acceptable to sneak off with a young man, unsupervised. You should have invited your gentleman friend to dinner with you and your parents or attended a church service with him instead."

Beth's annoyance yielded to amusement, but she suppressed her giggle out of courtesy. Mrs. Foster had over seven decades of religious teachings ingrained into her. There was no way to convince her that her views were old fashioned, nor did Beth have a right to devalue her opinions on the subject.

"When I return to Los Angeles, I'll be sure to let the studio know your concerns."

"Good. Meanwhile, you should stop in to see Reverend Redmond during your stay and repent. There may be hope for you yet." Mrs. Foster turned back to Mrs. Bates. "Barbara, it's nice to see you. I hope your Christian influence expels the sins from your daughter's soul and helps her see the light. I also suggest you educate Marie on the importance of asking God for guidance before she makes decisions that could ultimately damn her to Hell."

Mrs. Bates' lips twitched, indicating she held back laughter, too. "Yes, Lorraine. I will."

"Excellent. Good-bye!" With a hearty wave, Mrs. Foster took off down the street.

Beth cast a tentative glance at her mother. "My performance in *Sparkling Meadow* didn't shame you and Papa, did it? Mrs. Foster is radical in her opinions, but many of the older population in town share the same views."

Her mother's smile calmed her fears. "You've never brought shame upon our family. I'm proud of your performance and you should be, too."

"That means a lot to me, Mama. Thank you." Beth linked arms with her and they entered the market.

While they shopped, many townsfolk greeted them. Beth was asked about Los Angeles and various movie stars, and if she didn't have nice things to say, she fibbed so she wouldn't crush their excitement. As for her personal experiences, she kept her responses vague. It was still difficult to discuss Hollywood and the studio without getting upset.

Although Beth was grateful she was still welcome in Clarkson, she couldn't identify with many of the housewives she spoke to, even those close to her in age. While she discussed her film projects and purchasing her own house, the women discussed their children, their duties to their husbands, and what meals they were preparing for dinner with enthusiasm she didn't share. There wasn't anything wrong with their interests, and she certainly didn't think she was better than them. She too wanted a husband and children one day, but she also desired a career outside the home. This was the reason she'd left Clarkson in the first place.

While Beth wanted to see the world and explore her options, these women settled into small town life happily. Whether that was by choice or if they just didn't believe it was possible to do anything else, she wasn't sure. Perhaps her ambitions were farfetched, but she couldn't give up on her dreams. If she didn't return to acting, she would become a teacher, maybe attending college in Portland like her father suggested and relocating to another big city after graduation.

After gathering all the items on their grocery list, Beth and her mother made their way to the checkout. A fair-haired young woman stood in line, carrying a basket of produce.

Gentle in features, dainty in poise, and dressed in a conservative cotton dress, she radiated warmth and beauty that made even the cloudiest morning in Clarkson seem like a Southern California afternoon. Not Hollywood beauty, but honest-to-goodness prettiness that didn't require cosmetics or designer clothing for one to recognize and appreciate it. Beth couldn't believe her eyes. Emma Stacy hadn't changed one bit since high school.

"Emma!"

Emma's hand flew to her chest. "Marie, it's so good to see you!" She blushed. "Forgive me. Perhaps I should call you Elizabeth."

Beth hugged her. "Marie is fine."

"Goodness. There's so much to catch up on." Emma released her. "How long are you in town for?"

Beth's smile wavered. "I'm not sure."

"Well, we must get together during your stay. How about we meet at Mr. Kent's drugstore one afternoon. I'll give you my telephone number and you can ring me up when you're free."

Mrs. Bates stepped forward. "Marie, you and Emma should catch up now. I'll finish here and see you back at the house."

Beth motioned to her mother's overflowing basket. "Are you sure? I don't want to leave you to put all the groceries away on your own."

Her mother nodded. "Of course I'm sure."

"I can drive you home," Emma said. "I have the car because Neil is busy fixing our eaves trough. It's been leaking since God knows when—probably the turn of the century when the house was built!"

"Neil?" Beth's eyes widened. "Not Neil Russell?"

Emma giggled and raised her left hand to show off an engagement ring and a wedding band.

"My, we do have a lot to discuss." Beth kissed her mother's cheek. "Thank you, Mama."

Emma paid for her produce and they left the store.

Mr. Kent's drugstore was a smaller establishment than Schwab's Pharmacy and didn't attract any celebrity clientele, but his chocolate malts were the best Beth had ever tasted.

They claimed their usual seats at the far end of the counter and set down their belongings. Mr. Kent rushed toward them.

He'd always reminded Beth of James Stewart in *It's A Wonderful Life.* Not only did he resemble the actor in appearance, even though he was much older, but he was also gregarious and kind and always willing to go out of his way to help anyone in town like George Bailey did in the film.

"Marie, what a surprise! You look so grown up." He gestured to her with gusto. "Last I heard you were living in Los Angeles. What brings you back here?"

Again, Beth kept her reply simple. "I missed Clarkson."

"Really? I can't imagine you'd find anything interesting here after all the exciting things I'm sure you've experienced since leaving town." Mr. Kent placed two napkins on the counter. "So what'll it be? The usual?"

Beth and Emma nodded.

"All right. Two chocolate malts coming right up." Mr. Kent left to prepare their orders.

Beth was curious about what brought Emma back to Clarkson, but she also hoped taking control of the conversation would keep the focus off her. "So what's happened with you since we last saw each other?"

Emma's eyes twinkled. "Well, I attended the Portland Teaching School for Women for one year with the intent of staying in the city after graduation. But fate had other plans. I was walking home from class one afternoon and ran into Neil— literally. My books fell to the ground and he helped me retrieve them. He asked if I would like to have a soda with him. And the rest, as they say, is history."

"What was he doing in Portland?"

"He was on a delivery. After high school, he committed to working full time at his family's furniture business. I never gave him the time of day growing up—we seemed very different—but that afternoon changed everything. We got married six weeks later."

"Six weeks!"

Emma giggled. "Yes. We knew we were going to be together forever, so why not? After our wedding, since I was still in school, he visited me every weekend. Then two weeks before I graduated, he informed me that Mrs. Cooper passed away."

Beth gasped. "Oh, no. She was a lovely woman."

Emma nodded. "When she died, a position opened up at the Clarkson schoolhouse. I applied and they offered me the job right away. It was perfect because Neil's job is based here so I would've had to return regardless. I didn't mind moving back to town really, even though it wasn't my initial plan. I'd follow him anywhere."

"How do you like teaching?"

Emma's expression brightened with almost the same intensity as it did when she spoke about her husband. "Oh, Marie. Teaching is superb. I couldn't imagine doing anything else. It's been such a rewarding experience. It's also helped me become more comfortable around children, which I hope will come in handy when I'm raising my own kids someday." A frown crept upon her lips. "Neil and I have been trying to conceive for over a year. Unfortunately, we haven't been successful."

Beth placed her hand over Emma's. "Not too worry. I'm

sure it will happen for you soon."

"Thank you, Marie. You're such a dear friend." Emma shot her a smile, which made her smile, too.

When Emma left for Portland after high school graduation, they parted on positive terms and wished each other well in their future endeavors. Two months later, Beth left for Los Angeles. She assumed they'd never see each other again. She felt so relaxed around Emma, as if they'd never separated. Why hadn't they kept in touch? It was such a shame. She would ensure it didn't happen again.

Mr. Kent delivered their chocolate malts and two spoons and then greeted a young man who had just entered the drugstore.

"Enough about me." Emma picked up her spoon. "Tell me all about Hollywood!"

Beth's eyebrows drew together. "Life in Los Angeles is more fast-paced than in Clarkson. There's vibrant nightlife, everyone dresses fashionably, and the weather is beautiful practically all year round. It's a large city, but the entertainment industry is actually a close-knit community. So in that regard, it's similar to small town living."

Emma plucked the cherry off the top of her malt. "Neil and I went to San Francisco on our honeymoon and really enjoyed it. The vacation cost us much of our savings, but it was worth it. Maybe one day I'll have the opportunity to visit Los Angeles, too. You know, before Neil and I have children." She shook her head. "Gosh, how rude of me. I'm sorry for redirecting the conversation away from you."

Beth scoffed. "Are you kidding? I love hearing about your life."

"That's sweet of you to say, but I bet my life is boring compared to yours."

"It isn't boring. It's magnificent. You have a husband who loves you and you're working in your dream profession."

"Yes, but tell me about your dream, Marie. I was shocked when I heard you were working at a motion picture studio. Although, after watching *Sparkling Meadow*, it's clear you belong in the movies. Your performance was incredible, and I think your looks rival the most beautiful stars in the industry."

While many people praised others to be polite, Beth could always trust Emma to speak frankly. Consequently, she felt at ease offering a more candid view of Hollywood life than she'd shared with others previously.

"Thank you for the compliment on my acting. As for my appearance—well, you'd be surprised what professional hair, wardrobe, and makeup teams can do to someone average like me. Mostly, beauty in Hollywood is an illusion. Though, there are exceptions. Actresses like Constance Murphy, Ava Gardner, and Elizabeth Taylor look as stunning in plain old trousers as they do in lavish evening gowns."

"I'd truly love to hear what working for a movie studio is like." Emma leaned closer.

Beth swirled her spoon in her glass. "Well, the studio system is very structured. Everything is controlled, from the photographs and articles printed in the papers, to how we dress, what films we make."

"Still, Hollywood seems so glamorous. I wouldn't mind driving a flashy car, wearing fashionable clothing and expensive jewelry, and attending fancy soirées in designer outfits every night."

"That's what I thought, too, but . . ." Beth shrugged. "It's really isn't that great."

"But you get to hang out with famous movie stars. That must be fun. Although, now that you're a famous movie star yourself, I suppose it's pretty standard fare, right?"

Beth dropped her spoon into her glass. She'd lost her appetite. "Sure, there are some people I was truly honored to meet, but overall, the images presented to the public are just that—images. I know it's difficult to understand because most pull off their personas so well, but movie stars are just like everyone else, except we have faces that are known all over the world. Our true personalities, though, are not so public. We are whatever the studio wants us to be."

Emma frowned. "I see."

Beth didn't like dashing her friend's high hopes, but after putting on an act for everyone at the market, she preferred to tell the whole truth this time. "I don't mean to sound ungrateful. Most of my time in Hollywood was wonderful. It's just not the idyllic paradise it's made out to be."

"Are you happy you became an actress?"

Beth's answer was immediate. "Absolutely."

Emma pushed aside her glass. Sympathy softened her gaze. "Marie, I've known you since we were four years old. Please tell me why you're really back in Clarkson."

"Well, um . . ." Beth dabbed her teary eyes with a napkin.

Emma placed a hand on her shoulder. "I'm sorry. I didn't mean to make you cry."

"No, it's fine." Beth sniffled. "To be honest, my time at Starlight Studios has come to an end."

Emma gasped. "Why?"

"There was an incident . . ." Beth gathered the strength to elaborate. "It shattered the Hollywood dream for me and stressed that, although I love acting, I hate the studio system and the controlling studio boss."

"Is it possible to act in films without contractual obligation to a major motion picture studio?"

Beth placed her napkin on the countertop. "Actually, yes. I know of a man—my beau, in fact—who successfully acted in Hollywood without one. However, his circumstances were unique."

Emma clasped her hands. "A beau! That's swell, Marie."

"Well, former beau." Beth released an unsteady breath. "After the incident, he left and I haven't heard from him since."

"Did you love him?"

"Yes, and I still do with all of my heart. He's a good man." A fresh batch of tears sprung to her eyes.

Emma took her hand and squeezed. "Then everything will work out."

Beth regarded Emma hopefully. Her mother had said the same thing. What did they know that she didn't?

"How can you be certain?"

"Because you're a wonderful, kindhearted woman, and it's

only a matter of time before this man realizes he made a terrible mistake."

Beth dipped her spoon into her milkshake and collected the thick, chocolate dregs at the bottom of the glass. It would be a shame to let it go to waste. "I pray you're right, Emma. I really do."

"Well, golly!" The young man who was seated at the other end of the counter approached them. "You're Elizabeth Sutton, aren't you?"

Beth hesitated. Was she? Or was it time to forget about her for good and start over? For simplicity, she responded positively. "Yes, I am."

He removed his fedora. "I'm honored to meet you. You're my favorite actress."

Beth drew back from him. "Me?"

"Yes, Miss Sutton." A blush tinted his cheeks. "My name is Nelson Crop. I'm a traveling vacuum salesman. Never in my wildest dreams did I think we would cross paths. You're so talented and—if you don't mind me saying so—pretty, too. Pardon my curiosity, but what are you doing in this small town?"

"Well, I . . ." Beth frowned. How much did she want to reveal to this stranger?

When she had first arrived on the Starlight Studios lot, she never considered that the film industry wouldn't live up to her expectations. The young man looked so excited, she didn't want to put a damper on his mood like she did with Emma. Instead, she took a page out of Connie's book and committed to the glamorous image he had of her.

"Thank you, Nelson. You're too kind." She extended her hand and he shook it readily. "It's a pleasure to meet you. As for why I'm in Clarkson, I'm visiting friends and family before I fly back to Hollywood."

"To make another fantastic motion picture, I imagine." Wonder flitted across his face. "You've truly made my day. Actually, this is hands-down the best experience of my life. May I have your autograph?"

Beth presented her best red carpet smile. "Of course."

The young man produced a pen and an Electrolux receipt pad from his pocket. Beth signed her name, accompanied by a personalized a note.

He tucked away the items. "You've sure made me happy, Miss Sutton."

"Please call me Elizabeth."

"Wow, really? Thanks!" He placed his fedora on his head. "Enjoy your time in Clarkson, Elizabeth."

After he left the drugstore, Emma sighed. "Gee whiz. It must be nice to have such a positive impact on someone."

Beth focused on the front door as it closed, leaving her and Emma as the only patrons in the drugstore. Her smile widened. And it wasn't an act either. "Yes, I suppose it is."

While they finished their chocolate malts, they discussed what their fellow schoolmates were up to since graduation and other various goings-on in Emma's life. From time to time, Beth's encounter with the vacuum salesman entered her mind. Now the idea of returning to L.A. enticed her. Connie had urged her to think about rallying together with others to try to change the studio system. Was it at all possible?

When their glasses were empty, Beth offered to pay the check, but Mr. Kent declined her money. To compensate, she dropped a few bills into the tip jar when he wasn't looking.

Emma collected her belongings. "I'm sorry I have to leave. I just don't want Neil to worry."

Beth gathered her purse. "It's no problem at all. I'm glad we had this time together."

After saying good-bye to Mr. Kent, Beth left the drugstore with Emma. As they drove to her parents' house, she smiled at the passing scenery instead of tearing up like she did when she arrived in town yesterday.

Tomorrow she would call Olivia to discuss their return to Los Angeles. They had careers to revive and beaux to find, and she hoped they could make the journey together. As much as she loved Clarkson, she had to move on. She would visit more frequently, but it was no longer her home.

When they parked in the driveway, Emma shifted her gaze across the car. "Marie, I wish you all the best in California."

Beth's eyebrows rose "How did you know I was leaving?"

A fond smile overtook Emma's lips. "As soon as I saw you in the checkout line, I was convinced your rightful place was in show business. And that's a compliment. There's no definitive explanation as to why or how I know this. It's just a given."

"I'm going to miss you." Beth hugged her tightly.

Emma returned the embrace with much love and encouragement. "Me, too. Let's keep in touch this time, all right?"

"Definitely." Beth took down her address and they exchanged good-byes.

Once Emma drove off, Beth ascended the steps to the front porch. This time she walked right into the house instead of ringing the doorbell and met her parents in the kitchen.

Her mother smiled. "Did you have a nice time with Emma?"

"Yes, very much so." Beth cleared her throat. "Mama, Papa, I've made up my mind. I'm going back to Los Angeles."

At the appearance of her parents' frowns, Beth felt a twinge of regret. She shouldn't have revealed the truth so bluntly after all she had put them though, but skirting around her decision would provide false hope, which wasn't fair to them either.

"When?" Her father set down his coffee cup.

Beth maintained eye contact to convey her commitment. "Friday, depending on the available flights out of Portland. If it's all right, I'd like to spend some more time with the two of you before I depart."

"Are you sure it's wise to return so soon?" her mother asked.

Beth nodded. "I can't avoid the issues I need to sort out in my life. It's time to face them head on. I also don't want to give up acting as a profession."

Disapproval toughened her father's gaze. "What will you do for money if you can't get your contract reinstated?"

"Oh, I'm not asking for my contract to be reinstated."

His eyes widened. "That's absurd. How will you act without one?"

Beth shrugged with a lighthearted ease that surprised but also delighted her. "I'm not sure. What I am certain about is that something else awaits me in my acting future. I want to find a way to have more creative control over my career, and the studio system restricts artistic freedom. I have no place at Starlight Studios anymore."

Her father scowled. "Aidan planted those crazy ideas in your head. I will tell you the same thing I told him—there is no security in that way of living. I suggest you apologize to your boss and beg for your job back."

Beth shook her head. If her father were aware of what had transpired between her and Mr. Mertz, he would change his tune. While she appreciated his advice, she had to figure out everything on her own. "Please trust me, Papa. I suffered a setback, but I'm all right now."

Her parents traded hesitant glances. In the silence that followed, Beth was convinced they would dispute her position.

In a rather shocking turn of events, her father's expression softened with acceptance. "If you ever need to return to Clarkson, we will always welcome you, no matter what."

Beth flung her arms around his neck. "Thank you, Papa."

He rubbed her back. "It's wonderful to see you happy again, Marie."

Beth smiled so widely her cheeks hurt. It had been so long since this had happened. Goodness. She truly was happy, wasn't she?

Chapter Thirteen

The following afternoon, Beth spoke to Olivia over the telephone and they arranged their departures for Friday morning. After Beth hung up, her father offered to drive her to the airport, and the rest of her plans came together nicely. Over the next few days, she helped her mother around the house and spent time with her father in his shoe repair shop and in front of the television, watching his favorite evening programs.

On the eve of her flight, as Beth lay on her bed, her mother entered the room, holding two scrapbooks. Beth sat up and made space for her mother to sit next to her.

"Before you leave tomorrow, I wanted to show you a few things." Her mother opened the first album. Newspaper and magazine clippings labeled with the names and dates of the publications filled many of the pages. "I've saved mementos from your career since the beginning and I want you to have them."

Tears of gratitude flooded Beth's eyes as she perused the album. When she came across the *Life* magazine article from Aidan's race in Santa Barbara, she lingered on the photograph she took with him and her friends. The image had initiated the fiasco with Mr. Mertz, but it also proved that life could be beautiful.

Her mother flipped through the blank pages at the end of the album. "These are for when you reestablish your career."

Beth threw her arms around her mother. "I'm going to do it. I'm going to act again."

"I know you will, sweetie." Her mother held her tighter. "I never had any doubt that this town wasn't for you and you were destined for bigger things. It was confirmed when I saw your films. You've found your calling, and as I said earlier in the week, I'm so proud of you."

Beth pulled back to stare at her, to memorize her face again. Her fair complexion, smooth skin, and large brown eyes radiated youth preserved by a life full of purpose, passion, and unconditional love both for and from her husband and daughter. Her mother was proof that although this was not the place for Beth, there was still great honor in this way of life in Clarkson.

Remorse squeezed Beth's heart. Even though it had only been a few months since they had last seen each other, there were details she had forgotten, like the sprinkles of gold in her mother's brown eyes and the softness of her hair. Beth couldn't bear to lose them forever. The same fear occupied Aidan—only he would never have the opportunity to see his mother again, to reclaim the memories that had drifted away over the years.

It was important not to stay away from Clarkson for too long. Visiting her parents would allow her to ensure she always held on to Marie Bates, regardless of what happened in her career. It was just as important as reclaiming her identity as Elizabeth Sutton.

Beth wiped the tears from her eyes. "What's in the other album?"

Her mother set the second scrapbook on her lap. "Pictures to remind you of where you came from if you're ever feeling lost again."

On the first page was a photograph of Beth in her infancy, dressed in her baptismal gown. Photographs followed of her with her parents and friends. One photograph in particular, of her and Emma standing in the schoolyard and grinning for the camera, produced a giggle from her lips. From then on, she couldn't stop beaming as they looked at the rest of the album and reminisced about her childhood.

"Thank you so much, Mama."

Her mother stood from the bed. "I'll leave you so you can look at the rest in private."

"Before you go, I need to give you something." Beth reached for her checkbook on the nightstand and filled out the top check.

Her mother took the check. "For Emma Russell?"

"Yes. Can you please give it to her after I leave? She's much too humble to accept it from me personally."

Her mother nodded. "What should I say?"

"Tell her . . ." Beth smiled at a photograph of them on Halloween dressed as a pair of dice. "It's for a second honeymoon for her and Neil."

Her mother kissed her forehead. "Will do. Good night."

Beth pored over the albums again, revisiting the memories accompanying every page. She ended up lying on her bed with the first album opened to the Santa Barbara article and clutched to her chest. She stayed that way long after the sun set and the moon appeared, blanketing her bedroom in a silver glow. There were many blank pages left and she was determined to fill all of them, starting with the addition of the photograph of her and Aidan in New York City, which she had left behind in L.A.

Mrs. Foster was right about her compromising on her dignity, but it had nothing to do with her character's kiss in *Sparkling Meadow*. Luckily she still had a chance at redemption. But it would not come from Reverend Redmond. It would come from hard work and Aidan's love and the support of their friends.

Beth would make Aidan accept that they belonged together, even if she had to talk until she lost her voice. This was not the act of a weak and desperate young woman. Taking a proactive stance exhibited strength and courage. She would not allow Mr. Mertz's evil to destroy their relationship—something so pure, so real, amongst his immoral and illusory world.

The shrill cry of the telephone blasted throughout the house. Her father grumbled about it being too late for calls as he left his bedroom and walked downstairs. Beth placed the album aside and followed him into the living room. He tightened the belt on his flannel robe and lifted the receiver.

"Hello." His eyebrows knitted together. "No, I—" He sighed. "Well, all right, I'll accept the long distance charges."

Beth rushed to her father's side.

"Yes, this is John Bates. Who's this?" He directed his puzzled gaze at Beth. "One moment."

Beth grabbed the receiver from her father, forgoing the ladylike manners she was taught as a child. "Aidan? Aidan, is that you?"

"Beth, it's Nathan calling from Los Angeles."

A stitch of disappointment surfaced in her chest. At the same time, she was glad he'd called. "Nathan, it's lovely to hear from you. Have you spoken to Olivia in Portland?"

"She's in Portland?" The sudden hopefulness in his tone didn't last. "No, we haven't spoken."

"I'll give you her parents' telephone number—"

"Beth—"

"Don't worry. Once you two talk, everything will be all right."

Nathan cleared his throat. "Beth, are you sitting down?"

The color drained from her face. "No, why?"

"Perhaps you should—"

"Nathan, what is it? Tell me." She gripped the receiver tighter.

"Beth . . . it's Aidan." Nathan's voice shook. "There's been an accident. He's . . . he's . . ."

"No. Please, no!" Beth's knees buckled and she dropped the receiver. Her father caught her before she fell to the floor.

"What's going on?" Her mother rushed downstairs. "Marie! John! What's wrong?"

It was as if Beth was watching a movie and the projector

had gone haywire. Her surroundings spun, blurred. No longer did she stand on an even plane, like the universe had shifted and split wide open, determined to suck her into a black hole of grief and despair.

Wails—fraught and high pitched, akin to dialogue on fast-forward—burrowed into her brain. It was the most awful sound.

"Marie!" Mrs. Bates peered at her husband with wild, wet eyes. "John, help her!"

"Marie, stop!" Her father shook her madly. "Get a hold of yourself this instant and tell us what's the matter!"

Tears poured down Beth's face. Her throat burned and her stomach roiled, threatening to expel its contents. Oh, God. The wailing . . . it was coming from her.

"I'm getting to the bottom of this right now." Her father handed her over to her mother and picked up the dangling receiver. By the time he finished questioning Nathan and hung up, his complexion was ashen, his gaze detained by devastation.

Locked in her mother's embrace, Beth cried until she was unable to catch her breath. No, it couldn't be. Her father could fix anything. She'd turned to him in her youth whenever she needed help, and he'd never let her down. He could fix this, too. He had to.

"Papa, please!" She stumbled over to him and latched onto his housecoat. "I love Aidan, Papa. Please do something. I love him!"

Her father yanked her close. As his arms came around her, a sob rattled his sturdy form. "There's nothing that can be done, Marie. I'm sorry. I'm so very sorry."

Chapter Fourteen

Had the *Golden Gloves* company made it to Chicago to complete the film, Beth would have loved it there. The Neo-Gothic and High Renaissance churches, quaint residential streets, and Art Deco skyscrapers were an eclectic mix of enchantment and mystery. The sophistication of the metropolis's neighborhoods resonated from every city block, and the harbor provided awe-inspiring views of the sun's rays skipping across Lake Michigan. Unfortunately, the circumstances under which she and Olivia made their trip cast a shadow over everything.

As their taxicab drove through downtown, Beth's heart squeezed. Their overnight airplane ride from Portland was spent much the same way as her voyage now—grieving to the point of numbness and exhaustion, transforming her from the woman with newfound positivity she all-too-briefly became before receiving Nathan's telephone call two nights ago.

After Nathan called back to provide her with her travel information, she contacted Olivia. Thankfully, her friend insisted on accompanying her.

Upon their arrival in Chicago, they secured transportation

from the airport to the hospital without stopping by the hotel to check in and drop off their luggage. Beth didn't want to waste any more time away from her ailing beau.

Men and women wearing chic urban attire strolled along crowded streets, past fashionable storefronts, creating a bustle of action reminiscent of New York City. Beth longed to amble through Central Park with Aidan like they did on their first date, with the suburban feel of L.A., its steady climate, and unauthentic charisma nothing but a distant memory. Sadly, those days were far behind her now. The horrors awaiting her at the hospital were her reality.

When the taxi pulled up in front of Chicago Memorial Hospital, Beth was unprepared for the group of reporters huddled near the entrance, minded by security.

How did they find out Aidan was here? Nathan never would've alerted the press.

"This is your stop, ladies." The driver turned toward the back seat. "That'll be three-fifty."

Olivia opened her purse, but Beth had already handed over the fare and tip.

The driver opened the back door and they emerged from the cab. Beth secured her sunglasses as their luggage was retrieved from the trunk. The driver didn't seem to recognize her, but it was unlikely her anonymity would last much longer.

A brisk wind blasted down the street. She fastened the buttons on her coat and picked up her suitcase. Tears stung her eyes, breaking through her numbness. In Clarkson, she didn't think she'd be able to face the truth of Aidan's condition, but she had surprised herself. She had collected her remaining strength against the most disturbing circumstances, and now here she was, about to see him in person. Yes, it would be difficult, but quitting was not an option.

With a nod to Olivia, she began her trek to the hospital. The reporters recognized her immediately.

"Miss Sutton, is it true Aidan Evans is on his death bed after wrapping his Porsche around a tree?"

"Since *Golden Gloves* has been terminated, why was Mr. Evans in Chicago in the first place?"

"Are you here as a concerned costar or something more?"

"Can you confirm that a priest has been called in to administer the last rites to Mr. Evans?"

Beth kept her head down as security escorted her and Olivia into the hospital amongst camera flashes. Although she had been taught to always cooperate with the press, this time, she would not give them the courtesy of a response. Imagine trying to profit from someone else's misfortune. It was sickening.

Inside, Beth and Olivia were greeted by additional security, fronted by an older man wearing a dark suit and a tight frown. There was a kindness in his eyes that didn't seem forced.

"Miss Sutton, my name is Alfred Motts. I'm the head of security here at Chicago Memorial Hospital. Mr. Taggart informed me you'd be arriving this morning."

A sob escaped Olivia. She brought a tissue to her mouth and bowed her head to weep. Beth placed a hand on her shoulder. Hopefully she'd have the opportunity to thank Nathan for making all of her arrangements. She truly missed him and knew all too well how Olivia felt in his absence. A deep connection existed between Nathan and Olivia that could never be severed. The engagement ring on Olivia's left hand was proof she still loved him in spite of his betrayal.

Mr. Motts motioned across the lobby. "Please follow me. I'll take you to Mr. Evans' ward."

Beth removed her sunglasses and placed them in her coat pocket as they walked toward the elevators. Saint Raphael, immortalized in stained glass, filtered in the sun, bestowing the lobby with a warm and peaceful glow.

It had been ages since Beth had sought divine intervention. However, as she passed the Archangel, she grasped her diamond pendant and whispered words of mercy and forgiveness. Perhaps she was unworthy of acknowledgement, having turned to prayer only in times of need, but Aidan—her dear, dear Aidan—deserved salvation.

O great prince of the heavenly court, I beg you . . .

On the eighth floor, they exited onto a ward modest in furnishings and void of the comforting atmosphere from downstairs.

"Please wait here. I'll fetch the doctor." Mr. Motts walked down the corridor, leaving Beth and Olivia standing amongst the probing stares of nurses and orderlies. When he returned, a man with salt and pepper hair, black-rimmed glasses, and a long white coat accompanied him.

"Good morning, Miss Sutton. My name is Doctor Patrick Billings." He shook her hand. "I received Aidan Evans in the emergency room following his accident. I'm his primary care physician."

"It's nice to meet you." Beth offered a meek smile and gestured to her friend. "This is Olivia Weston."

"Good morning, Ms. Weston." Dr. Billings provided her with a handshake, too.

Mr. Motts stepped forward. "I will leave you to speak with Dr. Billings privately, Miss Sutton. If you need anything, please do not hesitate to summon me."

Beth nodded. "Thank you."

Mr. Motts disappeared into the nearest stairwell.

"Miss Sutton, our conversation would be better suited in my office." Dr. Billings turned to Olivia. "Ms. Weston, if you'd like to have a seat in the waiting room, I can send for you when we're finished."

Tears filled Beth's eyes. "Please let her stay. I cannot bear to be separated from her."

Sympathy flooded the physician's gaze. "As you wish."

Beth and Olivia followed Dr. Billings past the nurses' station, earning them more inquisitive glances and even some whispers.

Since Beth's first and last visit to a hospital was when she sustained her superficial head injury in December, she was unfamiliar with them except from what she'd seen in motion pictures. The reality was quite different from how they were portrayed onscreen. Chicago Memorial was meant to be a place of healing, but the white walls, acrid smell of bleach, and eerie quiet on the ward reminded her of suffering and loss.

Dr. Billings motioned for them to enter his office first and then shut the door upon his entry. A diploma from the University of Chicago Medical School presided over an oak desk covered with file folders, a table lamp, and a telephone. The blinds decorating the only window in the room were closed.

Dr. Billings took a seat behind his desk after Beth and Olivia placed their suitcases on the floor and claimed the two chairs on the other side. He adjusted his glasses, cleared his throat. Stalling, perhaps.

"First of all, I must say I don't know how the press found out about Mr. Evans' admittance. I assure you they did not hear anything from my staff. We pride ourselves on discretion here at Chicago Memorial. Hence, we have increased our security presence on the premises to fend off further unwanted intrusions."

Beth wrung her hands. "Thank you, Doctor."

"I'm not sure if you're aware, but Mr. Evans' father, Graham Evans, is a prominent member of Chicago Memorial's medical team."

Beth's eyes widened. "He is?"

Dr. Billings nodded. "Dr. Evans has been on personal leave for the past month. Since Mr. Evans' admission, I've tried to reach him over the telephone, but all of my attempts have failed. I stopped by his house yesterday, but no one was home, so I left a note on the door, requesting that he call me right away. Thankfully, we were able to contact Mr. Taggart, which is why you're here today. Nathan is a good man. He cares about Mr. Evans a lot."

Olivia removed another tissue from her purse and patted

her moist eyes.

Beth clenched her jaw, steeling herself. "Aidan . . . how is he?"

Dr. Billings folded his hands on the desktop. "Normally, Miss Sutton, I wouldn't disclose personal information to anyone other than family, but Mr. Taggart says you and Mr. Evans are . . . close."

All Beth could manage was a nod.

"I will be frank with you. Mr. Evans is in a coma. In a situation like this, however, a comatose state is actually best. It limits neurological activity, giving the brain a chance to rest and heal. Until he regains consciousness—that is, *if* he regains consciousness—it is impossible to predict how his injuries have affected his cognitive and motor abilities."

"So you won't know until he wakes up?" Beth chose to focus on when, not if.

"That is correct. Fortunately, Mr. Evans was wearing his seatbelt, which very well saved his life, so there is a chance he may make a full recovery. How much of a chance, though, I cannot say."

"That's fair, Doctor. Thank you."

"As for Mr. Evans' current condition, he is critical but stable. He's breathing on his own. Therefore, no mechanical ventilation is required. We inserted an intravenous line to deliver maintenance fluids and medication directly into his bloodstream instead of relying on intramuscular or subcutaneous injections. We are also monitoring him with a cardioscope. It's quite something, actually. It's a new medical device, which records a patient's heart rate and emits an alarm if it falls outside normal limits. We typically only use this machine in the operating room. However, we've found it helpful in Mr. Evans' case, given the extent of his injuries.

"Aside from the swelling in his brain, Mr. Evans broke his nose and two ribs. He also has multiple lacerations and contusions—cuts and bruises—on his face and torso, which took the brunt of the impact when he skidded off the road and crashed into the tree. We cannot rule out bruising of his liver and spleen either, although his lab work indicates no internal bleeding."

Beth placed her hand over her heart. It all sounded so complicated, so serious. "It's bad, isn't it? His condition . . ."

Dr. Billings frowned. "This is a Catholic hospital. I'm not sure if you're a religious woman, but considering how this could have turned out, I'd say someone is watching over him. To have survived a motor vehicle accident this severe . . . well, in my opinion, he is very lucky. Please do not repeat that to anyone, however. From a medical perspective, *lucky* is not a term I like to use when discussing my patients."

Beth could no longer hold back her tears. Olivia hugged her while the doctor expressed his deepest condolences, never breaking his professional poise.

Her crying did not last long; she made sure of it. This was not the time for weakness. Aidan needed her. She would not sit around, playing the victim, while her beau fought for his life.

She wiped her face with a tissue Olivia gave her. "May I see Aidan, Dr. Billings?"

His eyebrows furrowed. "I don't think that's wise right now, Miss Sutton."

"Please. I've come all this way."

"But—"

"Look, Doctor. I'm not leaving this hospital until Aidan can accompany me, alive and well." Beth served the physician a polite but pointed look. "So you might as well let me stay at his bedside."

Olivia squared her shoulders. "Me, too."

Dr. Billings stood. "As you wish, Miss Sutton."

Beth and Olivia left the office with their belongings and followed Dr. Billings to Aidan's room. He stopped in front of a closed door at the end of a quiet corridor.

"This is Mr. Evans' private accommodation. I must warn you, Miss Sutton, he has a significant amount of facial swelling, so you may be startled by his appearance. Rest assured, though, we are controlling his pain with medication. Let me know when you're ready."

Beth tightened her grip on her suitcase. She wasn't ready— she'd never be ready to face Aidan in any state of unwell. But this wasn't about her. "Let's go."

Dr. Billings opened the door. Olivia's hand flew to her mouth. Beth gasped and dropped her luggage. Bandages, dried blood, bruises, a pale, unmoving form . . .

"Oh, Aidan!"

Lightheadedness struck Beth hard, inciting a wave of dizziness that left her struggling for breath. The room shifted off-kilter, swaying her toward the doorframe. Yellow splotches fragmented her vision—they wouldn't disappear no matter how many times she blinked, no matter how desperate she was to remain strong for her beau. She felt herself drifting, sinking . . .

Dr. Billings grasped her arm and steadied her. "I'll have Mr. Motts arrange transportation for you and Ms. Weston to your hotel. You can see Mr. Evans another day."

Beth screwed her eyes shut, breathing deeply to fight the threat of unconsciousness. "No, I'm not leaving. I can't."

"Miss Sutton, you've had quite a shock. You mustn't aggravate your condition."

The floor beneath her seemed to stop moving. She cracked open her eyelids, testing her surroundings, assessing her situation. Yes, the vertigo was gone. Her mind was clearer, set to purpose.

She stood up straight and brushed the hair from her face. "I appreciate your concern, but I'm fine."

Dr. Billings released her slowly, watching over her as if she was the patient. "You cannot care for Mr. Evans properly if you neglect your own health."

"Being separated from my beau is what will hurt me the most, Doctor. This is where I belong."

Beth walked to Aidan's bed. Dressed in a hospital gown, he lay on his back with a blanket pulled up to his mid-torso and his hands folded at his waist. Bandages covered his forehead and nose. His face was puffy and battered. The subtle rise and fall of his chest was the only indication of life.

A rectangular device—the cardioscope, most likely—sat on a stand next to his bed. Its monochrome display revealed a green trace that looked like a bouncing ball with a comet's tail. The intravenous line Dr. Billings spoke of was inserted into Aidan's left hand. Below that, on his middle finger, was the ring she had given him for Christmas.

"Oh, Aidan." Her purse slipped off her shoulder as she fell to her knees. Tentatively, she touched his forearm. A shudder tore through her. Goodness, he felt so cold.

"Come on. Let's get settled." Olivia helped her to her feet and stowed her jacket and purse in the closet. They claimed the two chairs at Aidan's bedside.

"Can I do anything to help him in his recovery?" Beth regarded the physician with broad, desperate eyes.

Dr. Billings approached the bed. "Although there is no medical evidence to support it, I believe talking to him might do some good."

Beth leaned toward her beau. "Aidan, it's Beth. I love you very much. Please come back to me. Please."

"I'll leave you now. Send for me if you need anything." Dr. Billings patted her shoulder and left the room.

Beth tossed Olivia a teary glance. "He looks so helpless."

Olivia straightened Aidan's blanket. "He'll get well, especially now that you're here."

A knock announced visitors. Olivia opened the door and greeted Connie and Matthew, much to Beth's surprise and delight.

"We came as soon as we heard." Connie embraced Olivia.

"Beth and I just arrived. How did you know Aidan was here?"

Matthew exchanged hesitant looks with Connie. "Nathan called us. He told us about Aidan's condition and arranged clearance with hospital security so we could visit."

Olivia's lower lip trembled. "That was . . . nice of him."

Connie crossed the threshold. Her eyes widened when they landed on Aidan.

"Dear God." Releasing a sob, she threw herself at her fiancé and buried her face in his chest.

Matthew stroked Connie's hair and swallowed hard. A muscle in his jaw twitched.

His shimmering eyes met Beth's. Unspoken words of sympathy and sadness underscored the silence between them. The all-American crooner, with the dimpled grin he wore so frequently it became his trademark, looked on the verge of an emotional breakdown. There would be no friendly banter today. No laughter or song.

Once Connie regained her composure, she rushed over to Beth. "I'm so sorry."

Beth stood and hugged Connie in lieu of a verbal greeting. She didn't think she could get any words out without bursting into tears again.

"Do you think Aidan can hear us?" Matthew set their suitcases next to the door.

Olivia answered on Beth's behalf. "We're not sure, but the doctor says it doesn't hurt to talk to him."

Matthew approached the bed, holding his fedora with trembling hands. "Hey, Aidan. It's Matthew. Connie is with me. We've come to, uh—" He grimaced and turned away, but not quickly enough to hide the tear that tumbled from his left eye.

Using a silk handkerchief he pulled from his pocket, Matthew wiped his face on his hasty charge to the opposite side of the room. He stopped in front of the window with his back to the group. Head down, he stood there silently, the slump of his shoulders the only indication of the anguish broiling within him.

Beth took her seat. It was time to speak, whether it was hard for her or not. "Thank you both for coming." She sniffled. "Aidan appreciates it, too. I know he does."

Matthew faced the room again, his aggrieved expression belonging to a man who would use any means necessary to protect his friends, his family. "We're here for however long it takes until Aidan is well again."

At Beth's suggestion, the women gathered a washbasin, filled it with soap and water, and cleaned the dried blood on Aidan's face, around his bandages.

Alongside her friends, Connie rolled up her sleeves, tied back her hair, and performed basic care practices with the utmost dedication. She even bought flowers from a shop across the street to freshen up the place—surprising acts of kindness, given her rocky history with Aidan, but welcome nonetheless. They rallied together, just like old times, and the mood lightened. One look at Olivia, however, was a reminder that an important member of their group was still missing.

While Beth's friends came and went throughout the day, she refused to leave Aidan's room. She maintained a vigil at his bedside, speaking to him regularly and humming the song he wrote for her.

Sometime in the afternoon, Olivia squeezed her shoulder, drawing her attention from her beau. "Beth, we're going to the cafeteria to get you some food. You haven't eaten since we arrived."

"Any requests?" Matthew put on his fedora.

Beth's smile was faint but genuine. Come to think of it, she was famished. "Whatever you choose will be fine."

"All right. We'll be back shortly." Connie grabbed her purse and left the room with Matthew and Olivia.

Beth shifted her gaze back to Aidan. In slumber, he always looked so peaceful. The tension around his mouth was gone, the grooves in his brow smoothed out.

Aidan had driven to Chicago to talk to his father, she was sure of it, but it was a mystery as to whether a meeting had actually taken place. If it did, were a hostile confrontation and a hasty departure responsible for his accident? She hoped his return provided him with the same solace visiting Clarkson had granted her, but given the weathered man before her, it didn't seem promising.

Beth retrieved a container of petroleum jelly from a supply closet and applied it to Aidan's scabbed lips. When she was done, she slipped her open hand under his, not holding it for fear of hurting him, but just letting him know she was still there.

An older nurse with a nametag that read *Rita* entered and nodded a greeting. She replaced the nearly empty glass intravenous bottle with a new one and shifted Aidan's position in bed.

As Rita headed for the door, Beth cleared her throat softly. "Excuse me, ma'am."

She pivoted in the doorway. "Yes, Miss Sutton?"

"From your experience, do patients usually . . . I mean, if they're in a coma . . ." Beth gulped. "Do they usually wake up?"

Rita's eyes softened, revealing the compassionate nature suited to her profession. "We have a chapel on the main floor, adjacent to the lobby. Prayer is often comforting at a time like this." Following a glance at the crucifix hanging over Aidan's bed, she exited the room.

Beth slouched in her chair, tears obscuring her vision. She chastised her behavior using adjectives inappropriate for a lady, never mind a Catholic hospital, but the only ones that seemed to do her situation justice. She didn't want to cry—with all of her heart she wanted to remain optimistic—but the waiting, the seriousness of Aidan's condition, and the lack of assurance from hospital staff left her feeling defeated.

A knock, hesitant in its delivery, pulled Beth from her reflections. Her heart leapt when she saw who stood in the doorway. She barreled toward their visitor, wrapping him in the tightest hug possible.

"Nathan! Oh, I've missed you so!"

"Hello, Beth." He dropped his head to her shoulder and released a deep breath against her ear. "I've missed you, too."

Beth peered up at him, sharing a full-blown smile. While his neatly pressed suit and straight posture conveyed confidence, his weary gaze confessed the truth. Aidan's eyes were often bloodshot because of his insomnia, but Nathan's eyes rivaled the sun when it hovered over the horizon—so fiery red in color they burned her just by looking at them.

"I'm sorry, Beth. I know the words themselves are inadequate, but you must believe the sincerity behind them."

"It's not your fault, Nathan. None of it is."

"But I—"

"Guilt is useless when felt for no reason except to torture yourself and displace the blame from the true culprit. Connie went through it—Aidan, me, and now you. I won't stand for it any longer."

Nathan brushed his hand to her hair. "You're a strong woman, Beth. You've always been strong." Sadness settled on his face as his attention drifted to her beau. "I spoke to Dr. Billings upon my arrival. I'm glad Aidan's condition changed from grave to stable since my initial conversation with him."

"Me, too." Beth pressed her cheek to Nathan's chest, finding solace in his embrace. He had a calm and comforting aura about him, a fraternal quality that made her feel safe. She was so grateful he was here. Their group was now complete, reminding her of another detail of which he was probably unaware.

"Olivia accompanied me to Chicago. She's at the hospital cafeteria right now with Connie and Matthew."

Nathan drew back abruptly. "Liv is here?"

"Yes. She booked her airline ticket after you booked mine. She wouldn't let me come alone. By the way, thank you for making my travel arrangements. You really came through for me."

"It was the least I could do." Nathan adjusted his fedora. "Anyway, I should go."

Beth recoiled. "What do you mean? You just arrived."

Regret passed across his face. "Beth, you've been very gracious to me, but I don't believe Olivia will be as forgiving."

A frown descended upon her lips. "Olivia loves you. She'll want to see you."

Nathan's jaw set tightly. "She used to love me."

"She still does."

"I wasn't going to come to Chicago, but I needed to see Aidan's condition for myself and determine if there was anything more I could do to help." The fissures in his brow deepened. "I never planned on staying."

Beth took his hand. "Please do. We need you."

"I can't. Even if Olivia still loves me, I'm unworthy of her. My past is—"

"In the past."

Nathan wrenched from her grasp. "But I lied to all of you."

"It must've been for a good reason. You would never hurt us on purpose."

He bowed his head. "I truly didn't have a choice."

Beth cradled his cheek in her hand. "I forgive you and Liv will, too—"

A gasp erupted. Beth and Nathan stepped apart and turned toward the corridor. Olivia stood with Connie and Matthew, her face absent of color. She gaped at Nathan, as though she had difficulty accepting that he was there.

"My apologies. The last thing I wanted to do was upset you

all further." Nathan ducked his head and exited the room, avoiding eye contact with everyone. He made it halfway down the hallway before Olivia spoke.

"Wait!"

Nathan stopped. The silence that wedged between them was filled with hope . . . longing.

Olivia took a step toward him. Followed by another. And another. Nathan turned around. When tears toppled from her eyes, he darted over to her and captured her in his arms. He grimaced as sobs retched from her throat, as if each one was a slash to his heart.

Beth had never seen Nathan cry before, but as he held on to his beloved, tears flowed down his face.

"My darling. Why are you so good to me? I don't deserve it." Nathan framed Olivia's face in his hands, grazing his thumbs across her wet cheeks.

"Because I love you." Her voice broke. "I always have and always will. That dreadful Luther Mertz is to blame for your mistakes. You're a great man, Nathan. The greatest man I know."

"There are things I need to tell you—not to justify my actions but to shed light on why I let Luther control me, why I stayed behind when the rest of you fled." Nathan motioned toward Aidan's room. "I'd like you all to hear what I have to say, if you don't mind."

"Not at all." Matthew escorted Connie into the room and set the food they'd purchased on the bedside table.

Beth's hunger vanished, replaced by relief over Nathan's

return. As Nathan and Olivia entered the room hand in hand, she also felt something else she thought had abandoned her forever: optimism.

When she reclaimed her seat next to Aidan, she placed her fingers to his wrist and focused not on his injuries but how grateful she was to be reunited with him. All was not lost as long as he drew breath, as long as his pulse fluttered under her loving touch.

Nathan removed his fedora and hung it in the closet. "My mother isn't dead."

Olivia's eyes flared with shock and bewilderment. Beth didn't blame her friend. She, too, was stunned. It seemed inconceivable, based on Nathan's own statements to the contrary in the months since she'd met him. Instead of bombarding him with questions, she kept silent, allowing him to open up as he saw fit.

"Her name is Marion Taggart, but you'd know her best as Marion Whitney."

Recognition skipped across Connie's face. "The actress?"

Nathan nodded. "She's housed at a mental institution in New York City. She's . . . unwell."

"I remember her from my childhood." Olivia shared her comments gently. "My mother was a big fan of hers. She used to take my brother and me to see all of her pictures. I always wondered what became of her."

"My mother's mental illness progressed to the point where she could no longer work at the studio or function well on her own. Luther used his influence to have her admitted to Bellevue

Hospital in secret and paid for the best care money could buy, including silence from the medical staff. That's why the public never learned about her condition."

"Mr. Mertz thrives on exposing people's weaknesses and using them to his advantage." Connie regarded Nathan in confusion. "Why would he help her?"

Nathan's eyes dimmed. "Apparently, Luther and my mother were in love."

"In love?" Olivia's voice rose. "I don't believe it!"

"I had no idea until a few days ago." Nathan exhaled deeply. "After my father's death, I moved to New York in hopes of getting into journalism and to be closer to my mother—who I thought was living in an uptown apartment. The truth was she was homeless. After Luther had my mother admitted to the hospital, he reached out to me and blackmailed me into working for him, insisting that he would pay her medical bills if I did his bidding without question."

Olivia shook her head. "How awful."

"I swear I had no clue that Luther was making unsolicited advances toward his female employees and passing them off to men who worked for him. If I did, I would've severed ties with him sooner." Nathan tugged at the knot in his tie. "Typically, my jobs for him involved covering up scandals that jeopardized his financial investments into people's careers. What he tried to do to Beth, however, was damning to his moral character directly.

"I couldn't turn a blind eye anymore. I threatened to expose the man he truly is, using my contacts at the press, if he didn't step down from his position at the studio and let me quit. I hated resorting to his tactic of blackmail, but it was the only way to ensure that my mother remained in Bellevue's care and he'd never hurt anyone again."

Olivia's eyes flickered with expectation. "So you don't work for Mr. Mertz anymore? You're free?"

"My conscience is shackled to my past mistakes, so I don't consider myself completely free. But yes, my work with Luther has thankfully come to an end." Nathan sighed. "I didn't tell you all the truth about my mother for fear that my deal with Luther would be revealed. I didn't want to risk destroying the only financial support my mother had—which, of course, was before I knew he would've supported her no matter what because of his feelings for her. I'm not ashamed of my mother. I just want her fans to remember her as she was."

Nathan shifted his turbulent gaze to Connie. "I'd heard what happened to you years ago, but I assumed you chose that path to kick-start your career. I was foolish not to have realized what was really going on—that you were coerced into submission. I'm truly sorry."

Connie smiled—not the gleaming smile used to win over film audiences, but an unguarded, effortless smile that shone with genuineness. "I appreciate your concern, but you're not to blame for what happened. I'm just glad you're finally able to move on from Mr. Mertz."

Nathan shoved his hands into his pockets. A pout seized his lips. "I should've left Luther's office when all of you did, but I was terrified he'd be on the telephone with Bellevue right away, planning his retaliation."

"If you needed money, why didn't you come to us? We would've helped you."

The others nodded in support of Beth's statement.

Nathan shook his head. "The financial cost is too much to bear for a woman you don't know."

"But we care about you, Nathan."

"Regardless, I never felt right turning to others for help."

Matthew's brow wrinkled. "So Bellevue's fees are more than what you made working at the studio?"

Nathan dragged his hand along the back of his neck, dodging the curious stares of Olivia and his friends. "See, that's the thing . . . Luther never paid me a salary. He paid for all of my expenses. He gave me a house, a beach cottage, a car, a weekly allowance, more than any man would ever need, but I was never officially on the payroll."

Matthew frowned. "Why couldn't you have left the studio earlier and worked some place where you would've earned a salary? You're well established in the industry. I'm sure you could've easily found another employer who'd utilize your skills. That way, it wouldn't have mattered if Mr. Mertz stopped paying your mother's hospital bills."

"The way I rationalized it was, until the incident with Beth, I had no reason to leave. I wanted for nothing in the materialistic sense and my mother was taken care of. Sure, I wasn't always happy doing Luther's bidding, but I convinced myself it was worth it if she was safe. Only when I realized the extent of his treachery did I have the motivation and the means to quit."

"Now that you're unemployed, what's going to happen to your mother?" Connie asked.

"I called Bellevue before I left L.A. They told me her bills have been paid for the next six months in advance, nonrefundable, so that bides me some time to come up with a plan to earn the money to cover her stay."

"We'll all pitch in, and we won't take no for an answer." Matthew arched his eyebrows. "So what did Luther say when you told him he had to step down from his position at the studio?"

"He refuted the idea immediately, but in today's newspapers there's a statement from him, announcing his retirement." Pride permeated Nathan's posture. "It was inevitable he'd heed my warning in spite of his arguments to the contrary. The accusations alone, whether they could be proven or not, would raise questions. There's no way he'd risk public denouncement, not after how hard he worked to create the studio."

Beth couldn't believe it—a Starlight Studios without Mr. Mertz. What did this mean for the future of film industry? Would creative freedom no longer be impossible for actors? These were loaded topics. She made a simpler inquiry.

"Is someone going to take Mr. Mertz's place?"

"Three senior executives are vying for his job, but based on the number of studio employees trying to break free from their contracts, I don't know how long the old system can be maintained."

"You never made a salary." Olivia twirled her engagement

ring around her finger.

Nathan lowered his gaze. "Yes, I'm afraid even your ring was bought by Luther."

Olivia removed the ring and threw it in the garbage. Nathan grabbed at his chest, as if she'd dumped his heart along with it.

She shrugged. "Well then, you'll just have to get me another one. That is, if you still want to marry me." She peered at him hopefully.

"Oh, darling. Of course I do." Nathan made a move to embrace her but stopped before following through on it. "I have nothing to offer you financially. I'm confident I can find work elsewhere, but it will take me some time to get back on my feet. Even then, I cannot guarantee we will live in luxury like you've been accustomed to this past year, especially while I'm making payments to Bellevue.

"If not for my meager savings of my allowance, I couldn't even have afforded the fare for the cab rides to and from the airport. I was only able to purchase my airline ticket and Beth's ticket and hotel reservation because I made the arrangements using the studio's expense account before I announced my resignation." His shoulders hunched. "I'm sorry I'm not the man you thought I was."

Olivia wrapped her arms around him. "Nathan, when you asked me to marry you, I said yes because I'm in love with *you*. I couldn't care less about material possessions. Plus, I have my own money. I don't need yours."

"I will do whatever it takes to ensure you never regret your decision." Nathan placed a kiss to her temple. "And I will buy you another engagement ring, I promise."

Olivia shook her head. "Forget what I said earlier. I don't want one. It's you I need, not material possessions."

He caressed her cheek. "Liv, you would honor me if you wore a ring I purchased with my own money. Please reconsider."

"All right." A smile graced her face. "I would also like to meet your mother."

"But she—"

"She's your mother. It would be a privilege."

Nathan pulled her close, holding her like he'd never let her go. "I love you."

She clasped her hands at his nape. "I love you, too."

The couple shared a kiss.

"Is this great?" A grin sprung to Matthew's face. "Nathan's back. He and Olivia made up. Life couldn't get any better, huh?"

Sorrow spiraled through Beth, annihilating her delight over Olivia and Nathan's reconsolidation. She blinked rapidly, spilling tears down her cheeks.

Matthew stepped toward her, his expression warped with woe and shame. "I'm sorry, Beth. That was really insensitive. I was just so happy to see them back together, I wasn't thinking."

Beth accepted Matthew's handkerchief and dried her eyes. She placed her hand over her beau's, searching for the slightest sign he wasn't lost forever, longing for the day he'd return her touch.

"An apology isn't necessary. Aidan and I will get our happy ending, too." She focused back on her friends. "Why don't you all take the night off? There isn't much going on here. Plus, there's not enough space for all of us to sleep in the room comfortably. Nathan, you and Olivia can use the suite you reserved for me at the Blackstone."

Matthew folded his arms across his chest. "Forget it. We're not leaving you alone."

Beth pitched a fond look at Aidan. "I'm not alone."

Matthew traded hesitant glances with the others, gauging, deliberating. Finally, he sighed in acquiescence. "We'll return first thing tomorrow morning, okay? Call me and Connie at the Talbott Hotel if you need anything."

"All right." Beth walked her friends to the door. They gathered their belongings and hugged and kissed her good night. They even said good-bye to Aidan, strengthening her hope that he'd get better soon.

Once they were gone, Beth grabbed a blanket and a pillow from the linen closet and returned to Aidan's bedside. She was too tired to change into evening attire but removed her shoes for comfort before creating a makeshift bed out of the chair. She'd eat the food her friends bought for her later.

"I love you, Aidan, and I'm here for you always." She brushed her fingers through his hair and then settled in her seat for the night. Despite her efforts to stay awake, she ultimately gave into her fatigue and slept.

Low mumbles stirred Beth from slumber. She opened her eyes and waited for them to adjust to the dark. She was not sure how long she had slept, but moonlight seeped into the room through the open blinds covering the window. Incoherent murmurs spilled from Aidan's lips. His right hand twitched in hers.

Tears streamed down her face. "I'm here, Aidan. It's Beth. Please come back to me."

A shrill alarm blasted from the cardioscope—so ghastly in pitch she was surprised her ears didn't bleed. She jumped to her feet. Aidan stilled. The cardioscope's screen displayed a green line with low blips.

"No!" Panic launched Beth out of the room. Her eyes burned from the fluorescent corridor lights. "Somebody help him! Please!"

The door at the end of the hallway burst open, revealing a horde of doctors and nurses pushing a cart of medical equipment and medication. They stormed past her and entered Aidan's room.

"Summon Dr. Billings from the on-call room immediately," a young physician yelled. "Tell him we have an emergency involving Mr. Evans!"

Beth's legs gave out. She flew into the doorframe as a nurse left to locate the staff physician. After what seemed like an insurmountable amount of time, Dr. Billings raced into the room.

Beth charged at him and grabbed a fistful of his lab coat. "Save him! Please!"

The cardioscope's staccato alarm converted to a continuous

beep. The line on the screen fell flat.

Dr. Billings shrugged her off. "Get her out of here!"

A nurse pulled Beth toward the doorway. She fought back, screaming for clemency, until two more nurses helped extradite her from the scene. The door slammed shut, sealing the medical team inside Aidan's room, leaving her alone in the corridor.

Sobs retched from Beth's throat as she collapsed to the floor. "Please don't leave me. Please don't leave me." She pulled her knees to her chest and rocked back and forth. "O glorious Archangel Saint Raphael, I humbly pray you to heal the many infirmities of Aidan's soul and the ills that afflict his body . . ."

"Carotid pulse remains faint," Dr. Billings shouted. "Administer epinephrine one milligram!"

Beth peered toward the ceiling, her face streaked with tears.

Lamb of God, You take away the sins of the world; spare us, O Lord.

"He's seizing. Lorazepam seven milligrams now and prepare for endotracheal intubation!"

Lamb of God, You take away the sins of the world; graciously hear us, O Lord.

"Forty units of Vasopressin, stat!"

Lamb of God, You take away the sins of the world; have mercy on us.

"We're losing him!"

Beth squeezed her eyes shut.

Lamb of God, You take away the sins of the world . . .

The cardioscope fell silent.

Grant us peace.

Chapter Fifteen

Sunlight streamed into the kitchen as the sheer curtain billowed over the open window above the sink. The quaint room was familiar; so was the view of the meadow surrounding the property.

Aidan's brow creased in puzzlement. He was in his childhood home in Fairfield, Indiana. But given the worn blue jeans and white T-shirt covering his tall, muscular frame, he was a twenty-three year old man, not a boy.

Tentatively, he explored his surroundings. There was no dust, no clutter. No blood. No screams. The house was immaculate and quiet.

He peered through the kitchen window. Sparrows fluttered outside, chirping a merry tune, while the grass swayed in the zephyr. The luscious land seemed to stretch on forever, nothing but vibrant greenery and colorful flowers.

Life.

A warm gust of wind blew into the kitchen, ruffling his hair. He grinned. He'd forgotten how peaceful it could be here.

Drawn to the meadow, he left the house through the back

door and traveled across the porch to stand under the cloudless blue sky. Tilting his head back, he closed his eyes and reveled in the heat of the sun against his face.

"Aidan?"

He gazed out at the field. His grin widened.

Beth stood barefoot in the meadow, wearing a pristine white sundress. Her brown hair was set in loose curls, framing her rosy cheeks and broad smile. He jogged over to her.

"There you are!" She giggled. "I've been looking for you."

Aidan brushed the hair from her face. "You've found me, baby."

Beth took his hand and pulled him across the meadow. The wind played with her dress, the cotton fabric drifting behind her in an elegant train.

Releasing his hand, she extended her arms and twirled around, her twinkling brown eyes lifted toward the sky. Aidan watched in wonder as she spun faster and faster, her laughter ringing like church bells as her hair danced across her cheerful face. She was a spectacular vision in white. His little dove, innocent and pure.

With a frisky leap toward him, Beth clasped her hands behind his neck and pressed their bodies together. She treated him to a loving gaze. At once, Aidan captured her in his arms and kissed her. Their lips remained joined as he lifted her off the ground and spun, enveloped by the gentle breeze.

Dizzy with devotion, Aidan paused and guided her closer, sprinkling kisses along her throat. Amidst their passion, they lost their footing and tumbled to the earth, cushioned by the grass as they relaxed and caught their breath.

Aidan plucked a pink flower from the soil and trailed its petals down Beth's face. She smiled and settled in his embrace. Her eyelids wilted while the sparrows continued their sprightly song in the distance.

He tossed the flower aside and traced his fingers up along her hip and one supple breast, coming to rest at her nape. As she rested safely, he studied her quietly, her soft breaths swathing him in serenity.

"It's lovely here." Beth sighed and opened her eyes. "Must we leave so soon?"

"What do you mean?" He combed his fingers through her hair. "We can stay as long as you wish, little dove."

Her lips formed an alluring pout. He preferred her smile.

"Oh, how I wish that were true." She slipped from his arms and stood, brushing grass and dirt from her dress.

Aidan linked his hands behind his head and squinted against the sunlight. A grin stretched across his face. "You're beautiful."

Beth averted her gaze. A frown decorated her mouth. "It's time."

Without another word, she dashed toward the house.

Aidan leapt to his feet and ran after her. He took only a few steps and then halted midstride.

"Mother?" His voice carried on the wind, lost amongst the rustling foliage.

It was impossible. There was no way . . .

He blinked once. Twice.

Beth vanished, as though only a mirage. His mother remained. She stood in the meadow, her wavy auburn hair and flowery frock shimmering in the sunlight.

Somehow, he managed to walk up to her. She welcomed him with a smile. Before speaking, he took some time to commit her youthful appearance to memory. He wanted—no, needed—to remember her this way. Healthy and carefree.

"I'm sorry." Tears flooded his eyes.

"There's nothing to be sorry about, my son. I love you and I am with you always." Her smile adopted a wistful twist. "She's exquisite."

Beth.

A grin tugged at Aidan's lips. "Yes, she is."

"Go to her."

Dread catapulted his heart against his ribcage. "What about you?"

She cupped his cheek. "You cannot have both, my son."

A knot formed in his chest.

"I love you." Aidan placed his hand over hers for a moment, relishing their reunion. Then he sprinted toward the house.

Inside, Beth hummed the tune he wrote for her. His heart swelled. He was home.

A blinding white light greeted him as he yanked open the back door. He winced and swung his arm across his face, shielding his eyes.

"Aidan . . ."

He dropped his arm and blinked rapidly to try to clear his vision. Disoriented, he stepped into the light. Hopefully he wasn't too late.

"Aidan . . ."

"Aidan . . ."

"Aidan . . ."

Fighting against the haziness that enveloped him, Aidan opened his heavy eyelids and met a dark brown, watery gaze that looked familiar. Beth leaned over him, her features drawn together, exposing prominent lines of worry.

A thick piece of her hair danced in front of his face. He attempted to lift his hand to brush it aside but was unsuccessful. His arms felt like they were cased in cement. In fact, now that he was more lucid, he realized that his nose hurt, his chest hurt. Damn it. It even hurt to move his eyes.

Aidan racked his brain for answers. He remembered confronting his father, leaving the house, wishing to return to Beth right away, and then . . . nothing.

As he blinked hard, the details of his surroundings came into focus. Olivia, Connie, Nathan, and Matthew gathered behind Beth, their expressions alight with hope. His mother was not among them. His time in the meadow had been a dream.

Where exactly was he? He was lying on an uncomfortable bed—that much was clear—but his thoughts were jumbled and he couldn't put the rest of the puzzle together. Maybe this was a dream and the meadow was his reality.

Beth wiped away her tears. Aidan moved his fingers, but it was still difficult to lift his arms. It pained him not to be able to hold and comfort her. Nathan said something to Matthew, which Aidan couldn't make out, and then Nathan disappeared from his field of view. He heard a door shut soon after.

Aidan swept his gaze down his body. Something was taped over his nose, and a tube ran into the back of his hand. The blankets draped over him secured him so tightly he didn't have room to maneuver—which explained why he could wiggle his toes but not raise his legs—and wires slipped under his bedspread, connected to a machine that had a screen with green peaks traveling across it.

He opened his mouth to speak, but his tongue felt thick and dry and his voice wouldn't cooperate. He closed his eyes as dizziness overcame him.

"It's all right, Aidan." Beth touched the top of his head. Panic eased out of him, even though his mind raced with questions.

He moved his mouth in a chewing motion, desperate to wet his palate. Beth's hand disappeared. Fear plowed into him; something nearby emitted a rapid series of beeps. The machine with the green peaks, maybe?

"I'm here," Beth said from somewhere in his vicinity, and then he sensed her beside him again. The beeping ceased. "Have some ice chips."

Aidan licked the ice greedily, tasting not only water but also a coppery tang that reminded him of . . . blood? His lower lip stung, but his dehydration prevailed and he finished everything she offered him.

Prying his eyes open, he finally found his voice. "Beth."

Her hand flew to her mouth. "You know who I am."

His eyebrows furrowed. "Where am I?"

Beth set down the cup of ice and leaned over him, grazing her hand to side of his face. "Chicago Memorial Hospital."

The machine with the green blips exploded into a chorus of high-pitched beeps again as Aidan struggled to sit up, haphazardly reaching for the wires and tubes connected to his body.

Matthew darted to his side. "Whoa. Easy there, buddy."

He placed his hands on Aidan's shoulders and tried to ease him onto his back again.

"Why . . . hospital? No." Aidan struggled against Matthew's grip. The effort left him winded.

Beth's chin quivered. "Please, Aidan. Don't strain yourself."

His heart shattered at her sorrowful expression. The back of his head found the pillow and Matthew released him. Aidan was much too exhausted and sore to fight him anyway.

With his resignation, the machine next to him stopped beeping. The peaks traveling across the screen—did they correlate to his heartbeat?

He blinked rapidly, fighting against the fluorescent lights above him. "I . . . don't . . . understand."

Beth's eyes shimmered with tears again. "You were in a car accident."

He flinched. A car accident? Was that why he couldn't remember anything after he left his father's house?

He cleared his throat. "How long have I been here?"

Beth wrapped her arms around her midsection. "You've been in a coma for almost three days."

Chicago Memorial Hospital. How ironic that he was brought to his father's workplace following their confrontation. He didn't have to worry about running into the man again, though. It wasn't like his father would stop by with a get-well card.

Aidan screwed his eyes shut, hoping to clear his thoughts. After a few moments, he opened them slowly. Beth's angel pendant glistened like a prism, casting a rainbow of colors across the sheets covering him. His gaze jumped to his left hand. He blew out a sigh of relief. The ring she gave him was still on his middle finger.

"Your car hit a tree." Beth's voice wavered. "Your nose is broken as well as two of your ribs. You also have many cuts and bruises."

With a sob, she collapsed to her knees, grasping his hand and bowing her head to the mattress. Connie and Olivia dropped next to her, whispering words of solace Aidan wished he had the strength to utter himself.

Beth tightened her grip on his hand, her face hidden by her hair as she wept. Aidan inched toward her, desperate to get closer, regardless of the pain that surged through his body with the movement. He forced his other arm to swing across his body and drove his hand into her hair, finding her face and cradling her wet cheek in his palm.

"Don't cry, baby," he said hoarsely. "I'm here. I'm okay. Please stand up."

Beth lifted her head and sniffed. Aidan caressed her cheek, searching her bloodshot eyes for any signs of comfort. There were none.

Olivia and Connie also cried, and their puffy eyes suggested the tears weren't new. Even Matthew looked distraught, when he was usually the one to offer comic relief, finding the bright side of even the darkest situations.

It didn't make any sense. What the hell had happened to yield these reactions?

"Matt, help them up." Aidan's orders sounded shaky, but Matthew obeyed immediately, assisting the women to their feet.

When Connie and Olivia stood, Aidan took a good look at them. They didn't have any makeup on their faces, which he had never seen before. They wore no jewelry, except Connie had on her engagement ring, and their outfits and hairstyles weren't fussy. Matthew was dressed down, too, in an oxford shirt and trousers. Aidan didn't think he owned anything other than designer suits.

The incident in Mr. Mertz's office and the events that followed had stripped them all down to the essentials. Sure, they still had their material possessions in L.A. and money in the bank. However, when it came down to right here, right now, all they had was each other. Really, that was all they needed. It meant they could start fresh and do things right this time.

Aidan scanned the room—the white walls, fluorescent lights, and medical equipment. He recalled Beth's visit to the hospital in Los Angeles and his fright when he got the call from Nathan that she was hurt. Then there were the memories of his mother passing away in the hospital outside of Fairfield, succumbing to injuries brought on by a vicious stranger who had manipulated her good heart and trusting nature and brutally beat and stabbed her to death.

Aidan cursed. He despised hospitals and everything associated with them. If not for his determination to avoid frightening Beth further, he would've ripped out all the tubes and wires shackling him to the bed and bolted from the room, regardless of his condition.

The door to the room swung open, revealing Nathan and an older man dressed in a white coat. A doctor. Aidan's face tightened in defiance.

"Mr. Evans." The physician flashed a wide smile. "It's wonderful to see you awake. You gave us all quite a scare."

"He knows who I am," Beth said. "And Matthew, too. He also responded to his own name, so he knows who he is as well."

Aidan's eyebrows pinched together. Of course he knew who they were. As for his own name—well, that was obvious, wasn't it?

"Excellent." The doctor approached the bed. "Mr. Evans, can you move your arms and legs?"

Aidan's eyes narrowed.

The doctor frowned. "Mr. Evans, can you understand me?"

"Yeah, I understand. I just don't wanna be bothered by you right now." A series of coughs racked Aidan's body. He winced from the pain that detonated in his chest.

"Aidan, please."

His gaze shot to Beth.

"This is the man who saved your life."

The physician blushed. "Nonsense. The boy is strong-willed. It was all his doing."

Aidan rolled his eyes.

"My name is Doctor Billings, Mr. Evans. It's a pleasure to meet you officially."

Aidan lifted his hand in a dismissive gesture, but Dr. Billings misunderstood.

"Please, a handshake isn't necessary." The expansive grin never left the physician's face.

Aidan opened his mouth to spit out a cutting reply but closed it when he caught a glint of sincerity in the doctor's eyes.

Huh. Maybe the guy wasn't so bad, after all.

"We'll leave you alone." Olivia took Nathan's hand. "I'm sure you'd like to speak to Beth and the doctor in private."

"Aidan, do you know who that is?" Beth peered at him hopefully.

Aidan's eyebrows came together again. "Olivia." Man, now he was even more baffled. "And before you ask, the blond woman is Constance Murphy, and the other guy is Nathan Taggart."

Beth clutched her hands to her chest. "Isn't that great, Dr. Billings?"

"Indeed."

Connie placed her hand on Aidan's forearm, her blue eyes sparkling with tears and . . . kindness? No question. This had to be a dream.

"It's lovely to have you back. Truly."

"Uh, thanks." Aidan's reply came out sounding more like a query.

Olivia stepped forward. "Aidan, it's nice to see you, well, talking and stuff."

"Okay." He dragged out the word on account of his confusion.

His friends made their way to the door.

"Oh, and Aidan . . ." Matthew tossed a smirk over his shoulder, displaying the jovialness Aidan expected from him. "Don't die again while we're gone, all right?"

Beepbeepbeepbeepbeepbeepbeepbeepbeepbeepbeep . . .

The machine went crazy as the blood drained from Aidan's face. Dead? He couldn't have heard Matthew correctly.

His friends laughed, but he could tell it was forced. Beth didn't even crack a smile. Once they were gone, leaving Aidan with Beth and Dr. Billings, a young nurse—probably straight out of school—arrived.

"Miss Sutton, you'll have to leave." The nurse shot Beth a stern look. "It's not proper protocol—"

Dr. Billings lifted his hand. "Miss Sutton can stay during the examination, and for however long she likes afterward."

The nurse still didn't look pleased but said nothing as she stripped the sheets from Aidan's body. He cringed at the flimsy gown covering him. This was not the image he wanted to present to Beth. Maybe she should've left with their friends.

"What did Matthew mean with the comment he made on his way out the door?"

Although Aidan looked to Beth for a response to his inquiry, Dr. Billings answered instead.

"Last night, you were clinically dead, Mr. Evans." The

physician delivered the news as if it was no big deal. "You came back to us just after we stopped our resuscitation efforts and remained in your coma until now."

Beth collected a fresh blanket from the linen closet. It seemed like an avoidance attempt so Aidan wouldn't catch the fresh batch of tears pooling in her eyes.

Thinking about what she must have gone through killed him all over again. Now it all made sense: his friends' strange behaviors, Beth's excitement over him not forgetting anyone's name. They had assumed the worst—like the car crash might've tampered with his mind or something. Man, he hadn't realized how serious everything was until this moment.

Dr. Billings asked him various questions like where he was presently, the date, and what his last memory was. The only thing Aidan wasn't sure about was the exact day, but he got the month and year correct, which seemed good enough.

Next, Dr. Billings shone a light in his eyes and had him perform basic motor function exercises. Afterward, the physician announced with immense satisfaction that he presented no clinical signs of permanent brain damage. Apparently not remembering the crash was normal, given the gravity of the accident.

Some questions about what happened to him that night were also answered. Road conditions were slick because it was raining, and he lost control of his Porsche one mile from the freeway. His seatbelt had saved him from launching through the windshield and into the tree he hit.

He would never tell Beth that he was speeding back to L.A.

to see her. He didn't want her to blame herself for his carelessness.

"Hey, Doc. Is there something you can do about that damn machine?" Aidan jutted his chin at the piece of medical equipment with the green blips on the screen.

"The cardioscope must stay for now, Mr. Evans," Dr. Billings said as he jotted down notes in Aidan's chart.

Aidan cursed under his breath, ensuring that Beth didn't hear him. He looked at his hand and fiddled with the tube stuck into the back of it.

"And the IV stays, too. At least until tomorrow." Dr. Billings chuckled when Aidan scowled. "Not to worry. You'll be taking medication orally soon enough."

Aidan's attention was diverted as Beth set down the blanket she'd retrieved and sat at his bedside. Her withered face gave away her exhaustion. How long had it been since she last slept soundly?

The nurse shifted Aidan in different positions while Dr. Billings concluded the physical examination—which didn't help his pain situation— and his diet was changed to solid foods.

During the doctor's assessment, Aidan caught Beth's gaze on a number of occasions, and she always offered a smile that didn't reach her eyes. He longed to get her alone so they could talk about a few important things—like the incident with Mr. Mertz and his abrupt departure from L.A. Then there was Beth's career to worry about, and their future as couple . . .

Aidan's head spun, but he was also eager to get out of the hospital and fix everything. The physical healing was only the beginning.

Dr. Billings hung Aidan's chart at the foot of the bed. "Before I leave, how is your pain? You received your last dose of medication almost four hours ago."

Aidan lifted his shoulders flippantly, aggravating his broken ribs. The grimace that followed told Dr. Billings the truth.

"I'll have the nurse administer another dose. You'll feel better in no time."

Aidan shook his head. "I don't want any more medication."

"Please let the doctor help you." Beth placed her hand on his forearm. "I don't want you in pain."

If Aidan weren't already lying down, the torment behind her words would've brought him to his knees. "Fine, but only a little. I don't wanna fall asleep."

Beth pouted. "You need your rest."

"Yeah, well, so do you."

Dr. Billings grinned. "Yes, the pain medication will make you drowsy, Mr. Evans, but it's best to take it easy anyway. You don't want to push yourself too soon." He relayed some orders to the nurse before leaving the room.

"When am I getting out of here?" Aidan asked as the nurse swapped his IV bottle for a new one.

"Relax, Mr. Evans. You're in good hands. As the doctor said, there is no need to rush your recovery." The nurse paused in the doorway. "I'll be back soon to give you a bed bath and administer your pain medication."

Aidan cringed. He'd have to find some way to bathe

himself.

When they were alone again, Beth draped him in the blanket she removed from the closet.

Aidan took her hand. "I'm sorry for what I've put you through."

Her eyebrows furrowed. "Sorry for dying?"

He shrugged. "Yeah, that. And everything else, too."

She waved him away. "Let's get you well before we talk about what happened."

"No, baby. You gotta know that *I* know it was completely wrong for me to take off like I did. You and I are better together than apart."

Beth choked back a sob. "You obviously didn't think that at the time."

"I'd convinced myself that I was responsible for what happened between you and Mertz . . . that I was weak and should've done more to protect you. My only weakness was abandoning you. I think I just needed to sort out some personal stuff by myself in order to truly realize my mistakes. I promise I'll never leave you again, no matter what."

She sniffled. "You vowed that before—"

"This time it's forever." Aidan shifted in bed to make room for her. "Lay down with me?"

"I don't want to hurt you."

"You won't." He lifted his arm in invitation.

Beth snuggled up to him and cried into his gown.

Aidan held her tightly. "I love you, baby."

"I love you, too. I just hope you stay true to your promise

this time. I've told you repeatedly that you're a good man, but you never believed me."

"Things are different now."

"How are they different?"

"I talked to my father before my accident."

Beth's eyes widened. "You did?"

"Yeah. He works here, you know."

"Yes, I know." Beth looked away as she replied—which only meant one thing.

"He never inquired about me, did he? Or visit me?"

"No." Beth whispered the word, as if she didn't want to be the bearer of bad news. "To be fair, he might not know you're here. He's been on a leave of absence for just over a month now. The hospital's attempts to notify him of your admittance have failed. Yes, the media has covered your accident, but we can't assume he has all the correct details."

Aidan's eyebrows shot up. This news was more shocking than learning about his brush with death. Last month was the fourteenth anniversary of his mother's passing. His father never mentioned anything about taking time off work. Then again, they didn't exactly sit around and catch up on all the goings-on in each other's lives. As for his father not knowing he was here, Beth wouldn't be making excuses for the man if she knew the truth.

Aidan exhaled deeply. Since they were all about confessions today, it was only proper that she learn the full story. "The night of my mother's murder, my father was with Betty."

Beth gaped at him. "Together as in . . . romantically?"

Aidan nodded. "For years, I blamed myself. Meanwhile, he was out betraying my mother's trust. Our encounter the other night was anything but cordial, but out of the whole mess, I realized you were right. I beat myself up over my mother's death, but it was the drifter who took her life. Then there's my father, who should've been around more but wasn't. Hell, maybe I could've done more to protect her on my own, but I was only a kid and scared out of my damn mind."

He shook his head. "Basically, I've learned there are many factors that come into play, which if handled differently, would've changed the entire course of how things worked out. But things unfolded how they did, and no matter how painful it all is, I have no choice but to accept it. Either that or I spend the rest of my life hating myself and hating my father for placing the blame on me to ease his own guilt. Part of moving on was forgiving him for the affair."

"That's mature of you, Aidan. I'm sure it wasn't easy."

"And in terms of forgiving myself—well, I want to talk to an analyst." He looked at her hesitantly. Hopefully she didn't think he was taking the cowardly approach. "You and me . . . we have a second chance at a relationship, if you still want me."

"Of course I do."

Aidan grinned. "You have no idea how happy I am to hear that. So, you see, that's why I need to take this step. Your support is crucial to me, but I also know professional guidance is required if I finally want to win this battle against my past. I don't wanna mess anything up this time around. I want to focus on our future together, not guilt or sadness, just the joy spending the rest of my life with you will bring me."

"Oh, Aidan. I'm so glad. I'll see an analyst, too. I'm dedicated to our relationship and want to do anything I can to help us move forward." Beth wrapped her arms around him.

Aidan groaned as pain seized what felt like every bone, muscle, and organ in his body.

"I'm sorry." She tried to pull back.

"No. Don't let go." He held her tighter and brought his lips to hers, despite the difficulty his bandaged nose presented.

A knock sounded at the door. Beth leapt out of bed and straightened her dress. The nurse from earlier entered the room, holding a basin full of supplies.

"It's time for your bed bath, Mr. Evans."

Aidan tensed. "I'll wash myself."

The nurse scowled. "I don't see how that's possible."

"Ma'am, may I please bathe Aidan?"

All eyes shifted to Beth.

The nurse scoffed. "Absolutely not. You two are not married. It's unethical, against policy. You're not even supposed to be here. If not for Dr. Billings bending the rules for you—"

"May I bathe you?" Beth directed her request to Aidan.

As much as he didn't want the nurse to do it, Beth helping him seemed worse. "As I said, I'll bathe myself."

"It's not safe in your condition." The nurse glared at him.

Aidan glared back. "You can leave now."

"Fine. I don't get paid enough to deal with the likes of you." With a huff, she set the basin on the bedside table and stalked out of the room. The door slammed shut behind her.

Beth reached for the bath items.

Aidan took her hand, bringing her to a halt. "I won't allow you to bathe me. It's not right."

When tears reappeared in her eyes, he wished he hadn't refused her offer so bluntly.

"Please let me take care of you."

Aidan stared at his ring and their entwined fingers. He had felt so helpless when he took Beth home from the hospital. Bathing her had brought him his only relief. He never believed the act was enough, but now he realized it had actually helped them both heal.

"Beth, I'd be honored if you bathed me."

A smile swept across her face. Aidan couldn't help but grin again, too. He wasn't sure how a bed bath worked, but Beth gathered the basin, removed the supplies, filled it with water in the bathroom, and got right down to it like an expert. As he'd learned before, love was enough to make up for lack of experience.

When Beth removed his gown, the full extent of the bruises and bandages on his body were revealed all at once. Under her loving gaze, he wasn't ashamed. He could recover his physical being by giving himself time to mend and then returning to the gym. The important thing was he was alive and reunited with Beth.

Beth completed her task with the utmost dedication, soothing his battered body until his pain slipped away and all that remained was serenity. After his gown was changed, she climbed back into bed with him.

He studied her bloodshot eyes and frowned. "Baby, when was the last time you slept?"

She stifled a yawn. "Don't worry about me."

A suitcase sat in the corner of the room. One of the bedside chairs had a blanket draped over it and a wrinkled pillow cradled in the seat—details Aidan had missed earlier.

Damn it. She hadn't left the hospital since her arrival.

Part of him wanted to berate their friends for allowing her to stay here instead of checking into a hotel, but he knew better. Beth was stubborn and probably refused to listen to them. He chose a gentler approach.

"I understand your desire to take care of me, but you need to look after yourself, too."

Beth shrugged. "I'm all right."

"You can rest now." He kissed her forehead. "I'm not going anywhere, little dove."

After some additional encouragement, Beth fell asleep. While she rested in his arms, Aidan tried to ignore the throbbing pain that coursed through his body now that his bed bath was done and his medication had worn off completely. It got to the point where he was so desperate to ease the ache in his chest he would've stopped the beating of his heart if it were without consequence.

Shifting his position, calling for the nurse, and risk waking up Beth wasn't an option. Instead, he recalled his mother in his dream—all the details about her he thought he'd lost forever. For the first time in a long time, no sorrow accompanied his recollections. He had a feeling this was how it would be from now on.

About fifteen minutes later, the nurse returned. Her eyes drilled into Aidan and Beth lying in the bed. "You two better not have displaced any tubes or wires."

Aidan placed his forefinger to his lips, indicating for her to be quiet.

The nurse muttered something about protocol and indecency but didn't press the matter. "I've come to administer your pain medication. Or would you like Miss Sutton to do it instead?" She rolled her eyes.

Aidan shooed her away. "Not now."

"It's now or never."

"Then never."

Beth stirred and opened her eyes. "What's going on?"

Aidan silently cursed the nurse.

"You must get out of the bed, Miss Sutton." The nurse stomped across the room. "Mr. Evans will fall asleep when the medication takes effect. He doesn't need you crowding him."

Beth shifted in the bed.

Aidan tugged on her hand. "Stay."

Matthew stuck his head inside the room. A grin lit his face. "Oh, good. You're is awake."

The door swung wide open, revealing Nathan, Olivia, and Connie. Beth pulled out of Aidan's grasp and stood, rubbing her tired eyes. He groaned. Bad timing for a reunion.

"You're looking much better, Aidan," Nathan said as the group entered the room.

Aidan glanced at the nurse. She'd already started

administering the medication. He took Beth's hand again. "Baby, I want you to stay at a hotel tonight."

"No. I'm not leaving you."

Aidan opened his mouth to protest, but a yawn won out instead. "Then stay with me . . . in my bed," he said, trying to fight the fatigue that attacked him. He would rather sleep on the chair than have her sleep there anymore.

Beth replied, but he couldn't make out what she said. His surroundings grew fuzzy and then faded into bright white nothingness. His muscles relaxed . . . his pain disappeared.

Aidan's eyelids dropped, and he felt himself slipping away. Panic hit him, mimicked by the cardioscope. Nothing would be more terrifying than if this was all a dream. He would rather go through everything he'd experienced since his visit with his father and end up in the hospital, battered and bruised and in the company of Beth and his friends, than wake up alone and in perfect health. The trauma of his accident was worth it as long as it reunited him with the people who meant most to him.

Aidan tried to remain lucid, but when Beth squeezed his hand, calmness enveloped him and he willingly submitted to his exhaustion.

Chapter Sixteen

A bright yellow light shone into Aidan's eyes as he emerged from his drug-induced sleep.

"Hello, Aidan." Beth stood before him, her back to the window. The sun cast a halo atop her head, presiding over welcoming eyes, rosy cheeks, and a stunning smile that was broad enough to eclipse it all.

"Hey." Aidan winced as he shifted in bed. "How long was I out this time?"

"Almost twenty-four hours." Beth's eyebrows knitted together. "Are you in pain?"

"It's not that bad."

She frowned.

He found a more tolerable position. "Really, I'm fine."

Matthew, Nathan, Connie, and Olivia entered the room, looking cheerful and well rested. Aidan lifted his hand in acknowledgement. Beth looked better, too, which was the biggest relief. She had changed into a red belted dress, and her hair was brushed and shiny.

Beth fixed his pillow and then handed him a glass of water.

The affectionate glance she gave him awakened a certain part of his anatomy, which thankfully wasn't affected by the accident.

"That must've been some drug they gave you. Dr. Billings mentioned the oral pain medication you'll get today won't have the same effect, so you can get back on a regular sleep schedule."

Aidan took a long drink to quench his thirst. Beth set the empty cup on the bedside table. He looked her over again, and his craving for her flourished. Yeah, he was definitely feeling better. "Did you get some sleep, too?"

"Yes." Her cheeks flushed more. "I slept in the bed with you."

"Now I know why I feel so good this morning." Aidan pulled her into his arms and brushed his lips to hers, which was easier than yesterday since the bulky bandage on his nose had been replaced with a less obtrusive one.

The absence of an alarm to give away his elevated heart rate drew his attention to the new free space next to his bed. The cardioscope was gone. He checked his left hand, and the day got even better. The IV was gone, too.

An orderly entered the room, carrying a meal tray. Connie positioned the bedside table so he could eat comfortably.

Aidan flashed a genuine grin. Part of his emotional recovery included talking to Connie once he was out of the hospital. There were a ton of things that needed to be said. Right now, he started with, "Thanks."

"You're welcome." With a smile that also seemed genuine, Connie retreated to her former spot next to Matthew.

Beth lifted the lid off his . . . breakfast? Lunch? Aidan glanced at the clock. Breakfast. There was only enough food for one, however.

"Are all of you going to eat as well?"

Matthew nodded. "We're heading to the cafeteria now. We'll grab something for Beth so she can stay here with you."

Beth sat on one of the bedside chairs and conveyed her gratitude with a smile.

Aidan put the lid back on his meal. "I won't eat until you do, Beth."

She wagged her finger at him. "Oh, no. You need your strength."

Aidan's grin emerged, despite his effort to suppress it. "Sorry, baby, but that's how it's gonna be."

Beth crossed her arms and glowered at him, but her smile eventually broke free, too.

After their friends left the room, Dr. Billings checked in on Aidan and relayed what the electroencephalograph—described as a brain wave recorder—revealed yesterday while he was asleep. It was all good news. In fact, he was healing better than expected.

Aidan owed Dr. Billings a lot. The physician had gone above and beyond his medical duty, supporting not only his patient, but also Beth and their friends. Maybe it was time to revisit his opinions on hospitals and medical personnel.

Dr. Billings monitored Aidan as he hobbled to the bathroom without assistance. He didn't want to know how they'd managed to empty his bladder while he was comatose. It felt great to be on his feet again, even though his legs shook the entire trip and by the time he got back into bed his body ached even more.

A nurse he'd never seen before administered his next dose of pain medication, which he swallowed with ease. Dr. Billings reassured him that this one wouldn't make him as tired as the intravenous one. Then the physician left with the nurse, granting Beth and Aidan some alone time.

As promised, Aidan didn't take one bite of his meal until their friends returned with Beth's food. His breakfast wasn't too tasty, but he was so hungry he devoured it like it was a prime cut steak dinner.

The group conversed on various topics until Aidan's curiosity got the best of him. He considered the most delicate way to bring up what was on his mind, but in the end went for the direct approach.

"What happened with Mertz after I took off?"

Gazes darted around the room. A throat cleared. Beth shifted in her seat.

Nathan stepped forward. It took him a few seconds to make eye contact. "Before I explain, there's something I need to tell you, Aidan. My mother is alive."

Aidan's eyebrows launched upward. He had braced himself for one hell of a response when he asked his question, but nothing as lofty as this.

If there was a definitive look of guilt and despair, Nathan had it down pat as he confessed who his mother was and how Mr. Mertz had blackmailed him into working at the studio. It cleared up a lot of things, but also fostered jealousy.

Aidan had connected with Nathan on a unique level because he believed they had both lost their mothers. Now that bond was severed. At the conclusion of Nathan's confession, however, Aidan understood why he'd withheld the truth. Aidan also insisted that an apology was unnecessary. Though, to placate Nathan, he accepted the one offered to him.

Then Aidan was delivered another surprise: Mr. Mertz had announced his retirement, and the future of Starlight Studios, including the standard seven-year contract, was in jeopardy.

Studio employees were excited over the possibility of a new approach to movie making. They didn't know exactly what had transpired in Mr. Mertz's office, just enough to credit Aidan with initiating the revolution. That was all fine and dandy, but Aidan and Beth still faced a major problem. The focus of the new men competing for Mr. Mertz's job was the completion of the films already in production when Mr. Mertz stepped down. Since Mr. Mertz had pulled the plug on *Golden Gloves* prior to leaving, the picture was probably never going to be finished. Also Beth, Connie, and Olivia's contracts were officially terminated, with no options for reinstating them, which complicated things further.

Minutes after their friends left to stretch their legs, the door swung open. Aidan's jaw dropped. The man with the greatest passion and artistic vision in the entertainment industry entered the room. If there was an Academy Award for perfect timing, he'd win it hands down.

"Mr. Kazan!" Beth rushed toward the director and flung her

arms around him.

"Hey, kid." Kazan grinned and patted her back. "I would've come sooner, but I had to get all of my information from the papers. Then it took some time to weed out fact from fiction. Christ, there are a lot of reporters outside. Luckily the head of security recognized me and escorted me up here."

Beth took his coat and hat and stowed them in the closet.

Kazan strolled across the room. "Aidan, I heard you died on us."

Beth's gaze fell to the floor. Her shoulders sagged.

Aidan's eyes narrowed. Out of respect, he softened his criticism with politeness. "Please watch what you say around her, Gadg."

Kazan cringed. "Sorry. Sometimes I blurt out inappropriate things. It's how I cope, you know?"

Beth presented a shaky smile. "It's all right. Aidan is on the mend now. That's all that matters."

"When I heard the news . . . " Kazan hung his head. "I'm glad you're okay, Aidan."

Aidan stuck out his hand to his mentor, the closest person to a father he'd ever had. "It's good to see you, Gadg."

The sorrow unloaded from Kazan's eyes as he shook Aidan's hand. "You, too."

Beth approached the bed. "Mr. Kazan, I apologize for only leaving a short note before fleeing to Clarkson. I should've called."

For the millionth time today, Aidan's eyebrows went skyward. So Beth had returned to Clarkson. Hopefully her visit with her parents had gone better than his visit with his father.

"You've had plenty to deal with, Beth. I don't blame you one bit." Kazan sat in an available chair. "I have something to share with the two of you. Since Luther Mertz shelved *Golden Gloves*, thus relinquishing his rights to the picture, I've taken it upon myself to get the project up and running again. After reaching out to my industry contacts and dipping—or more like plunging head first—into my personal savings, I've gathered all the footage we shot already and the resources required to finish the film without Starlight Studios' involvement."

Aidan flung into a sitting position. His medication hadn't kicked in fully yet, but his excitement over Kazan's news eliminated the pain resulting from the abrupt movement. "Gadg, are you serious?"

Beth clasped her hands. "My goodness. That's splendid!"

"If *Golden Gloves* doesn't explode at the box office, I'll be in debt up to my eyeballs for the rest of my life, but it's worth the risk to see this brilliant script up on the big screen." Kazan crossed his legs, knee to ankle. "We won't make a summer opening, but depending on Aidan's recovery, we may be able to swing a fall premiere."

"A fall premiere for sure," Aidan said. "I won't allow myself to be sidelined for long, not when I have a job to do. I'll also contribute whatever you need financially."

Beth nodded eagerly. "Me, too."

"I've talked to the rest of the cast and crew already. They're on board as well. Even the union has permitted it. So when you're both good to go, I'll finalize our filming schedule and everyone will meet us here in Chicago."

When Nathan, Olivia, Connie, and Matthew returned, they were updated on *Golden Gloves*' revival, and Aidan's room transformed into a temporary production office. Olivia agreed to stay on as the film's designer. Nathan offered to help Kazan with the behind-the-scenes organization, and Matthew offered to write and record a new theme song, since the studio still owned the original version. There were no salary negotiations, no contracts to sign. They merely shook hands to seal their partnerships.

After providing the name of his hotel and promising to stop in again tomorrow, Kazan grabbed his coat and hat and left.

As the day wore on, Aidan encouraged Beth and the others to take a break from the hospital and have a fun night out on the town. Beth refused, but he ended up convincing the others. They, too, promised to visit tomorrow.

Once they were alone again, Beth crawled into the bed upon Aidan's invitation. They shared a pillow, resting face to face, their hands linked and their noses touching.

"How was Clarkson?"

Beth beamed. "It was lovely. That is, before I got the call from Nathan about your accident."

Her frown appeared for only a moment before Aidan prompted her to share the good memories, not the bad ones. "How are your parents? How did you spend your days?"

Her lips curled upward. "My parents are well. I spent most of my time catching up with them, helping around the house, and venturing into town with my mother. I also caught up with my childhood friend, Emma. You'd really like Clarkson, I think. You should visit with me one day."

The tears that sprung to Aidan's eyes were unexpected but long overdue. He'd never had a normal childhood after his mother died and his family life vanished, and now Beth was offering to share hers with him.

He swallowed back the emotion that crawled up his throat. "I'd like that a lot."

Beth nuzzled his cheek. "Aidan, you seem very nonchalant about what transpired between you and your father. I know you two weren't close, but doesn't what you discovered about him bother you even a little?"

Aidan shrugged, but his composure was on the verge of crumbling. He didn't understand it. Why now? Life was good again. "Deep down, I guess some part of me would've liked to reconcile with my pop. He's my only living relative. But blood doesn't make family. You're my family—Kazan, Nate, Matt, and Olivia. Even Connie. So what if my past isn't worthy of a weekly sitcom? I'm grateful for everything I have. It's a waste of time to focus on everything I don't have."

"What about your accident? When you found out what happened, were you scared at all? I'm not bringing up everything to upset you. I just want to make sure you're not bottling up your emotions like before."

Aidan kissed the bridge of her nose. "What scared me most was seeing how distraught you were when I woke up from my coma. You concealed it well, but I could still tell you'd been through a lot. My waking up didn't erase all that. As for me, well, I was unconscious. So compared to what you dealt with—"

The memory of his mother in the meadow barraged him without warning. He blinked hard and his emotional dam broke, flooding his face with tears.

Beth pulled him into her arms as he bowed his head and wept over the loss of his mother, rejection by his father, but above all else, gratitude for his second chance at life—which brought to mind another topic he needed to discuss with Beth.

Aidan drew back so he could read her reaction as well as hear it. "Will you move to New York City with me?"

Her response was instantaneous, backed by a twinkle in her eyes that no amount of stars could compete with. "Absolutely."

Aidan chuckled. Leave it to Beth to turn his sorrow into joy with just one word, one look. "That's it? You don't need time to think about it?"

She giggled. "Not at all. I loved our time together in New York. Although you've rented a place there for a while, I feel like it would be a new beginning for us."

"I think so, too." Aidan grinned. "It's a done deal, then. Once *Golden Gloves* is finished, we'll move."

"I can't wait."

Longing softened the cheerfulness in Beth's expression. Mindful of his bandages, she worked her hands into his hair and brought their lips together. Aidan reciprocated like a man in optimal health. Car accident be damned. Nothing would prevent him from kissing and touching his girl when and how she wanted him to.

Afterward, they snuggled under the blanket, their heads

resting side by side on the pillow again.

"While you were unconscious, I hummed the song you wrote for me." Beth stroked his cheek. "I wanted you to know I was here for you."

Aidan closed his eyes. Her soft breaths and touch drifted across his face, swathing him in serenity.

She's exquisite.

Go to her.

He opened his eyes. "I love you so much, little dove."

Beth's smile was more perfect than lying in the most vibrant meadow under the warmest afternoon sun. "I love you, too."

They settled in for the night, moonlight gracing them with a lone spotlight as they slipped off to sleep.

Chapter Seventeen

Aidan was released from Chicago Memorial Hospital three weeks after his admission. He spent his twenty-fourth birthday in the hospital, quite the departure from the elaborate plans Beth and Nathan had made in the earlier part of the year, but his circumstances didn't impact his special day. People who loved him surrounded him. That was all he needed.

Upon his discharge, Beth and Aidan bought everything they required during their temporary stay in Chicago. They also rented a downtown apartment, where they'd reside until the *Golden Gloves* shoot concluded. Beth took care of Aidan alongside a home health nurse who visited daily, and within no time, he was ready to return to the set to finish the film.

Once Beth and Aidan told Olivia, Nathan, Connie, and Matthew about their decision to move to New York permanently, their friends decided the city was perfect for them as well. Olivia was interested in designing costumes for Broadway and Nathan wished to be closer to his mother at Bellevue Hospital. Connie grew up in New Jersey and already preferred the East Coast to the West Coast, and RCA Victor,

Matthew's employer, had offices on both coasts, which meant he could relocate without difficulty.

While Beth and Aidan remained in Chicago to wrap *Golden Gloves*, Connie and Matthew flew to Los Angeles to get their affairs in order, and Olivia and Nathan set up temporary residence at the Waldorf Astoria in New York City—using Olivia's savings—during their search for a new apartment and an office for Nathan's new business venture.

Before Olivia left for New York, she fashioned a wardrobe for *Golden Gloves*' remaining scenes. Her original designs remained in L.A. and belonged to Starlight Studios, and she didn't have time to make new ones. Instead, she visited thrift stores in Chicago and purchased everything she needed on a small budget.

By mid-June, Aidan felt well enough to fly to New York City and attend the Heavyweight Boxing Championship at Madison Square Garden—Beth's Valentine's Day gift to him. They landed just three hours before the start of the event and flew back to Chicago the following morning for a script meeting with *Golden Gloves*' full cast and Kazan, but they enjoyed their short trip and looked forward to moving there for good.

During their overnight visit, Beth suggested they sleep at Aidan's rented studio apartment on the Upper West Side. Although Aidan had been hesitant, he eventually agreed—but only for that one night. When they returned to New York after *Golden Gloves*' completion, he insisted they stay at the Waldorf Astoria, like Nathan and Olivia, until they found an apartment. Beth accepted his compromise.

As soon as Dr. Billings gave Aidan the all clear to return to the gym, he scheduled daily training sessions with Rocky Marcello, with a promise to Beth that he wouldn't push himself too far. A few weeks later, his hard work and dedication had paid off. He was back to his ideal weight, with just enough muscle to convince the film's audience he'd never been injured in the first place. His nose also healed well, giving no indication it had been broken.

Although newspapers all over the country covered Aidan's discharge and the news that *Golden Gloves* would be released in the fall, the public's paramount interest was in Beth and Aidan's relationship. Aidan confirmed they were in love when Beth wheeled him out of Chicago Memorial and into the crowd of reporters, photographers, and curious bystanders gathered on the street. He was in a good mood that day—not only was he finally able to leave the hospital after weeks of restlessness, but he was also on new pain medication, which made him a little loopy and extra chatty.

Since then, Beth and Aidan had graced the cover of all the major movie magazines, with headlines boasting various catch phrases that announced their love to the world. So far, they'd received an outpouring of public support, proving their popularity didn't decline with their full disclosure. To keep up with demand, the press requested exclusive interviews, but Beth and Aidan declined. They wanted to focus on Aidan's recovery and finishing *Golden Gloves* and also preferred not to overexpose their private lives.

Venus Rising was released in late April, but Beth didn't

attend the premiere because she refused to leave Aidan in Chicago. The film was a smash hit at the box office, and she received polite reviews for her dancing, which was a lovely surprise.

According to reports from Hollywood, Ronald Victor, one of Mr. Mertz's executives, was now in charge of Starlight Studios. Nathan predicted Mr. Victor would do a great job filling the role, and so far, everything was business as usual. However, rumors circulated that many actors and actresses were consulting with their attorneys to get out of their contracts.

Although big changes were occurring at the studio, Beth and Aidan were too preoccupied with other matters to concern themselves with most of the gossip. As soon as Aidan felt well enough, Beth contacted an analyst, Dr. Erik Johansson, who was recommended by Kazan. Dr. Johansson lived and worked in New York City, so their once-a-week sessions with him had to be conducted over the telephone on a secure long distance line until they moved to Manhattan permanently and could see him in person.

Even though they had only been talking to the analyst for a month, Aidan was doing much better in coming to terms with his past. He didn't suffer from nightmares or daytime visions like he used to, and he felt stronger emotionally. He also no longer feared that attending therapy would negatively affect his acting abilities.

Forgiveness was a crucial part of his transformation. When he shared the details of what happened during his confrontation with his father, Dr. Johansson praised his actions, stating he'd shown maturity and courage. The analyst was impressed with Aidan's work toward forgiving himself for his mother's death as well. Meanwhile, Beth dealt with what happened with Mr. Mertz and what Dr. Johansson described as her self-discovery while amalgamating her Marie Bates and Elizabeth Sutton identities.

Dr. Johansson also encouraged Beth and Aidan to open up about their pasts and how they felt their individual histories affected their relationship. They talked about the mistakes they had made with each other and what they hoped to achieve together from now on, and were well on their way to working through their issues.

It seemed the old adage that time heals all wounds was true, after all. With Aidan's body mended and his battle with past demons finally behind him, he and Beth looked forward to the future and plenty more opportunities dedicated to focusing on each other.

Chapter Eighteen

In mid-July, on her first day back on set in over three months, Beth paced her trailer, reciting lines. It was approaching midnight, but she was too jittery to be tired. Beyond the cast read-throughs over the last month, she had rehearsed privately with Aidan every evening. Still, she was concerned it hadn't been enough, so she continued to review her script obsessively at every opportunity, even though she already knew it by heart.

Eventually, Beth swapped her stuffy trailer for a breath of Chicago night air. Multiple trailers lined one side of the quaint residential street. Aidan's trailer was parked next to hers, but his door was closed. He was probably still preparing for his scenes.

Kazan chose to film the street scenes overnight when there were fewer people and less traffic to pose interference. In spite of the late hour, however, a crowd had gathered across the road. Right now, the trailers shielded Beth. When she moved down the street to film, she and the entire cast and crew would be in plain view. Security guards were called in to ensure no one trespassed onto the set, but if the enthusiastic reactions she and

Aidan received upon their arrival were any indication, it would be a challenge to keep the fans under control without falling behind schedule.

"Hey, Beth." Kazan approached her with grin so fresh no one would ever know he'd been there all day, preparing for tonight's shoot. "You look beautiful. Olivia really came through for us with the costumes. She won't have any trouble getting work in New York. I've put in a good word for her in the Broadway circles, but her reputation in Hollywood speaks for itself."

Beth smiled. "She really appreciates your assistance."

"It was my pleasure." Kazan shoved his hands into his pockets. "You know, I never thought much of that fiancé of hers because he worked so closely with Luther Mertz, but Nathan is actually a stand-up guy. Damn smart, too. He helped me a lot with *Golden Gloves* in the month after Aidan's accident. He'll have no problem getting back on his feet."

"He's working on a great business idea," Beth replied. "I have faith in him as well."

"I was just on set. The lights are up, and we've planned the route you and Aidan will take during the scene. We'll start with the conversation Mary and Joe have regarding his championship bout, and then Aidan and Wade will film the opening scene of the film. We'll tackle George and Joe's arrival at the gym last. That should bring us to about seven o'clock." Kazan guided her out of the way of a crewmember who raced past them, carrying a fan. "I came by to see if you'd be ready soon. Did you have anything to eat? I told Keith to bring you a sandwich and a cup of juice."

Beth frowned. "He came by, but I don't have much of an appetite. Thank you, though." She changed the subject before Kazan could voice concern. "Have you seen Aidan recently?"

"I spoke with him about ten minutes ago. He's still running through his lines. I don't see the benefit. He's the master of improvisation. He could complete every scene perfectly without rehearsing, based on instinct alone." Kazan gestured to the brownstone across from her trailer. "Why don't we have a seat while we wait for him?"

"Sure."

Kazan sat next to Beth on the front stoop, his shoulders hunched and his hands clasped between his knees. "I've always hated my nickname, Gadget. It was given to me in my Group Theater days in the 1930s. I love the theater, but my acting is terrible, and back then I hadn't considered directing as a plausible career path. So I accepted the role of a stagehand, the go-to guy who fetched stuff for others. A gofer, if you will."

He shrugged. "I've gotten used to the nickname. Now it's a term of endearment my friends use, often shortened to Gadg. It wasn't given to me under those circumstances, though. Anytime I think about it—and I mean *really* think about its origin—it makes me so damn mad. I spent too many years agreeing with others, plastering a smile on my face when all I really wanted to do was tell 'em off. There are certain social graces that are expected, but sometimes it's important to stand up for yourself and say what's really on your mind to save your dignity."

The quiet street was disturbed by commotion from the

crew, but Beth's attention was riveted on her director. Although she had always gotten along well with Kazan, they'd never shared deep conversations like he had with Aidan. Insight into this private man was a rare gift she didn't dare take for granted.

"Do you know John Steinbeck?" Kazan shot her an inquisitive glance, making eye contact with her for the first time since they sat down.

"I read *The Grapes of Wrath* when I was in school and *East of Eden* is one of my favorite novels."

"Two years ago, John and I were walking down the Champs-Élysées in Paris—have you ever been to Paris?"

Beth shook her head. "I've never been outside of the United States. Traveling abroad has always interested me, though."

"Well, we'll be flying to Europe to promote *Golden Gloves*, and Paris will definitely be a stop on the tour—London, too, Madrid, and most likely, Rome. If you love Manhattan, you'll love Paris. They're my favorite cities in the world. Anyhow, in 1952, I went to Paris to get away from Luther because he was driving me nuts over a film I was making for him called *Viva Zapata*. I met up with John, who took the train in from London. He was going through a bout of depression, and I don't know, I guess misery likes company. Over coffee, I told him how frustrated I was with Hollywood and how I should've stayed in New York and stuck to Broadway and the Actors Studio."

Beth giggled. "You sound like Aidan."

Kazan grinned. "Yeah, well, Hollywood is tough to stomach when you've been trained in the theater first. No offense. Anyway, after John told me all about the stuff he was dealing with—writer's block, trouble with his wife—I told him about the script revisions Luther wanted for *Viva Zapata* because he thought my portrayal of the main character would anger the Mexican people—which, by the way, was an unfounded accusation.

"Do you know what John said to me?" Kazan chuckled. "Keep in mind, this is after I gave him a diplomatic response to his problems. He told me I had to get back to myself, that my main goal should be to find myself again. He said I'd changed a lot since entering the entertainment industry and had become the worst thing of all—a nice guy! I was so busy getting people to like me and approve of me that I'd lost myself, who I was, what I wanted to be, my true identity. I'd become careless with my desires and wishes and positions. I'd become so used to sacrificing them, I no longer knew it was happening.

"Then he got to my nickname." Kazan's eyes twinkled with mischief. "That goddamn name is not you, he said. That's not what you're like. You're not a handy, friendly, adaptable little gadget! You made yourself that way to get along with people, to be accepted, to become invisible. He called it a neuter nickname, a piece of self-effacement that was useful for everyone but myself."

The humor faded from Kazan's face. "John's solution was for me to find out who I was and what my place was in the world. He said it was the only creative source I had. I had to claim it for my own and not let anyone take it away."

"I don't understand how you got that nickname in the first place now that I know its original meaning." Beth's eyebrows drew together. "I never thought of you that way at all."

Kazan's eyes lost focus as he slipped into contemplative silence. Oh, how precious it was, seeing this stoic man unguarded. Beth would be forever grateful that he'd initiated this discussion with her.

When he met her gaze, wisdom earned through patience, passion, and experience shone in his face. She felt closer to him in that moment than she ever had and ever would again. "Beth, I look at you and all you've gone through, how you stuck up for yourself and triumphed, and I think what an inspiration you are. You had your own nickname thrust upon you—Elizabeth Sutton—yet you didn't conform to it. You owned it. You made it adapt to who you really are.

"Then there's Aidan." Kazan's grin returned. "That goddamn kid brought down one of the most powerful men in the entire world—albeit, not in the best way—but still, he proved Luther wasn't invincible and set the ball in motion for drastic changes in the industry, including a system in favor of the performers, not executives sitting in corner offices pretending they know what it's like to film a movie. He did what I wanted to do back in '52 when I was battling Luther over *Viva Zapata*. He stood up to him. Meanwhile, I ran off to Paris."

"But you never let Mr. Mertz control you, Mr. Kazan. When you, me, and Mr. Stern were in his office the day I was informed I was cast in *Golden Gloves*, you put him in his place when he tried to tell you what to do."

Kazan rubbed his jaw. "Sure. But it wasn't always that way. Only after I got that wakeup call from Steinbeck did I take action and change my ways. After I left Paris, I arrived in L.A. with a renewed sense of what I had to do if I wanted to be respected in Hollywood. I demanded to Luther that the *Viva Zapata* script remain the way I wanted it. And damn it, it worked!

"But for so many years prior, I accepted my nickname and lived up to what others expected of me because of what *gadget* meant by definition. I compromised and wasted so much time acting like a coward. I was a fool. My pupils at the Actors Studio have always regarded me as an authority figure, an instructor who knows all. However, Lee Strasberg, Harold Clurman, Cheryl Crawford—my peers, the people who were part of the crowd who gave me the nickname in the first place—always thought they were above me, even though we all started out in the Group Theater and had once called each other equals."

Just the notion that Kazan would be considered anything less than a brilliant director and teacher was incomprehensible. He'd taught Beth a lot in only a few months. And Aidan . . . well, Aidan worshiped Kazan so much he'd strike down any man who disrespected him.

Kazan was too modest to accept grandiose compliments, so Beth took a more subtle approach to sharing her high opinion of him. "The important thing is you learned to stand up for yourself and took conscious action to execute change. You found your own way after feeling frustrated with the industry and Mr. Mertz's controlling ways. Meanwhile, I was forced to stand up for myself unexpectedly because I was thrust into a vile situation I never thought I would be in—one that I had to get out of even if it meant the end of my career. Our circumstances were very different. Your actions are admirable. Mine were the result of not having any other choice."

Kazan's eyes held hers. There was something about the way he looked at her that made her feel important, valued, and more talented than a novice actress who hadn't yet left her teen years.

"In my forties, I accomplished what you and Aidan accomplished in your late teens and early twenties, respectively. Regardless of how you came to the realization you deserved better than the treatment you received from Luther, you made it.

"Even though people don't know the real reason Aidan went after Luther, he still holds all the glory for what's going on at the studio right now—not that he asked for it. They believe he fought for more creative freedom, which by default resulted in him fighting for everyone in the industry. Never forget, though, you deserve credit, too. You set a great example for the other actresses who fell victim to Luther's control. You prevailed, despite the negative experience you endured."

Nathan and Connie had also prevailed over difficult circumstances and played important roles in forcing Mr. Mertz's resignation, but it was not Beth's place to address their private struggles with others. She and Aidan had opened up to Kazan because they respected and trusted him, thus she could appreciate her friends' trust in her to keep their secrets.

"I'm afraid you're giving me too much praise, sir."

"I'm proud of you, kid, and you should be proud of yourself. You're a force to be reckoned with, but still as sweet as ever."

Kazan placed his hand on her shoulder, his stubborn gaze softened by paternal approval. "Today is a monumental occasion, an incredible achievement—the start of the end of a project we thought we'd never finish. And we're doing it without Starlight Studios' involvement. You and Aidan have long careers ahead of you, as long as Aidan keeps his temper in check." He laughed and Beth did, too. "So don't be nervous today. You're gonna do a great job."

Beth blushed. "Thank you. Your confidence is much appreciated."

"You know, the Actors Studio would benefit from your membership." With a wink, he withdrew his hand from her shoulder. "You must audition, of course, but I don't see why Lee wouldn't agree with me. And if you get in, you'll be part of a very small group of performers who've made the move from Hollywood to our institution instead of the other way around."

Beth's eyes widened. "I would love to audition. As soon as *Golden Gloves* wraps, I'll write a scene to perform and—gosh, I'm so excited!"

"I look forward to it." Kazan stood and offered his hand. "Let's get that boy of yours, shall we?"

Beth and Kazan descended the stairs to the sidewalk. Wade met them halfway to Aidan's trailer, dressed in character and holding a magazine.

After they exchanged greetings with him, Kazan turned to Beth. "I have some stuff to sort out before we begin. You and Wade get Aidan and meet me on set in twenty minutes."

Beth nodded.

Upon Kazan's departure, Wade thrust the magazine in her face. "Have you seen the latest issue of *Modern Screen*?"

"No. Why?"

Beth accepted the periodical from him. On the cover were two unrelated close-up portraits of her and Aidan, which had been superimposed together to make it look like they gazed lovingly at each other and were about to kiss. Aidan was dressed in his *Spike Rollins* attire—his trademark red jacket and white T-shirt—and his green eyes had been colored to enhance their vibrancy. Beth was dressed in character for *Sparkling Meadow*, her hair secured in a ponytail, her wide brown eyes radiating innocence and submission.

The photograph was accompanied by a byline:

The girl-next-door ingénue captured the heart of the bad boy Method actor—and tamed him! Inside: How you can snag your very own rebel and experience a thrilling, everlasting love like Beth and Aidan!

"In the editorial section, there are readers' comments from the last issue—which you two were on the cover of as well—and they're all positive." Wade flipped through the magazine and pointed to the page in question. "The article in this edition praises your passionate relationship and calls the two of you a match made in movie heaven—a promising new love affair that proves opposites attract off screen, too."

Beth shook her head, but her face glowed from her broad smile. "Gosh, what will they think of next?"

"You know if the readers of *Modern Screen* think you're a great couple, then it must be true." Wade flashed a grin. "Oh, I almost forgot. They also printed the results of a poll where Aidan was named the actor female readers would most like to date."

Beth giggled. "What did you do, read the entire magazine?"

Wade's ears reddened. "I had some spare time after hair and makeup."

"I see." Beth's eyes gleamed with amusement. "Well, I'm sure Aidan will be ecstatic when I tell him the news."

"Ah, come on. You must love the attention." Wade draped his arm over her shoulders. "Did I mention you were voted Most Beautiful Actress this month?"

Beth shrugged. "A lot of the stuff they print is made up to sell more magazines and movie tickets. There's no point in letting it get to your head."

"You're too humble for your own good." Wade sighed dramatically. "Anyway, I'll leave you to get Aidan on your own. I'm sure he'll appreciate it more if you show up at his door alone instead of with me in tow. See ya soon." He took off down the street.

"Wait! You forgot your magazine." Beth waved the periodical in the air.

Wade pitched a grin over his shoulder. "You keep it. Frame it and give it to Aidan as a gift."

Smiling, Beth ascended the stairs to her beau's trailer and knocked twice. The door opened, and her mouth dropped. Aidan welcomed her with unruly hair, smoldering eyes, and a cocky smirk. Despite his conservative, checkered, button-down sport shirt and dark gray trousers, and his studious accessories—the script in his hand and the pencil tucked behind his ear—he looked so wild, so dangerous. But goodness, he wore it all so well.

"Hey, baby." Aidan propped his forearm on the doorframe above his head and leaned forward. His gaze held promises of a good time, the type of good time only he could provide her.

She gulped. "Hello."

He moved aside and extended his hand. Their fingers entwined and he led her inside with a soft kiss on her lips.

Beth held up the magazine. "A gift from Wade."

Aidan rolled his eyes. "What does this one say?" He tossed his script and pencil onto a nearby table and pulled her close.

Beth set down the periodical and brought her arms around his neck. "Oh, something about me taming your rebel ways."

Aidan's lips drifted toward hers. "Hmm, I don't know about that."

Beth whimpered as his tongue slipped into her mouth and his strong hands pressed to her back, bringing her body flush against his. If the *Modern Screen* cover corresponded to the first image on a storyboard, this kiss would have completed the sequence.

Aidan dragged his lips to her neck. "I may still be a rebel..." He placed a kiss to her jaw and then her cheek. "But I'm forever a one-woman man."

Beth gasped as he nipped at her earlobe. "Lucky woman."

Hot, heavy breaths played with her hair. "Baby, I'm the lucky one."

Their lips reunited.

When they were officially called to the set, Beth had to fan herself with Aidan's script for several minutes before she was able to leave the trailer with steady steps and a steady heart beat.

Security escorted them down the block. Once they passed the row of trailers, the spectators erupted into frenzied screams, unconcerned with the late hour or disturbing the neighbors. Beth and Aidan waved in acknowledgement, which only spurred their excitement.

They weren't the only ones excited. Following Aidan's accident, Beth had been so preoccupied with his well-being to think about anything else. Although she had always wanted to finish *Golden Gloves*, she didn't realize how much acting defined her until tonight. Sharing her return in front of the camera with Aidan made the occasion all the more special.

The cast and crew broke into applause, welcoming the couple back to the set and praising Aidan for his strength and effort toward his recovery. Then Kazan brought out a cake decorated with the phrase, *Happy Belated Birthday, Golden Boy*. Beth's eyes filled with tears as Aidan thanked everyone for their support.

Kazan cut the cake. Beth and Aidan handed out slices to the crew and the rest of the cast before claiming their own pieces. They sat in their reserved chairs along the curb, laughed with their colleagues, and smiled and waved to the crowd until their plates were clear.

In preparation for the night ahead, Kazan walked Beth and Aidan through the first scene, showing the path they would travel and where they would stop. He also set the context for their characters' discussion and planted the seed of what was expected, but as always, left enough unsaid to allow them to cultivate everything according to what felt right while filming the scene.

As Beth and Aidan conversed with their director and the first unit camera operator, the enthusiastic screams of the spectators turned into chants that quickly gained momentum. Kazan sent additional security across the street to try to calm the crowd, but it didn't work.

Eventually, Kazan threw his hands up in defeat. "Do you two mind greeting the fans so they quiet down? Or else we're going to be here well into the morning, which won't work for the scenes we have to film."

"No problem, Gadg." Aidan shrugged. "I mean, if Beth feels up to it."

She nodded. "Of course."

Kazan summoned three security guards to accompany them. Curious neighbors, easily identified by their casual evening attire and perplexed expressions, surveyed the commotion from afar as Beth and Aidan posed for photographs and penned their signatures.

The crowd consisted mostly of teenagers, especially young men dressed in jeans and T-shirts, copying Aidan's *Spike Rollins* wardrobe. Other bystanders included parents with younger children who were up way past their bedtimes. Even older adults stopped by to wish the couple well. Beth appreciated all the fans, whether they liked her in particular or were simply enthralled by the mystery and glamour of movie making in general.

After greeting everyone and appeasing all autograph and photograph requests, Beth and Aidan asked for quiet so they could commence filming. Some people dispersed, but those who remained pledged their cooperation.

Beth and Aidan received so many gifts, security had to help carry them. The couple offered the treats to the crew and brought the rest to Aidan's trailer so they could sort through it all later and decide what to donate to the local children's hospital.

After an hour delay, which thankfully Kazan had planned for because of the cake surprise, the cast and crew were ready. Once Beth and Aidan were clear about their directions, they walked toward their starting positions. The crowd stayed true to their promise and watched quietly, giving not only the *Golden Gloves* company a break, but security, too.

Aidan escorted Beth up the front steps of the brownstone that was supposed to house their characters' apartment. Spotlights stood on either side of them, lighting the way into the still of the night.

Beth squeezed his hand. "It's so wonderful to be back on set with you."

"Just think, *Golden Gloves* is almost finished." Aidan's widening grin warmed her heart, melting away her sadness over the conclusion of their film. "I never thought we'd make it, but here we are."

Beth beamed. "We have a lot to be thankful for."

"Damn right we do." Aidan placed a kiss on the back of her hand.

The first unit camera was positioned in front of them. A boom microphone appeared above their heads.

"Places, everyone! And quiet now, please and thank you." Kazan folded his arms across his chest and surveyed the set with a critical eye. He gave a satisfied nod.

The clapperboard sounded off.

"And . . . action!"

Mary and Joe descended the stairs and strolled down the block.

"A walk was a lovely idea, honey." Mary snuggled under her husband's arm.

"I suggested it because I wanna talk to you." Joe cast her a tentative glance. "I figured the fresh air would do me some good. You know, help me share what's on my mind more clearly."

"This is about your fight tomorrow night, isn't it?" Mary's voice carried a softness to cover up her trepidation over what she was about to hear.

"Yeah." Joe sighed. "I feel guilty about returning to the ring."

Her eyebrows furrowed. "Why? You're not to blame for the death of your former opponent."

"I know. I've come to terms with that. It's more like . . . well, I feel guilty because I get to box again, whereas he'll never have the chance. Stepping into that ring . . . man, there are very few things in life that give me such a thrill. I feel energized, alive, and ready to tackle anything, especially with you in my corner." Joe's lips plunged into a frown. "But Mary, isn't it wrong for me to feel happy? I mean, shouldn't a part of me always mourn what happened so his memory isn't lost forever?"

Mary stopped walking and grasped Joe's hands, gazing into striking green eyes, which after so many years of torment finally shone with self-worth. "Because of what happened, you have a renewed appreciation of life, how precious it is. Many people go through life without any passion, and that's the biggest shame— *that* is something to feel guilty about. Living life to the fullest is how you honor his memory properly. So please embrace this second chance and accept you're a good man who deserves happiness and an opportunity to earn the championship title. You've worked hard and you're a skilled fighter. I'm proud of you."

"I always want you to be proud of me." Joe brushed his hand to her hair. "You encouraged me to return to a sport I love and supported me as I trained. You stood by me as I tackled my demons, believed in me no matter what, and helped me heal. I've made it this far, and I'm so afraid I'll let you down if I lose the title."

Mary smiled. "Oh, Joe. Don't you see? You've already fought the toughest battle and triumphed. Regardless of what happens tomorrow, you'll always be a winner to me."

A broad grin stretched across his face. "You have no idea how much those words mean to me, Mary. Thank you for never deserting me."

Mary linked her hands behind his neck. "I love you, Joe."

"I love you, too. Forever." Threading his fingers in her hair, he bowed his head and pressed his lips to hers in a tender display of dedication and victory.

"Cut! Print that one."

Beth and Aidan stepped apart. The crew dispersed, setting up for the next scene.

Aidan surprised Beth by taking her face in his hands and placing a firm kiss on her lips. Across the street, the crowd went wild.

When he pulled back, his expression burst with joy. "We did it, Beth. Damn it, baby. We did it."

Beth wrapped her arms around him and hugged him tightly. "That we did, Aidan." She tossed a wistful look to the stars. "We mostly certainly did."

Chapter Nineteen

Beth and Aidan's Central Park West apartment was full of boxes. They didn't transfer much furniture east—opting instead to donate most of their items and buy new pieces in Manhattan—but much of what they did keep still needed to be unpacked. Beth's Cadillac and Aidan's Triumph motorcycle arrived from L.A. earlier in the week, followed by his mother's piano from Chicago. The piano now sat in their parlor, the focal point of the room. Aidan played the instrument every day, his melodies loud and joyous.

Following completion of *Golden Gloves* at the beginning of August, Beth and Aidan, along with their friends, flew to New York in search of the perfect home. Each couple found an ideal apartment on Manhattan's Upper West Side. The units were vacant, so they were all able to move in almost right away and put their prior residences on the market. Aidan also terminated the rental agreement on his uptown studio apartment.

It was unconventional for Beth and Aidan to live together out of wedlock. But after being forced to hide their relationship for so long, Beth refused to let anyone, or society in general, dictate what she and Aidan were allowed to do anymore.

Beth and Aidan's penthouse boasted two floors, with a grand staircase off the main atrium, a study, a parlor, five bedrooms, four bathrooms, two stone terraces—one on each floor with views of Central Park—a library, gym, sun room, media room, living room, dining room, and many other rooms to which they hadn't even assigned a purpose. Additional amenities included a security guard stationed in the lobby around the clock and valet parking.

Nathan and Olivia owned a similar suite in the adjacent building, which they purchased with a small mortgage qualified through Olivia's finances and Nathan's new business collateral. Matthew and Connie lived four buildings down the street in a duplex that originally belonged to a famous Broadway producer.

Just as they were all settling in, Nathan and Olivia surprised everyone by lawfully becoming husband and wife. Nathan had purchased a new engagement ring with his own money and proposed again. Olivia called and told their friends to meet them at City Hall the following morning. A Justice of the Peace married them in a quaint ceremony with little fanfare. They exchanged gold bands and proclaimed their personally written vows, followed by a delicious brunch with their guests at Tavern on the Green.

The next day, Nathan took Olivia to meet his mother at Bellevue. The new Mrs. Taggart was honored to meet the elder Mrs. Taggart, and she and Nathan now visited the hospital weekly.

Nathan and Olivia experienced great financial success since

moving east. Nathan found a reasonably priced office space in downtown Manhattan, and after some renovations, he opened his own public relations firm. Given his solid reputation at Starlight Studios, he immediately signed many notable names, including Beth, Connie, and Aidan. Business was booming. He even had to hire a personal secretary to manage the bevy of client appointments and run the office efficiently.

According to Nathan, this was the first time he felt he'd truly accomplished something on his own, adding honorable mention to his new wife, who supported him every step of the way. Most importantly, he looked forward to representing his clients respectfully, having learned from past mistakes.

As Kazan predicted, Olivia quickly established herself in the Broadway design community. Currently, she was contracted to provide the costumes for three up-and-coming plays staged by the Actors Studio.

Connie and Matthew's careers thrived as well. Connie signed on to star in a new motion picture, which would start filming in New York next week, while Matthew was hard at work writing the new *Golden Gloves* theme song. In the midst of all the activity, they decided on a September wedding, less than a month away.

Saul Stern referred Beth and Connie to an agent based in New York named Jay McGill. Mr. McGill would also manage their financial affairs as well as Aidan's. They thanked Mr. Stern for his service and for setting them up with someone on the East Coast who had their best interests in mind like he did.

Golden Gloves' official release was scheduled for October

eighth. Once they completed the publicity for the motion picture at the end of the year, Beth and Aidan had many film options to choose from, but they weren't yet sure in which direction they wanted to head. Beth cherished her newfound professional freedom and wanted to weigh all options before committing to another project.

The latest news out of L.A. was the permanent collapse of the old Starlight Studios system. Seven-year contracts were now a thing of the past. Actors were buying out their agreements and working as freelance artists like Beth, Aidan, and their friends, and independent production companies were obtaining permits to film in various soundstages on the Starlight Studios lot. However, all the money generated from these transactions and contract buyouts still didn't guarantee that investors wouldn't have to step in to keep the institution functional, since location shoots were becoming more and more popular.

Despite the drastic changes, the movie industry as a whole showed no indication of slowing down. Productions no longer needed to receive consent through a difficult studio boss. Directors and producers now financed films directly through the banks, so more projects were being green lighted than ever before on both coasts.

Living permanently in Manhattan was an adjustment for Beth, but the support of Aidan and her friends made it easy to fall in love with her new home. She looked forward to experiencing her first snowfall in two years and discovering what else the city offered with her beau by her side.

This morning, Aidan returned to New York after ironing

out the final postproduction details for *Golden Gloves* with Kazan in Chicago. He had been working hard since he got home, as if he hadn't spent most of the last two days traveling. Besides unpacking, they had a lot of wallpapering and painting to complete in almost every room, but they chose to pace themselves so they didn't get overwhelmed.

After unpacking cutlery in the kitchen, Beth was startled to see moonlight seeping in through the window above the sink. She couldn't believe it was so late already.

Before she could venture into the living room to suggest they finish for the day, Aidan entered the kitchen with a flushed face and hair wilder than usual—products of his stubbornness and frustration. Acting came to him with freewheeling ease. Setting up electronics did not. Not that he would ever admit it.

"Hey, baby."

"Hey, yourself." Beth nudged him playfully. "Did you finally win the war with the television?"

Aidan smirked. "How did you know we were fighting?"

She giggled. "You were uttering profanities at it for the last hour."

"Yeah, well, I had to show it who's boss." He wrapped his arms around her and brought their lips together.

Beth released a whimper, welcoming his tongue, his breath, everything he offered her.

Something else that came to him with freewheeling ease? The ability to sweep her off her feet with just one kiss. Oh, how she'd missed him these last couple of nights.

With a lingering moan, Aidan pulled back. "How about we

take a walk through the park?"

Beth placed her hand to his cheek. His suggestion appealed to her, but the dark circles under his eyes made her reconsider. "Are you certain you're up for it? You must be exhausted from your travels."

Determined green eyes fastened on her. "I'm never too tired to spend time with you. Plus, fresh air would be nice after being cooped up in here most of the day."

"All right. If you're sure, then we'll go."

Beth wore a pink cotton blouse and black pedal pushers. Her hair was proper, pulled back and curled, and her angel pendant was secured around her neck. She considered adding mascara and lip-gloss but didn't want to fuss over her appearance for only a casual stroll.

"I'll fetch my shoes and meet you by the front door."

"Okay. I'll be there in a minute." Aidan headed for the stairs. "I need to change clothes first."

Beth's eyebrows knitted together. He was dressed in a clean pair of jeans and a T-shirt. Nothing needed replacing. Maybe the addition of a sweater to combat any evening cool down was appropriate, but that was it. "You look great in what you're wearing."

"Thanks, baby." Aidan returned to her side to brush his lips to her cheek. "But I'm still gonna change."

After turning off all unnecessary lights, Beth chose her footwear and waited for her beau in the foyer. When Aidan rounded the corner, desire forged with happiness, inspiring a vivacious beat to her heart. His dark gray sport shirt, black dress pants, and black leather shoes were too stylish for a walk in Central Park. Well, not for Nathan or Matthew—or Cary Grant, for that matter—but for Aidan, yes. But goodness, she definitely wasn't complaining.

No wonder Aidan's picture adorned the bedroom walls of young women all over the country. He was the personification of a movie star, the type of man one could only dream about—so handsome, charming, and irresistible, he couldn't possibly exist outside the pages of a magazine. Yet here he was, all warm flesh and warm breath, staring at her like *she* was the most beautiful person in the world.

"Ready to go, baby?" He removed their house key from his pocket.

She frowned. "Are you sure I shouldn't change as well?"

Aidan raised his hand to drag it through his hair—which had been tamed during his trip upstairs—but at the last moment, he didn't go through with it. Instead, he brought his arm around her waist. "You look perfect the way you are."

"But I—"

He abolished her self-doubt with a knee-buckling kiss, and then they were on their way.

The late-August air was rich with a humidity that was absent in L.A. and took some getting used to, but the wind was gentle and stars blanketed the city, creating the perfect atmosphere for a walk.

They traveled along Central Park West to the traffic lights upon Aidan's insistence, despite the lack of cars on the road and Beth's suggestion to jaywalk in front of their building.

With his hand placed against her lower back, they crossed the street and entered the park via a narrow stone staircase, which brought them to a quaint pathway lined with elm trees. Black cast-iron lamps lit their route, guiding them deeper into the park.

Tucked safely under Aidan's arm, Beth sighed contently. What a treat it was to share this time with him after rushing around the apartment all week, trying to get everything in order. "We had so much fun in the park on our first date. I've missed it here. It's too bad we didn't have time to visit during our trip to the city in June."

Aidan kissed the top of her head. "I'm sorry, little dove. I should've brought you back sooner."

"Remember our conversation with the hot dog vendor?" Beth giggled into Aidan's shirt. He smelled like nature and mint aftershave—hardworking, robust male. "You pretended you weren't who you really are, even though he was convinced you were."

Aidan chuckled. "What I remember is my shock when you insisted we eat hot dogs, especially after I told you I'd take you to any restaurant in the city." His face contorted on a yawn, which he tried—rather unsuccessfully—to smother.

Beth paused under the lamplight. "If you want to go home, let me know. We can return to the park another day."

He shook his head. "Don't worry about me. I slept on the plane."

"But it's such a short flight. It couldn't have been a sufficient amount of rest."

Aidan scratched behind his ear, his gaze drifting to blackness beyond the pathway. "I'm fine, really."

Beth shrugged. "All right. I won't press the matter."

She reclaimed her spot under his arm and they commenced their walk.

Aidan seemed to have a destination in mind because every time they came to a fork in the road, he knew which direction to take immediately. It wasn't long before Beth recognized their surroundings as well. Although she hadn't been in the park in almost a year, the path unfolded before her as though she had traveled along it only yesterday.

They stopped at the top of a vast stone staircase, one of two presiding over Bethesda Terrace. In the center of the vacant courtyard, the Angel of the Waters fountain reflected the moonlight, glowing like a spaceship from a science fiction film, ready to take flight.

Beth took in the view with wide eyes, as if she was seeing it all for the first time. "It's just as beautiful as I remember. Thank you for bringing me here again."

"You're welcome." Aidan gazed at her in evident satisfaction. Never mind the scenery. His grin alone was worth the return trip.

They descended the staircase, arm-in-arm. Fortunately, there was no one else around, like the park was open only for them. The splendor of the moment and how grateful Beth was to have Aidan safe and back in her life overwhelmed her.

She clasped her hands to her chest. "I'm so happy I feel like . . . I feel like dancing!"

"Dancing?" Amusement fluttered across Aidan's face.

She nodded. "I know I wasn't much of a dancer in *Venus Rising* compared to the pros, but having this gorgeous terrace all to ourselves inspires me to just let go."

Aidan motioned to their surroundings. "Go ahead. You don't have to hold back on my account."

Beth beamed. She spread her arms out at her sides, tilted her head toward the sky, and spun with laughter. The gentle breeze toyed with her hair and tickled her skin. She felt liberated and oh, so content. She could dance, she could sing, she could do anything or nothing at all. She was finally free.

The funny thing was she no longer possessed the desire to fly away like she did when she lived in Clarkson. She was completely satisfied with her life and didn't want to be anywhere else in the world than with Aidan at the Bethesda Terrace right now.

With flushed cheeks, she stopped spinning and dropped her arms, struggling to catch her breath and establish her bearings. She wobbled on her feet, but Aidan was next to her immediately, steadying her with a tight yet tender arm around her waist.

Beth giggled. "I'm sorry. I bet I look pretty silly."

"Not at all." Aidan tucked an errant curl behind her ear, admiring her with a devoted twinkle that rivaled the stars. "You reminded me of a dream I had. We were at my childhood home in Fairfield. You were wearing a white dress, and I watched you spin in a field of wildflowers . . ." His musings faded to pensive silence.

He took her hand and walked backward, luring her toward the fountain. The angel hovered behind him, her Romanesque wings framing his gentle face.

When they reached the rim, he gathered her in his arms again. "Do you recall the story behind the fountain?"

"Some of it. It's from the Gospel of John, correct?"

Aidan nodded. "In one hand, the angel carries a lily, the symbol of purity, while her other hand blesses the water below. She represents the angel who bestowed healing powers on the pool of Bethesda in Jerusalem."

Beth smiled. "Now I remember. Legend has it that similar to the fountain in Jerusalem, this fountain has the power to save people from their ailments."

Aidan looked up at the statue. It appeared as though the angel gestured directly to him. "Beth, earlier we mentioned what we remembered most from our time in the park during our first date. We brought up the hot dogs and the vendor, but I gotta tell you, my most poignant memory was sitting at this fountain with you, reciting the Angel of the Waters story. There was a kindness in your eyes I'll never forget. You gave me hope that I wasn't such a lost cause, after all—that I could be healed eventually as well, even though on that day and for many months following, I rejected the notion.

"I always thought the legend was a bunch of nonsense, but after meeting you . . . well, I'm now a believer. Because just like the fountain, I, too, have been blessed by an angel. However, my angel doesn't exist in the water or in Heaven, but with me right here." He placed her hand over his heart. "Beth, my angel is you. But you're more sacred than any biblical tale, any fountain of healing. I couldn't imagine going through the rest of my life without you as my friend, my lover . . . my wife."

"Oh, my gosh." Beth brought her hand to her mouth.

Aidan dropped down on one knee and removed a black box from his pocket. "For so long, I was broken, desiring to be a man worthy of your love, free from guilt and torment. I kept working toward this goal, even though I thought it was too far out of my reach, because I couldn't bear to lose you."

He took her left hand in his. "When I abandoned you at the studio, I had given up on myself, but you hadn't given up on me. You've taught me so much, and after everything we've been through together, I'm proud to say I kneel before you now a changed man—the man I always wanted to be. I believe in myself. I believe in your power of healing. I also believe in the power of us. Baby, I love you with all of my heart and I will cherish you always."

Beth trembled as he popped the lid, revealing a large European cut diamond set upon what looked like a platinum band.

He peered up at her with broad, hopeful eyes. "Elizabeth Sutton, will you marry me?"

Beth lunged at him, wrapping her arms around his neck. "Yes. Yes!" She shrieked and jumped up and down. "Of course I'll marry you!"

With steady hands and a dedicated gaze, Aidan removed the ring from the velvet interior and slipped it onto the proper finger. He rose to his feet and hugged her. "You've made me the happiest man in the world."

Beth graced him with a sensual kiss. "Although you've always been a man of worth to me, I'm glad you waited until you believed it, too, before you proposed. I want you to enter into this next stage of our lives with the utmost confidence, without secrets or reservations."

"While we're on the topic of secrets . . ." Aidan cringed. "Baby, I have to confess something. I hope you won't be mad at me."

She flashed a teasing smile. "Well, that isn't the best way to start off our engagement."

He chuckled, but then his expression dimmed with solemnity. "You know how I went out of town this week . . . well, I didn't go to Chicago."

Beth's eyebrows furrowed. "You didn't?"

He shook his head. "I went to Clarkson to ask your parents for your hand in marriage."

Beth gaped at him. "You traveled across the country for that? You could've called them."

"No." His lips pulled into a frown. "I needed to do it the right away, talk to them face to face so they know how serious I am about you."

Beth cupped his cheek. "That's one of the loveliest, most thoughtful things you've ever done."

Aidan sighed. "You have no idea how relieved I am to hear that. I hated lying to you, and I didn't even do a good job. I thought for sure when I slipped up and talked about getting enough sleep on the airplane, you thought something was up."

Beth giggled. "Well, it was perplexing, but I never questioned your whereabouts. And I certainly didn't have any inkling you were going to propose. One day, I hoped you would. But I assumed if it did happen, it would be after our *Golden Gloves* promotional tour or once we're more settled here."

Aidan kissed her forehead. "I considered that, but my accident gave me a new perspective on things. I didn't want to put it off any longer."

Beth smiled. "I can't believe it. I'm going to be Mrs. Aidan Evans!"

All traces of levity plummeted from Aidan's face. His eyes flared, burning with a fierce, primal obsession. "Damn it, baby. You say that one more time and I'm not gonna be able to control myself."

Beth's heart pounded. The thrill she received from his look and touch torched her blood. "I'm going to have your name. Everyone is going to know I'm yours—that I belong to you. Mrs. Aidan Evans."

Aidan dipped his head, licked his lips. He was close. So, so close, she couldn't handle it. "You're wrong, baby. You're the one who owns me. You've always owned me."

His mouth claimed hers. Beth shuddered and collapsed against him. The ache was too much, her need for him too zealous. If she weren't so greedy, so intent on having him all to herself all night long, she would've begged him to take her right there in the middle of the park.

She whimpered against his lips, pawing at his hair, his clothes. "Take me home, Aidan."

Without delay, he swept her across the terrace. His heated hold on her conveyed just how far gone his own restraint was.

The walk back to their apartment took much less time than the reverse trip did. Somehow they kept their hands to themselves in front of the security guard in the lobby of their building and the elevator operator who brought them to the top floor. But as soon as they entered their apartment, all bets were off.

Their lips met frantically, making up for their brief separation. Although it was dark, they maneuvered through the apartment as if they had always lived there. When they reached the master bedroom, their clothes were discarded quickly and Aidan lifted Beth off the floor and reunited their lips.

Beth's legs came around his waist and her back met the wall between two open, floor-to-ceiling windows overlooking Central Park. Amidst a mild summer breeze and a spotlight courtesy of the moon, Aidan positioned between her thighs. She gripped his shoulders and deepened their kiss, hanging on to him with everything she had as the sheer curtains rippled and billowed like sails on a ship, enveloping them in white satin. He possessed her mind and soul completely. There would never be enough of this—of his words, his kisses, his caresses, his—

With a grunt, Aidan entered her. Beth threw her head back and squeezed her eyes shut. Her grasp on him tightened as he rocked his hips in a dedicated rhythm . . . again and again and again and again and—oh, the sensations, the desire he ignited in her . . . it was all so intoxicating, so consuming. Needy, gentle, passionate, this was the moonlight serenade of a man in love.

"Baby, you mean everything to me." He thrust again, filling her all the way.

"Oh, Aidan!"

And again.

"Baby . . .

And again and again . . .

"Baby . . . baby . . ."

Aidan carried her across the room and set her down on the mattress, which lay on the floor because their new bed arrived tomorrow. Beth reached for her diaphragm on the nightstand and inserted it with ease. Her lips parted on a sigh as Aidan traced his finger down her throat and circled her breasts. Then he was on top of her—panting, sweaty, and perfect—and their bodies reconnected.

Cushioned by crumpled cotton sheets and pillows without slipcovers, Aidan pressed his mouth to the center of her chest and dragged sideways to capture her nipple between his teeth. With a tug from his lips, Beth's control slipped. She moaned and tangled her hands in his hair as he moved inside her, deeply and powerfully connecting them beyond their physical position.

Showering her with reverent kisses, Aidan grabbed her hands and entwined their fingers. Palm to palm, he placed their linked hands beside her head on the pillow and they came together faster, pushing and pulling, searching for the soul-connecting release they both desperately needed.

Beth felt pressure building. One more grind of his hips caused her to gasp and arch against him. Her orgasm arrived with earth-shattering intensity, bringing with it an explosion of starlight behind her closed eyelids and a feeling of floating, of weightlessness.

Aidan held her tight while he threw himself into her once, twice, before he tensed and came undone, too. They cried out each other's names. The tremors that blasted from their bodies seemed to shake the entire apartment.

They drifted back down together, their labored breaths calming and their racing hearts slowing. Then Aidan settled next to her on the mattress and pulled her close. When Beth rested her hand on his chest, her engagement ring caught the moonlight.

He lifted her hand and kissed the diamond. "I love you, little dove."

"I love you, too." Beth exchanged smiles with him, followed by kisses and caresses that continued well into the morning.

Although they still had a lot to unpack, their penthouse didn't feel bare at all. Because even after they painted, wallpapered, and filled every room with furniture, the greatest asset to their apartment would always be their devotion to each other and the opportunity to cultivate their relationship without boundaries. For even the most opulent fixtures could not compete with love's ability to truly make a house a home.

Chapter Twenty

"Ladies and Gentlemen, we are gathered here today to unify this man and this woman in holy matrimony before God, this church, and all of you, the couple's distinguished guests."

Aidan stood across from Beth with the largest grin on his face. They had rehearsed the service, but now that it was official, the additional weight attached to the priest's words—the significance, the sanctity—really sunk in.

When Aidan initially entered the church, he was concerned he didn't belong. However, united through his friends and fiancée, he believed in his goodness and his right to be here today, even when the ceremony wasn't focused on him at all.

"Matthew Bartholomew McKenna, do you take Constance Annette Murphy to be your wife? Do you promise to be true to her in good times and in bad, in sickness and in health, to love her and honor her all the days of your life?"

Matthew nodded. "I do."

"Constance Annette Murphy, do you take Matthew Bartholomew McKenna to be your husband? Do you promise to be true to him in good times and in bad, in sickness and in health, to love him and honor him all the days of your life?"

Connie's eyes glistened with tears. "I do."

The priest acknowledged their declared consent to be married, and then Aidan and Nathan—as Best Men—handed over the rings to be blessed.

Matthew slipped Connie's ring on her left hand. "My dearest Constance, take this ring as a sign of my love and fidelity, in the name of the Father, and of the Son, and of the Holy Spirit."

Connie secured his ring on his finger. "Matthew, take this ring as a sign of my love and fidelity, in the name of the Father, and of the Son, and of the Holy Spirit."

Aidan's gaze wandered to Beth. Blanketed by stained-glass-filtered sunlight, she looked resplendent in her dark blue dress and upswept hair. One day soon, this would be their reality. For so long, acting was the only thing that defined him. Now there was no greater role than that of her husband.

When Aidan traveled to Clarkson to ask for her parents' permission, his nervousness rivaled his guilt over withholding the truth from her. His first meeting with Mr. and Mrs. Bates had been shaky—to put it mildly. Now he was showing up at their door unannounced, hoping they would recognize his honorable intentions and accept him as their son-in-law.

His feelings for Beth prompted him to open his heart. Surprisingly, Mr. Bates gave his blessing right away and even apologized for his abrasiveness during their initial encounter. Mr. and Mrs. Bates told Aidan they appreciated his candidness about his past. They also believed him when he promised that his family values were very much intact, even though he was estranged from his father, and that he would cherish Beth and commit everything he had to their marriage. Mrs. Bates then prepared dinner and the three of them enjoyed casual conversation well into the evening.

Matthew and Connie scaled down today's affair considerably from the circus they had planned in partnership with Starlight Studios, despite continued pressure from various publications to turn their nuptials into a grand spectacle. Only their close friends and family were present.

Matthew and Connie signed the Declaration of Marriage, and then the priest recited a prayer. Connie had chosen a Catholic ceremony because she had been baptized Catholic, attended church regularly while growing up, and desired to reconnect with her religious roots after abandoning them upon her move to L.A. While she found her religion in the Catholic Church, Aidan found his in Beth. Love often made people believe in a higher power, but in his case, there was nothing greater than what he felt for his fiancée.

"In the name of the Father, the Son, and the Holy Spirit. Amen." The priest made the sign of the cross along with everyone else. "What God has joined, man must not divide. I now pronounce you husband and wife. Mr. McKenna, you may kiss your bride."

Matthew lifted Connie's veil and brushed his lips to hers. The room erupted into cheers, and the organist commenced a tune. As the newlyweds rushed down the aisle, Aidan focused on Beth again. She fastened a dazzling smile back at him.

Behind Nathan and Olivia, he escorted her out of the church amongst the photographers hired to record the event. It was the ideal weather for a wedding—sunny and warm, complete with a bright blue sky and a temperate breeze.

Reporters and spectators lined the quaint Southampton street, peacefully minded by local police. Society papers as well as notable trade publications reported on the wedding for weeks, in spite of Matthew and Connie's efforts to keep it secret. The crowd was respectful, though. They tossed rice and cheered as the bride and groom walked to the limousine, which was decorated for the occasion with roses and a *Just Married* sign mounted on the trunk. Aidan and Beth were showered with rice, too, as they made their way to their chauffeured Bentley.

As the car pulled away from the church, Beth pressed her head back against the headrest and sighed. "That was such a lovely ceremony."

"Yeah, it was." Aidan removed grains of rice from her hair, admiring her pink cheeks and thoughtful smile. Unable to resist, he brought their lips together. He didn't care if their driver was getting a show. He'd wanted to kiss her properly all day, and in the quietest moment they'd had in hours, nothing was going to stop him.

When they arrived at their destination, even Aidan was impressed with the reception hall's décor. There were no indications that Matthew and Connie had arranged everything on a modest budget, especially the head table, which was decorated with a three-tiered wedding cake, bottles of champagne, and elaborate flower arrangements.

Aidan and Beth sat at a table with Nathan and Olivia, Matthew's agent, Mervin Lewis, and Merv's wife, Lois. Traditionally, the wedding party occupied the head table with the bride and groom, but this alternative arrangement allowed Connie and Matthew's parents to sit there instead and spend time with their children.

A quartet played pleasant music, waiters served appetizers, and photographers made the rounds. Aidan wasn't one for small talk, but with everything going on, he wasn't tied up with the same people for long. He and Beth exchanged words with Matthew and Connie, too, but overall left them to their other guests, whom they didn't see regularly.

Matthew serenaded his new bride and they shared their first dance as husband and wife. Connie threw the bouquet, which her sister caught, and then she danced with her father. When they were done, Matthew waltzed with his mother, sweeping her across all corners of the dance floor, while a photographer captured the moment.

Aidan watched them with a foreign sense of calm. He would never dance with his mother at his wedding—in fact, he would have no family in the traditional sense present when he married Beth next year. Six months ago, that would've destroyed him.

He really had come a long way, hadn't he?

Following dinner, Connie and Matthew cut the cake and guests of honor were due to give toasts. Matthew had spoken at Nathan and Olivia's post-wedding meal at Tavern on the Green, and Nathan would speak at Aidan and Beth's wedding. Therefore, at this soirée, Aidan would say a few words. Initially, improvisation seemed like a good idea—as he was famous for in his profession—but now he wished he'd written something down.

Connie's mother was the first speaker. Alice Johnson looked a lot like her daughter—voluptuous, platinum blonde, and elegant. She declared how proud she was of Connie and how happy she was to have Matthew officially join the family. Given all Connie had been through to finally be free from Mr. Mertz's control, Aidan could tell her mother's praise meant a lot to her.

Before long, it was his turn. He claimed the podium next to the head table and acknowledged Matthew and Connie with a nod before casting his gaze to the audience.

"I first met Matthew at The Brown Derby just over a year ago through our mutual friend, Nathan Taggart, at a time when I was really wary of the whole Hollywood scene and yet on the cusp of superstardom. Matthew demonstrated with great poise how to deal with fame and take this peculiar life we lead in stride by focusing on the good even in not-so-good times."

Aidan wrung his hands to keep from raking them through his hair. Somehow, the words came to him without hesitation. Maybe following his heart like he'd done when communicating with Beth's parents really did inspire articulacy, after all.

"Matt became not only a mentor to me, but also a dear friend. He was there when I landed myself in the hospital, tossing out jokes to lighten the mood, yet treating his duty as my self-proclaimed brother with seriousness, love, and enthusiasm. Without a doubt, I'm a better guy for having met him.

"Now, Constance . . ." A grin formed on Aidan's lips. "She and I didn't exactly start off on the right foot, but I think she's a swell broad and, well, I didn't know Matt before he met her, but I see the way he is when they're together and she really brings out the best in him. Connie has proven time and time again that she's a special, strong woman, and I'm really glad to know her, too."

Aidan looked toward the back wall, hoping to better his chances of reining in his emotions. Opening up in front of the camera or onstage was cathartic. In other circumstances, it was downright nerve racking.

"These last few months have been difficult. The six of us— Beth, Connie, Matthew, Nate, Olivia, and I—left L.A. when everything was one heck of a mess at the studio, and we stuck together through it all. I know I speak for the other three when I say, if not for Matt and Connie's support, we wouldn't have recovered as well as we did.

"The magazines declare them an attractive couple, the epitome of Hollywood glamour, and that's true. But a side of them that's often overlooked is that Matthew and Connie exemplify the essence of generosity and true friendship. It's a great honor for me to stand up here today and speak on behalf of a room full of people who hold them so near and dear to their hearts." Aidan pitched his grin at the newlyweds. "I wish you both the very best of everything, including a long, fruitful marriage filled with happiness and love."

Amongst polite applause, he walked back to his table and

sat down.

Beth welcomed him with a smile. "That was wonderful."

Aidan shrugged in an effort to convey indifference. Honestly, he worried he hadn't done the couple justice. "Thanks. It's hard for me to, you know . . ."

She took his hand and squeezed. "It was perfect."

Aidan squeezed back. He valued her unconditional support more than he could ever express verbally. Even though they had been seeing an analyst, he believed Beth was the most integral part of his transformation. Without her, he'd be no better off than he was before he came to Hollywood—a lonely pessimist, hiding out in a dark apartment, leaving only for work; a shell of a man without genuine human connection or a true purpose in life.

When the quartet resumed playing, Aidan asked Beth to dance. Following her consent, he guided her to the sea of couples already on the floor. Holding her close, he showed her the best moves he had. One song turned into four. The fifth tune was a fast one and not in his comfort zone, so he led her back to their table, where he obtained the attention of a waiter and ordered two flutes of champagne. Once they finished their drinks, Beth announced her departure for the restroom.

A slow song commenced as she left the table. The dance floor was still busy, and all around Aidan people engaged in animated chatter.

While Matthew spoke with a well-known record producer, Connie sat at the head table alone, watching her guests with her famous movie star smile. But this wasn't the same smile that had graced the big screen or red carpets on countless occasions. This one burst with happiness, lending it a sincerity rarely seen on her previously.

Aidan walked over to her and extended his hand. "Would you care to dance?"

Her eyebrows rose. "You want to dance with me?"

He smirked. "Yeah, well, don't get used to it or anything. It may never happen again."

She giggled. "In that case, yes. I accept your offer."

Aidan ushered her to the dance floor. The other guests dispersed, allowing them the middle all to themselves. Once they reached a prime spot under a sparkling chandelier, they faced each other in proper form.

Connie blinked rapidly. Tears toppled down her face.

Aidan's eyes widened. "Are you all right?"

"Yes." Her lower lip trembled. "I don't mean to cry. I must look frightful."

"No, you don't. You make a beautiful bride, Connie." And he meant it. Draped in white satin and lace, she looked prettier today than she had in any of her motion pictures.

She sniffled. "Thank you, Aidan."

They picked up their pace in time with the music, but Connie's persistent frown made Aidan stop them midstride. "If you wanna go back to your table, you can."

She shook her head. "I'm enjoying your company. It's just been an emotional day. It doesn't help that I haven't gotten much sleep while planning the wedding." At her instigation, they continued dancing. "Aidan, I want to apologize for how I treated you. You've been wonderful to Beth. Nathan and Matthew love you, and Olivia told me so many times to give you a chance, but I refused. I let my past with Luther Mertz get in the way of a possible friendship between you and me. It was wrong and I'm sorry."

Aidan shrugged. "Hell, you don't have to apologize. I wasn't exactly cordial with you either. I thought you were a spoiled, untalented contract star. I never gave you the benefit of the doubt or made an effort to get to know you better."

Connie shared a sheepish smile. "I guess we both made mistakes, huh?"

Aidan chuckled. "I used to do a lot of that."

"Me, too." Her eyes lost focus.

At the start of the second verse, Aidan lifted his arm and twirled her. His attempt to cheer her up worked. With lighthearted laughter, Connie completed her rotation. They replaced their hands, returning to form.

"Thank you for helping me realize I deserved better than what I experienced when I first came to Hollywood, Aidan. Also, that I was worthy enough to find happiness again, even though my behavior years ago wasn't honorable."

Aidan looked down at his feet, but he wasn't monitoring his steps. There was a lot of baggage that went along with what happened in Mertz's office. It was difficult to talk about; difficult to look someone in the eye and admit wrongdoing. However, to officially make amends with Connie, she needed to know he was sorry as well—that he was ashamed he had been so quick to judge her. His past struggles perpetuated his standoff nature and negative behavior. He should've recognized the same in her, too.

"With every punch I threw at Mertz, I was really battling with my personal pain, punishing myself for my mistakes while simultaneously hoping to displace the blame on someone else. Mertz is far from an innocent party in all this, but I used what he did to Beth as an excuse to lash out at him. Sure, I did it to defend her, but I'm ashamed to say she wasn't the sole reason for my attack. I've been seeing an analyst, you know. He made me realize a lot of things and I'm not angry like I used to be."

Connie sighed. "When you hit Luther, I saw my own hurt in your eyes. That's why I went after him as well. I felt united with you then, as silly as it sounds. It was in that moment I realized you and I are a lot alike, only I buried my pain for years while yours was palpable."

"Because you're stronger than me."

Connie clasped his hand tighter. "That's not true. You showed remarkable strength and courage when you confided in Beth. I was too scared to open up. Foolishly, I thought everything would go away if I ignored it long enough. You're also right that inflicting pain upon Luther wasn't the answer. I had to search within myself for redemption and to reclaim my self-worth."

"You're an honorable woman, Connie." This time, Aidan didn't hesitate to look her right in the eye. "Beth told me how you dragged her out of my house and encouraged her to continue on in my absence, how you supported her at the hospital, took care of me, and helped clean me up."

"When Matthew and I flew to Chicago and saw you . . ." Connie grimaced. "All I could think about was how much I wished I could apologize to you and set things right between us. I worried I'd never get the chance."

"Even if I didn't wake up from my coma, you would've earned my respect, Connie. I owe you a thank you for everything you've done for me and Beth."

"It's what friends do. I'm just glad our suffering is behind us and we have the opportunity to start anew." Connie placed her head on his chest and closed her eyes. Her brow smoothed out with the arrival of her smile.

Aidan held her close and slowed their steps to fit the music. If the old Aidan Evans were allowed a glimpse into his future, he would've denied its authenticity. Never would he have predicted that he and Connie would be friends—and slow dancing together, of all things.

The song came to an end. When Aidan looked around, an uncharacteristic blush leapt into his cheeks. Every guest had cleared the dance floor. Applause broke out. Beth brushed tears from her eyes.

Aidan took Connie's hand and kissed it. "I'm honored you granted me this dance."

She curtsied in a grand and beautiful way, as only she could. "And I'm honored you consider me a friend."

Aidan brought Connie back to her husband. He and Beth wished the newlyweds a lovely honeymoon in Europe, made dinner plans with Nathan and Olivia for next week, and then exited into a tepid fall night.

Last night, Aidan and Beth had checked into the Seaside Inn, where the rest of the wedding guests resided. As nice as those accommodations were, they didn't feel like staying there again. Their *Golden Gloves* promotional tour would make them extra accessible to the public in the coming months. Tonight, they desired to spend time alone together in a place where no one could find them.

Several blocks from the reception hall, tucked away on an unassuming side street, they stumbled upon a charming motel. Aidan paid the desk clerk extra money to keep their whereabouts a secret, and he and Beth blissfully, passionately, slipped into temporary obscurity.

Chapter Twenty-One

Beth and Aidan strolled along Broadway before dawn, the echoes of their footsteps the only sounds on the typically busy New York City street.

Fourteen hours from now, *Golden Gloves* would premiere at the 46th Street Theatre. Fans, friends, industry peers, and notable members of the press would crowd the area for red carpet festivities, and their idle footfalls would fade amongst the chaos. Right now, they could enjoy their togetherness without interference and exercise their renewed outlook on their careers and relationship: Life is a journey, not a destination.

Beth and Aidan both took unprecedented paths in their professions and prevailed. Most importantly, they achieved individual redemption and reclaimed their self-confidence because of what they found in each other. They didn't worry about what lay ahead for them. Everything would turn out all right, regardless of any future obstacles they faced. Love empowered and saved, and brightened people's days during the darkest storms, as long as they put in some hard work along the way, of course.

Newspapers all over the country predicted *Golden Gloves* would break box office records. The media dubbed the film as their acting debut as a couple, which piqued the public's interest, but it was the glowing reviews from critics granted advance screenings that really fueled the buzz. The film opened nationwide next week, and theaters expected lineups hours before tickets went on sale. Aidan and Beth were grateful they could finally share Joe and Mary's story with the world.

This morning, their walk had brought them to many landmarks from their courtship, including the famed Actors Studio. During Beth's first visit as a guest, she'd completed a scene with Paul Newman. Then, much to her shock and excitement, Aidan had risen from his chair in the back of the room—the epitome of the gorgeous, brooding rebel—to take the blue-eyed actor's place. But it was for other reasons she would remember that day forever. Aidan had asked her out on their first date that afternoon, and it was also the first time they'd performed together, marking the start of their professional partnership.

Aidan exuded energy, passion, and realism during their scene, demonstrating in a raw and captivating way what acting was truly about. Watching his incredible gift onscreen was awe-inspiring. Live? Well, there was nothing like it.

From then on, Beth had viewed their profession with more esteem. To self-reflect, to tap into emotions buried deep within oneself in order to pull off an authentic performance, was no easy feat by any means, whether an actor was a natural performer like Aidan or someone who needed continuous coaching to achieve his greatest potential. Beth was honored to be a member of the Actors Studio now and to have the opportunity to nurture her craft alongside acclaimed professionals in theater and film.

Before long, the couple arrived at the 46th Street Theatre, which was already decorated for the premiere. The film's title and their names in equal billing lit up the marquee. The velvet ropes were secured and a sign erected on an easel at the entrance announced the event information.

Beth and Aidan huddled together against a brisk wind in front of a *Golden Gloves* promotional poster, one of many mounted on the theater's exterior. In the advertisement, Joe was dressed for a fight, his gloved fists raised and his narrowed eyes fixed ahead. Mary stood in the background with a gentle grip on his shoulder.

While Joe's features were set tightly, hers were softened by hope and adoration. In spite of these differences, their united front was unmistakable. Mary's subtle gesture proclaimed their love for each other and determination to triumph over their troubles as a couple more effectively than if they shared an intimate embrace.

Mary supported Joe through it all. Whether physically or in spirit, she was always in his corner. She was with him as he slaved away at the factory, as he trained at the gym all day, every day, improving his mental and physical well-being . . . when he entered the ring for his first bout since his former opponent's demise, and every bout after that. She was there during every punch he threw, every hit he took, and kneeled beside him whenever his guilt and torment brought him to the mat.

But her greatest influence? Allowing him to stand back up on his own. Because any real woman—a woman who truly wanted to support her husband and exemplify the good wife—recognized the value of a man's self-worth and encouraged him to find his own way. Only Joe, and Joe alone, had the power to knock out his demons and keep them down for the count.

"Once our film is no longer in theaters, we should collect some of the posters and hang them up in our home." Aidan's eyebrows rose. "What do you think, baby?"

Beth giggled at his joke. "Oh, sure. In fact, I think we should convert our apartment into a *Golden Gloves* art gallery and charge the public admission."

"Is that sarcasm I detect?" Aidan smirked. "So does that mean you wouldn't want a picture of me half-naked mounted above our bed?"

Beth tapped her chin in faux contemplation. "You know, I always thought our amazing acting abilities generated all the interest in *Golden Gloves*, but perhaps the attention is really due to women all over the world wishing to see you shirtless."

A grin spread across Aidan's lips, gracing his face with boyish splendor. "Are you saying I'm nothing but a sexy beefcake whose sole purpose is to satiate the carnal sexual desires of the entire adult female population?"

Beth clasped her hands behind his neck, presenting her best demure look while trying to hold back a smile. "Well, you are on the cover of *Photoplay*'s special Movie Star Hunks issue this month, voted number one by the magazine's female readers."

Aidan's gaze floated down her body, radiating a heated admiration that communicated he'd be more than happy to see *her* without a shirt on. Unlike the *Golden Gloves* poster, however, she'd be for his eyes only. "The only thing I care about is whether I satisfy your carnal desires."

The threat of a smile evaporated as Beth's longing skyrocketed, fueled by cherished memories she hoped to replicate when they returned home. "I'd say our lovemaking in the foyer prior to our walk, and our two romps in the parlor yesterday evening . . . oh, and our christening of the kitchen table yesterday morning thoroughly demonstrate your wondrous sexual prowess and how well you entice me and satiate my every need." She kissed him softly. "I love you and cannot wait to marry you."

Aidan's expression sobered, his playfulness transforming to tenderness. "I love you, too, Marie."

Beth drew back from him. Her lower lip quivered, her eyes grew moist. Goodness, she never thought hearing him address her by her given name would yield such joy. "You haven't called me Marie before. Why now?"

Aidan framed her face with his hands. His gaze bore into hers, strengthened by sincerity. "Because I want you to know that I love every part of you, past and present, and I will also love the woman you'll become in the future."

Tears trailed down her cheeks. "Elizabeth Evans is the name I will wear most proudly."

Taking her hand, Aidan ushered her away from the theater's lights. They pressed up against the vacant box office, two anonymous shadows locked in a fervent embrace, their lips caressing and uttering promises of forever.

Before heading home, they paused in front of the *Golden Gloves* poster again. Beth placed her hand on Aidan's shoulder and squeezed. Their reflections in the glass merged with the faces of their movie counterparts—a time capsule of youth, a reminder of all they had been through and attained.

At dusk, they would walk the red carpet together, smiling for the cameras and openly sharing affection, marking yet another important moment in their relationship. Beth would dedicate a section in her scrapbook to the premiere and document every new milestone until every page was full like she had dreamed about on her trip back to Clarkson—the first stop on her renewed flight as Elizabeth Sutton, a lifelong journey that would always be made in the company of her beloved.

Chapter Twenty-Two

February 1959

Beth awoke to find the other side of the bed empty and the apartment strangely quiet in light of recent events. She looked toward the nightstand. The clock displayed three in the morning.

Dressed in a silk negligee gifted to her by her husband, she slipped out of bed and walked barefoot into the hallway. The door to her right was ajar. She crept up to it and poked her head inside the room.

Aidan stood in the darkened nursery before a floor-to-ceiling window overlooking Central Park, clad only in a pair of worn black jeans. A flurry of snow fell outside, dusting the glass with thick, white flakes. His sleep-tossed hair glowed copper in the moonlight.

Two-week-old Hannah Catherine Evans lay in his arms, held to his bare chest in a manner at odds with the strength flaunted by his physique. Aidan's head was bowed to his sleeping daughter, who looked so tiny in comparison, dressed in her finest satin nightgown. He rocked her gently, humming the lullaby he wrote for her on the piano.

Although they had been married for over three years, Beth's pregnancy came as a surprise. Aidan was moved to tears by the news, although he later confided that he worried about his ability to be a good father. He wanted desperately to give his child all the love he had missed out on after his mother died, but felt the pressures he put on himself were so great he couldn't possibly meet his own expectations. His biggest fear in life was failing as a parent now that he was more confident in his role as a husband.

Moments like these reinforced what Beth had assured him throughout her pregnancy. When Hannah was born, unconditional love and instinct took over, making up for all of their doubts and inexperience.

Aidan was an excellent father. In fact, he spoiled Hannah. It was endearing, especially since he still had the reputation of the surly, rebellious young actor from *Spike Rollins* who enjoyed racing his sports cars and motorcycles through the streets of Manhattan—though he had toned down his speeds when he learned of Hannah's impending arrival.

If Beth thought Aidan was overprotective during their courtship and marriage, it was nothing compared to the guardianship he showed his daughter. The bond between them was already impenetrable. Beth often admired the two of them, wondering what she did to deserve such a blessed life.

The nursery fell silent as Aidan brushed his lips to

Hannah's forehead. "My beautiful girl," he whispered. "I love you and your mother so very much."

Following a gentle kiss to Hannah's nose, Aidan turned his head to rest his cheek on her forehead. He closed his eyes and resumed his song while he swayed with her against the backdrop of the storm outside.

Beth smiled and tiptoed back to bed, where her husband's lullaby ushered her into her own peaceful sleep.

$\mathcal{E}$pilogue

October 1985

"Thank you, Mrs. Evans. It was a pleasure working with you."

"The pleasure was mine." Beth stood and shook the hand of Lester Harold, the CEO of the company publishing her memoir.

With the release of *Taking Flight: The Journey of Elizabeth Sutton* fast approaching, Beth was excited but also nervous. She'd toyed with the idea of writing her life story thus far for a while, but the task always intimidated her. Gathering over fifty years of memories was a tough feat. However, when Nathan Taggart put her in touch with Mr. Harold two years ago, they hit it off right away, giving her the motivation she needed to begin.

Mr. Harold's assistant had recorded Beth's experiences as she dictated them, and then he transcribed them. To assist her with the accuracy of some events, she referred to the journals and scrapbooks she'd written and compiled over the years.

Once the book hit shelves, Beth would embark on a ten-city North American promotional tour, participating in in-store signings as well as television appearances on all the major networks. The buzz for her memoir was overwhelmingly positive, which was welcome news. There were times during the writing process when she wondered if anyone would care to read about her life. Advance sales had already put her at the top of the *New York Times* Best Seller list. She couldn't wait to get on the road and meet her fans.

Although Beth remained truthful in her memoir, she didn't cover all the larger events in her life, such as what happened between her and Luther Mertz. She mentioned Mr. Mertz's contention concerning her relationship with Aidan, but she didn't broach the subject of his blackmail. Some details needed to stay private. Her autobiography was not a sleazy tell-all. If she didn't have something nice to say about someone, she either referenced them in passing or skipped certain stories entirely. All of her milestones were covered, so she didn't feel as if she cheated her readers out of anything important.

Mr. Harold accompanied Beth to the door and they exchanged good-byes. A Lincoln Town Car waited for her in front of the midtown office building. Her driver, Sam, already had the back door open. For the last fifteen years, Sam had been a valued employee—honest, hardworking, and kind. Beth and Aidan had lucked out when he applied to work for them after retiring from a thirty-year career in law enforcement.

Gripping her coat closed to shield herself from the crisp October wind, Beth greeted Sam with a smile. "I hope you weren't waiting long."

"Less than five minutes, Mrs. Evans." He shared a grin, accentuating the lines in his face. "How did it go with Mr.

Harold?"

"Wonderful." A gust of wind blew down the street. Beth pushed the hair out of her eyes. "I still can't believe I'm only a week away from the book's release."

"I must say, I'm looking forward to reading it."

She patted his forearm. "I hope you enjoy it."

"I have no doubt I will."

"Ms. Sutton?" A young woman approached, smiling broadly. "I'm sorry to bother you, but I really wanted to say hi."

Beth smiled back. "Don't worry. You're not bothering me."

"My mother and I saw you last year on Broadway. You were amazing." The young woman wrung her hands. "I've caught some of your films on television as well. I'm a huge admirer."

"Why, thank you." Beth moved closer. "What's your name?"

"Marcia. Marcia Potts." She blushed. "A lot of my friends like Bo Derek and Farrah Fawcett, but you're my favorite actress."

"What a compliment." Beth giggled. "I never thought I'd be placed in the same category as a perfect *10* or one of Charlie's Angels, especially at my age."

"My favorite movie of yours is *Golden Gloves*. You and Aidan Evans have such great chemistry. No wonder you've been married for so long."

Beth's smile widened. "I'll make sure to tell him that. He'll be flattered to know people still enjoy his earlier work."

"Mr. Evans is a terrific actor and the original rebel. He truly paved the way for Warren Beatty, Jack Nicholson, Robert Redford . . . the list is endless."

Beth laughed. "Aidan has always been a rule breaker, that's for sure."

Marcia removed a pen and note paper from her purse. "Do you mind if I get your autograph?"

"Not at all."

While Sam waited patiently, Beth wrote a personalized note to Marcia and signed it. Legally, since April 1955, she was Elizabeth Evans. Professionally, she still went by Elizabeth Sutton. Marie Bates would always be a part of her, too, though she'd dropped the name long ago.

Beth handed over her autograph. With a parting wave, Marcia continued down the street.

A doting twinkle danced in Sam's eyes. "That was nice of you. Not many people are so gracious to their fans."

Beth shrugged. "If not for them, I wouldn't be in the position I'm in today. I never forget that."

Once she was settled in the backseat, Sam shut the door and sat behind the wheel.

With the fall season officially settling into Manhattan and Halloween approaching, residences and storefronts were decorated accordingly. Even after all this time, Beth adored New York—the energy, the culture. But most of all, the places in the city that held her favorite memories.

They drove past the Marriott Hotel, which had been built after the Astor Theater was demolished in 1982, twenty-nine years after it premiered *Sparkling Meadow*, the film in which Beth played a young farm girl. Hollywood didn't make many motion pictures like that anymore. Nowadays, grittier films dominated the box office. It was a trend that began in the 1960s—a decade, in her personal experience, that had seen the greatest change.

The 1960s started with The Beatles singing songs with innocent titles like "I Want To Hold Your Hand". By the latter part of the decade, sex, drugs, and edgier rock and roll reigned supreme. Artists were creating music beyond what anyone had experimented with previously, resulting in some of the most exciting songs in history. The end of the space race in July 1969 also forever changed people's perceptions of what was possible. Neil Armstrong's walk on the moon proved that mankind's potential wasn't limited to the sky, but the infinite space beyond.

Clarke Gable died in 1960, and Marilyn Monroe in 1962, taking with them much of the glamour of past eras. The assassinations of President John Kennedy in 1963, followed by Martin Luther King Junior and Robert Kennedy in 1968, further challenged the American dream. The Vietnam War divided Americans politically, and the hippy movement escalated, celebrated by countercultural events like Woodstock in 1969.

Hollywood changed as well, following the shift in culture. After the shocking and horrific Tate-LaBianca murders in 1969, celebrities no longer felt safe. Although Beth and Aidan hadn't lived in Los Angeles in years, they felt the effects when they traveled there for business.

When they'd resided in L.A., most celebrities lived in houses lined along the street with their front doors easily accessible from the sidewalk, and they rarely worried about an invasion of privacy. Celebrity homes bus and trolley tours existed then, too, but the organizers and tourists were always respectful. Unfortunately, the entertainment industry was no longer a close-knit community in L.A. Celebrities lived in mansions surrounded by high hedges, stone walls, or wooden fences and were guarded by security teams, hiding from photographers, and sadly, their fans.

The newer, rabid style of journalism out there today also contributed to the need for seclusion. Since the fall of the studio system, it had become popular to expose the darkest secrets of celebrities. As a result, the press's tactics grew more aggressive.

Beth and Aidan lived low-key lifestyles void of gossip-worthy stories, despite their popularity and success, but many others suffered greatly from these so-called exposés. It began with *Confidential Magazine* in the 1950s and worsened during the hunt for photographs of Elizabeth Taylor and Richard Burton. Now there were dozens of tabloids competing for the most revealing stories and pictures.

Politics merged with the entertainment industry in recent decades as well. The Civil Rights Movement, the Women's Liberation Movement, and the 1981 inauguration of former Starlight Studios contract star Ronald Reagan as President of the United States were some examples. But the ultimate illustration of this merger was former President John Kennedy.

It didn't matter what type of man President Kennedy really was, only what he displayed to the public. People sensed a change on the horizon in the early 1960s and felt apprehensive about it. They needed a leader to whom they could turn for reassurance and believed the affluent Senator from Massachusetts was the ideal man for the job.

President Kennedy's untimely death marked an end of a magical era. It was a slow demise, which began with the fall of the fantasy, illusory world of Mr. Mertz's studio system years earlier. After his assassination, President Kennedy achieved popularity of mammoth proportions, much like celebrities who pass away before what's considered their time. The question of what could have been was the mystery that fueled this exaltation. Because of the unknown—what great things President Kennedy might have accomplished for the country had he lived—the American people admired him more than they probably should.

Elia Kazan wrote the following after President Kennedy's assassination:

One look at Jack told me he was an actor, too. He understood our way of life, shared our values, our morality. He was one of us. He even possessed the poise that an actor needs to carry a play, as well as that old leading man quality, dash.

Like those fellows who walk into Sardi's and make every head turn, he enjoyed the adulation showered on him. He enjoyed being who he was. And now he is dead. A miserable, jealous little extra killed our leading man.

The Bay of Pigs? Forgotten.

Khrushchev and Vienna? So what?

Not since President Roosevelt's death has there been such a catastrophic blow to the show people.

President Kennedy's assassination changed the country drastically and left people feeling hopeless and adrift. It wasn't just the death of a handsome, charming person who possessed leading man qualities with which Presidents Lyndon Johnson and Richard Nixon could never compete that affected the American people so much, but the loss of all he represented.

The American public related to President Kennedy. Yet at the same time, they thought he was above them. It was the ideal balance for a leader to possess, similar to what people admired about their favorite movie stars.

From her years in the entertainment industry, Beth had learned that the formula for success depended on performers' abilities to display both perfection and vulnerability to their audience. These qualities gave people hope. Politicians—any public figure, for that matter—were no exception.

In some ways, Beth missed the days when movie stars were enigmas who provided the public with an escape from everyday life. She didn't prefer studio contracts and Luther Mertz's reign, but she did prefer the type of films they made compared to now. Anyone could watch the less desirable aspects of real life on the nightly news. The cinema was supposed to be full of fantasy and fun. Yes, Starlight Studios had made many excellent, more dramatic motion pictures as well, but a line was drawn to ensure the storylines weren't too graphic and many ended happily ever after. Consider *Spike Rollins*. It was ruled as groundbreaking at the time and wasn't centered on an idyllic paradise, but the conclusion of the film still gave people hope.

Magic and intrigue were missing in public figures and films

today. Now society wanted scandals and seedy truths. Why would people want to take away the one piece of innocence they could always rely upon in trying times, those that brought them so much joy and awe in their youth: the uplifting stories shown in motion pictures? Why did they now want violence, corruption, and deceit in films when it existed so prevalently in real life?

Then again, perhaps the perfect public images created by the Starlight Studios system contributed to actors like Marilyn Monroe succumbing to the perils of alcohol and substance abuse. Many performers upheld their façades when all they wanted was to reveal their true selves and have people love them for who they really were.

Beth was fortunate. Under contract, she was able to remain true to herself because it coincided with Mr. Mertz's plan for her as *his star*. If she had been made to adhere to an image that was unlike her real personality, maybe she would have met the same fate as many of her colleagues. Maybe then she'd have a different opinion on the matter entirely. Either way, they could not go back. As a society, they had seen too many truths—they knew too much—and the pubic still craved more.

And now Beth was days away from the release of her autobiography, about to provide intimate—albeit limited— details of her personal and professional lives to strangers. The irony was not lost on her.

While Beth and Aidan lived in New York City, they kept in touch with their friends from Hollywood. Directors Preston Adams and Alistair Graves retired after long, successful careers and were still living in L.A. Elia Kazan lived in Manhattan with his third wife, Frances, whom he married in 1982. Molly Kazan died unexpectedly at the age of fifty-six from a cerebral hemorrhage in 1968, and Barbara, his second wife, passed away from breast cancer in 1980. Mr. Kazan retired from directing in the late 1970s and now spent his days writing fiction. He also considered penning his autobiography. Beth offered encouragement on the subject, given her own positive experience.

Jack Peters and Ryan Sawyer were no longer a couple. In the late 1950s, Ryan was encouraged to marry his agent's secretary, much like Rock Hudson's façade, to strengthen his "manly" image. The engagement was arranged after a rumor about Jack and Ryan began floating around the industry. Ryan panicked and ended their relationship immediately, scared of what would happen to his career if the truth were confirmed. The secretary, Laura, divorced him after three years of marriage. Beth last heard that Ryan had purchased a ranch in North Dakota, where he now spent his days alone, tending to his horses.

Jack left the film industry in the late 1970s after his newly diagnosed arthritis made it difficult for him to dance. His breakup with Ryan had devastated him, but fortunately he met and fell in love with another man, Jonathan, with whom he currently shared a home in Santa Barbara.

Beth's former costar, William Everett, married four times and fathered five children, all of whom were not conceived with his wives. His popularity dipped in the 1960s and 1970s, but given his persistence and his penchant to take any acting gig offered to him, he always managed to stay in the limelight.

Luck struck in 1982 when Will landed the lead in a new series, *Mason*, launched on a major television network. With his deeply tanned skin, polished veneers, toupee, and newly lifted face, he was now the highest paid actor on the small screen.

Mason featured a wealthy Los Angeles private detective named Chase Mason, who lived a glamorous life, wore flashy gold jewelry, and managed to catch all the bad guys by the end of every hour-long episode without creasing his silk suit, scuffing his shiny dress shoes, or having one lock of hair fall out of place. Each episode ended the same way, with Detective Mason celebrating his victory amongst a bevy of scantily clad beauties at his Malibu beach house and drinking champagne.

Beth had seen Will many times over the years. He still lived in Beverly Hills, and as usual, always had some younger busty pinup on his arm. Although the world had seen many shifts over time, some things never changed. She was glad he was doing so well.

Wade Henley achieved moderate success following his role as Sal in *Golden Gloves*, but a few years later,= he decided to leave the movie industry to pursue a career in real estate. He currently operated out of a beachside office in Santa Monica. He was the father of three boys and married to a cosmetician he met on the set of his final film.

Beth's childhood friend from Clarkson, Emma Russell, was still happily married to Neil. When Neil's father passed away unexpectedly in 1956, Neil took over the family's furniture business and expanded the company into a popular local chain. He established new headquarters in Portland, where they resided now. Despite their initial difficulties, Emma and Neil became parents to two beautiful girls, Susanne and Heather, both of whom became teachers like their mother. Beth and Emma corresponded through letters and telephone calls and saw each other at least once a year.

Luther Jensen Mertz died of attack in 1971. The obituaries called Mr. Mertz a movie mogul and pioneer, and that was by all means true. An impoverished Polish-Jewish immigrant, he had arrived in America in the 1910s and managed to create a successful motion picture studio from nothing and make thousands of films now considered classics. Given that Beth chose to omit why she despised him in her memoir, she had no choice but to accept the public's high opinion of him. But she would never forget the man he truly was behind closed doors: a callous, corrupt tyrant.

Sam pulled up in front of Beth's apartment building near the intersection of Central Park West and West Seventy-Second Street and opened her door. After bidding him farewell, she entered the building. Beth and Aidan had lived in the same apartment since the summer of 1954 and had never considered selling. Nowhere else would feel like home.

When Beth exited the elevator on the top floor, a familiar melody greeted her in the corridor. She blushed like a young woman on her first date as she entered the apartment and hung her coat in the foyer closet. Humming along with the song Aidan wrote for her years ago, she traveled to the parlor but stopped just outside the door. He played so beautifully she didn't want to interrupt him.

She took a detour into the library and approached the fireplace mantel to admire her favorite photograph from their wedding on April sixteenth, 1955. The ceremony was a quaint gathering in Manhattan, with only their dearest friends and her parents present. Beth wore a lace, organza, and taffeta gown, designed by Olivia, while Aidan wore a black tuxedo. She'd never forget his tears as she joined him at the altar and they exchanged custom-made rings and personalized vows. It was one of the greatest moments of her life.

Another photograph showed Beth dancing with her father during the reception. Her parents still lived in Clarkson and were in optimal health. She visited them regularly and they often visited her as well.

The photograph from Beth's first date with Aidan was next on the mantel. She brushed her fingertips to the glass. Memories of their time at the Bethesda Fountain and the Waldorf Astoria mingled with the notes Aidan played in the parlor.

There was also a photograph of Aidan's mother, Catherine Evans. Encompassed by an antique gold frame and protected by glass, Catherine looked like a movie star posing for a professional portrait with her broad smile and eyes full of tenderness and mystery. She reminded Beth so much of Aidan.

Aidan never resolved his feud with his father. After Graham Evans' death in 1974, his widow, Betty, sorted through his belongings and discovered this photograph of Catherine and others of Catherine and Aidan together locked in his office desk. She mailed them to Aidan right away. At that time, Aidan hadn't seen his mother's face in over three decades. When he received the photographs, he wept, but he also seemed at peace.

Presently, Betty lived in Sarasota, Florida. Since his father's death, Aidan wrote her every month, and in each correspondence, he included a check. Betty never cashed them, but he continued to send them anyway. The money was Aidan's attempt to make up for his inability to provide her with the stepmother/stepson relationship she had wanted and deserved. Although he liked Betty and had forgiven her for the affair, she was connected to a negative time in his life he didn't want to revisit.

As Aidan ushered the song into the third verse, Beth walked to the oak hunch embedded in the wall, surrounded by books. She admired the music box Aidan gave her for her nineteenth birthday at the end of their first date in New York. There was also a collection of photographs of their children taken over the years.

Hannah Catherine Evans was born February seventh, 1959, and Nicholas John Evans arrived on March fifteenth, 1962. Neither Hannah nor Nicholas ever showed an interest in acting as a profession. Beth and Aidan never pushed them either way, preferring them to explore all types of hobbies while growing up and follow their own paths.

Like her father, Hannah had high cheekbones and green eyes so vibrant she was often asked if she wore colored contacts lenses, while her full lips, narrow nose, and dark brown hair resembled her mother's features. Poetry, painting, and music were Hannah's passions. She had learned piano from Aidan and had also taken up the violin and flute in her youth. Currently, she worked as a music teacher at an all-girls private school uptown.

While Hannah was an extrovert who poured her energy into the arts, Nicholas was far more reserved and had an interest in technical knowledge and mathematics. He took guitar lessons during his Joe Strummer phase a few years ago, but never stuck with it. Like Beth, he wasn't musically inclined.

During his teenage years, Nicholas exhibited a lot of his father's rebellious tendencies, including talking back to his teachers and a penchant for fast driving. When it became clear that Nicholas could not be deterred from racing altogether, Aidan enrolled him in professional lessons to allow him to hone his skills safely and limit his daredevil driving to the racetrack.

Thankfully, in his senior year of high school, Nicholas settled down and got serious about his studies, though he and Aidan still raced each other for fun at a track outside the city. Twenty-three years old now, he lived in an apartment near Union Square and studied architecture at New York University.

Beth took only six months off work after each child was born. She loved her family, but being a stay-at-home mother and housewife didn't appeal to her. It was the reason she had left Clarkson to begin with. Instead, she strived for the best of both the personal and professional worlds. Typically, when Hannah and Nicholas were younger, she and Aidan accepted jobs away from home only if they could take the children with them. When the children were in school, this meant during summer breaks. When that wasn't possible, one of them stayed home while the other filmed on location.

Hannah and Nicholas were well traveled and had attended the finest schools in Manhattan, but through their charity work and constant reminders of their family's humble roots, they didn't act superior or entitled because of their parents' fame. In fact, Beth and Aidan were often told how grounded their children were. It was one of the greatest compliments they could have received.

Six Academy Awards sat on the hutch's middle shelf. Two of the statuettes were from Beth and Aidan's Best Actress and Best Actor wins for *Sparkling Meadow* and *Spike Rollins*, respectively. The next two were top honors for their work in *Golden Gloves,* which continued a successful run in theaters for weeks after its release and earned Elia Kazan an Oscar for Best Director. Then there was Aidan's Best Director Oscar for his 1976 third directorial effort, *Segue,* for which he also wrote the screenplay. And finally, Beth's third Best Actress Oscar for her role in that same film.

Over the years, Aidan had been both in front of the camera and behind. It was his desire to return to his theatrical stage roots that encouraged Beth to work with him on Broadway. They had costarred in several productions over the years and were even each nominated for a Tony Award.

Beth and Aidan were active members of the Actors Studio until 1964 when Aidan came to her with an idea to start an organization to help ill children. They talked it over in earnest and then left the Actors Studio to focus on bringing his dream to fruition.

By that time, the Actors Studio wasn't the same anyway. Elia Kazan had left, and under the sole rule of Lee Strasberg, the organization became more about celebrity than talent alone, superseding its original philosophy and making it an ideal time for Beth and Aidan to resign. However, they still applied the knowledge they'd gained as Actors Studio members to every one of their acting projects.

One of Beth and Aidan's proudest moments occurred in July 1965 when they attended the grand opening of the first Golden Warriors Camp for Children, named after Aidan's role in *Golden Gloves,* the film where his character beat the odds and triumphed, despite his hardships.

The Golden Warriors Association, also known as GWA, was a non-profit organization that served children and their families coping with cancer. Its mission was to ensure that kids didn't have to compromise on their childhoods because of a serious illness.

Over the last twenty years, GWA had grown substantially, thanks to contributions from individuals and corporations. Presently, Beth and Aidan were fortunate to receive support from more than one thousand annual donors. They donated portions of their own incomes as well and continued to play an active role in its operation.

In the beginning, GWA consisted of a single camp in Ashford, Connecticut. Today, the organization oversaw twelve full member camps in eight states, six new camps in various stages of development, and five global partnership initiatives in Africa and Asia. At camp, children enjoyed horseback riding, boating, swimming, fishing, arts and crafts, sports, music instruction, and acting instruction, which included participation in an end-of-summer play.

Although Aidan had purchased a Steinway grand piano—which he currently played in the parlor—he loved his mother's scuffed upright piano most. Therefore, it was fitting he had the instrument restored and then donated it to GWA.

When they visited the camps, Aidan gave piano lessons to the children. Watching him teach the young boys and girls was a treat. He shared his musical gift without a hint of fear, sadness, or apprehension—an amazing transformation from the tormented twenty-three-year-old man who played for Beth in Lou's Music Shop in Los Angeles.

Tonight, the Lincoln Center for the Performing Arts was hosting a benefit to celebrate the twentieth anniversary of GWA, with Beth and Aidan as the guests of honor. Arrangements for the event had been ongoing for months, with their dear friends, Olivia and Nathan Taggart, and Constance and Matthew McKenna at the helm. Although the exact anniversary date was in July, they wanted to hold the benefit after the camps finished for the year so planning wouldn't overlap with camp preparations and activities. This evening's event was less about personal recognition and more about the additional exposure it would provide their cause. Every ticket had been sold, with one hundred percent of the profits going to GWA.

When Aidan drew the song to a close, Beth tiptoed into the

parlor but stayed near the door. Sunlight streamed in through the window, gracing her husband with a spotlight as he launched into "Moonlight Serenade", another one of her favorites.

As Aidan delved into the chorus, he noticed her standing in the doorway. A large grin sprung to his face, and the passion in his performance strengthened. He injected love and devotion into the tune until the final notes faded, immersing the apartment in silence.

Beth smiled as Aidan stood and approached her. Faint lines decorated his face and some gray was scattered amongst his brown hair, but his dazzling grin and affectionate gaze were as youthful and fervent as when they first met. Even after all these years, he never failed to take her breath away.

"My beautiful little dove." He took her hand and kissed it. "When did you get home?"

"About ten minutes ago."

Aidan wrapped his arms around her. "How was your final meeting with Lester?"

"Very productive." She rested her cheek against his chest and closed her eyes.

Aidan pressed his lips to the top of her head. "You committed a lot of time to writing your memoir. Your fans will love it. I know they will. And I can't wait to read it either."

Beth looked forward to Aidan reading it as well. Unbeknownst to him, she had written a forward, dedicating the entire book to him and their children.

The grandfather clock in the corner chimed, reminding

them of the time. Hand in hand, they walked upstairs to their bedroom to start getting ready for the benefit. While Aidan showered and shaved in their en-suite bathroom, Beth applied additional makeup, striving for an elegant evening look. She also changed into a shimmering navy blue gown with an open back and intricately patterned beading on the bodice.

Beth still considered herself slim, but curvier than she'd been in her late teens, which was only natural after thirty years and bearing two children. She was proud of her womanly figure. It showed that she was loved as both a wife and a mother.

In addition to selecting her favorite diamond earrings, she decided to wear the diamond angel pendant Aidan had gifted her on their first Christmas together. Carrying the necklace, she opened the double French doors leading outside. A gentle fall breeze greeted her as she stepped barefoot onto the terrace, presiding over a panoramic view of Central Park.

Beth sensed more than heard Aidan's approach. Her skin tingled, her heart sped up; she felt his burning gaze. When his arms encircled her waist from behind, she leaned back and sighed contently.

"You look stunning," he whispered.

Beth turned around. His hair was wild, damp, and wavy, and his bow tie was undone, the loose ends hanging down his chest. He was the only man she knew who could pull off sexy, rebellious, as well as handsome while wearing a tuxedo.

She held up the necklace. "Can you put this on for me?"

Aidan's eyes blazed with approval. "Absolutely."

Beth placed her back to him again and lifted her hair,

exposing her neck. Aidan draped the pendant over her chest and worked the clasp in the back, his fingers caressing her nape. When he was done, he held her close. They took a moment to watch the sunset and then returned inside.

After Beth fixed Aidan's bow tie, he disappeared into their walk-in closet and emerged holding the ring she'd bought him on the same Christmas he'd purchased her necklace.

He held out the ring. "Would you do me the honor?"

"Of course." Beth took his left hand and slid the ring on his middle finger, next to his wedding band. They shared a tender kiss and then ventured downstairs where Aidan helped Beth with her coat.

In the lobby, Benjamin, the full-time night security guard, greeted them. "Good evening, Mr. and Mrs. Evans. Do you need a car or have you arranged chauffeured transportation this evening?"

"I'm driving us." Aidan tossed Beth a sly glance. "I think we'll go for a Porsche tonight."

"Which one, sir?"

"The '55 Spyder."

Benjamin grinned. "Excellent choice, Mr. Evans."

Beth and Aidan waited outside. Within minutes, Dean, one of the building's valets, drove up in Aidan's favorite Porsche. Aidan had purchased the car in the summer of 1955 to replace the one destroyed in his accident. It was his most prized possession in his collection of almost twenty cars and motorcycles.

Aidan opened the passenger door and ensured Beth was

settled before taking his seat behind the wheel. After they snapped on their seatbelts, they were off, choosing to leave the rain top up for the drive.

When Aidan turned onto Columbus Avenue, his lips twitched into a smirk. "How about some speed, baby?"

Beth shrieked with delight as he gunned the engine and raced down the road. Just like old times.

"Honey?" She sat up straighter, squinting ahead. "What's going on up there?"

Aidan decelerated. "I don't know. There's a bunch of people gathered—"

"You don't suppose . . . ?"

Aidan's eyebrows furrowed. "Nah. The Lincoln Center isn't for another few blocks."

When they completed their next turn, Beth's jaw dropped. Pedestrians gathered on the sidewalk, at least ten people deep, guarded by local police. The crowd grew in size the closer they got to the Lincoln Center.

Aidan stopped the car at a police checkpoint and rolled down his window. An officer peered inside. His eyes alighted with surprise.

"Mr. Evans, Miss Sutton, I expected you to arrive in a chauffeured limousine or something."

Aidan nudged his chin at the crowd. "What's with the crowd?"

The officer's brow creased. "Why, they're here hoping to catch a glimpse of you two, of course."

Beth's eyes widened. "My goodness. I can't believe it."

"My colleagues and I were dispatched here this morning when people first started to congregate," the officer said. "We may end up closing this part of the street altogether if the crowd continues to grow. We're happy to help. After all the good you've done with GWA, it's the least we can do." He gestured ahead. "Have a great night."

Aidan parked at the valet stand in front of the Lincoln Center and they emerged from the car. The crowd roared.

Reporters stood along the red carpet. Their flashbulbs illuminated the path to the entrance, which was packed with guests dressed in their best evening attire, channeling old Hollywood glamour. Beth and Aidan appeased as many of the reporters as possible as they made their way across Lincoln Plaza, answering questions about GWA and posing for photographs.

At the front door, a Lincoln Center employee handed them a program, outlining tonight's schedule. When Aidan removed Beth's coat at the coat check, his eyes feasted on her everywhere, as if he hadn't already seen her in the dress at their apartment. Her heart palpitated as he pulled her in for a gentle kiss packed with the promise of more intimacy when they returned home later tonight.

Recent arrivals greeted the couple. Two of the guests included Lydia Dale and her son, Thomas.

Beth embraced him. "Thomas, it's great to see you again."

Aidan nodded. "Yeah. It's good to see you, Tom."

Thomas shook Aidan's hand. "I'm honored to be here."

Lydia hugged Beth. "Congratulations."

"Thank you." Beth returned her embrace.

Lydia offered her hand to Aidan. "You, too."

He shook her hand, grinning politely. "Thank you for coming tonight."

"I wouldn't miss it for the world." A flicker of past pain shot across Lydia's face as she looked at her son.

In January 1968, Lydia had reached out to Beth and Aidan when Thomas was diagnosed with cancer at the age of ten. Beth hadn't spoken to Lydia in years until she showed up at their apartment with puffy, red eyes, looking so broken and frail, on the brink of bankruptcy and begging for a moment of Beth and Aidan's time. At first, Beth was suspicious of Lydia's motives, but the desperation behind her former costar's plea encouraged her to invite Lydia into her home.

Seated in their parlor, Lydia spoke about the deterioration of Thomas's health and spirit and how she wanted him to attend the Golden Warriors camp in Connecticut in the summer, following his first round of chemotherapy. It had taken a lot of courage to come to them. She admitted she was fearful they'd turn her away. Regardless of their history, Beth was determined to help.

Becoming a mother had changed Lydia in the best possible way. She was no longer the selfish, conniving woman they once knew, though she did have a difficult few years before Thomas's arrival.

Lydia never found a love like Beth and Aidan's. She had been married three times, the second marriage lasting no more than two months. She also battled alcohol addiction in the mid-

1950s. Finding out she was pregnant had encouraged her to seek treatment, and thankfully she had been sober since.

Lydia never married Thomas's father, which was a big scandal in 1958. When Thomas was diagnosed with cancer, she abandoned acting to remain at his side. Her third husband offered no support and instead took off on frequent trips to Las Vegas, disappearing for weeks at a time and gambling away her money. It was after Lydia divorced him that she approached Beth and Aidan.

Thomas had been in remission since 1970, having beaten the bleak odds set against him by his doctors. He currently studied medicine at Columbia University, with a focus in oncology. Since he turned sixteen, he had also volunteered as a counselor at many Golden Warriors camps nationwide.

Lydia's career took a negative turn throughout the 1970s when she tried to make a comeback after Thomas's recovery. She appeared in many low budget films that lacked substance and were major box office flops. However, she persevered, drawing strength from her son, and in the last five years she made a triumphant return to the industry via the Broadway stage.

Beth's attention was redirected as Hannah and Nicholas arrived.

"Dad!" Hannah flung her arms around Aidan.

He returned the hug with equal excitement. "Hey, butterfly."

Hannah's nickname came from the character she'd played in her only stage performance: a kindergarten play. In true

Method acting style—though she was only five years old at the time—she insisted on wearing her costume around the house and being called butterfly in the weeks leading up to the production. Although her enthusiasm toward acting didn't stick, the nickname did.

"Hi, Mom!" Hannah hugged her mother next.

"Hi, sweetie." Beth stepped back to admire her daughter. "You look beautiful."

Her compliment wasn't biased in the slightest. Hannah wore a gold-colored dress that complemented her dark curled hair, creamy skin, and slim figure. Beth couldn't believe how fast the years had passed. It seemed like only yesterday she was reading her daughter bedtime stories. Now Hannah was an accomplished adult, living on her own—though, much to her parents' delight, residing just a few blocks away from their apartment.

"Hey, Mom." Nicholas flashed a half grin that transformed his usual intense expression into one belonging to a devoted son who was happy to see his mother.

Nicholas was handsome by the highest standards, with the same defined jawline and wavy brown hair as his Aidan, though he wore it in a shaggy style popular with young men these days. His good looks, combined with his intelligence, made him a sought after bachelor. Times had changed, however, and going steady at his age was no longer the norm. Nicholas dated regularly but was not linked to any woman specifically—at least, as far as Beth knew.

"Hey to you, too." Beth embraced him tightly. At over six

feet tall, he had to lean down to hug her properly. "I see you took the plunge and put on a tuxedo."

Nicholas chuckled. "I figured if Dad could do it, so could I."

As Nicholas greeted his father, Beth observed them fondly. Though Nicholas had inherited a mix of his parents' physical features, Beth saw more of Aidan in him. Their mannerisms were so similar, from the confident yet casual way they carried themselves, to their baritone laughter and the way they messed with their hair whenever they were deep in thought or nervous.

Beth's gaze skipped to Thomas. Thomas watched Hannah with the same intensity often seen in Aidan's eyes whenever he looked at Beth over the years. Hannah and Thomas had spent time together whenever he was a camp counselor and she dropped in to the camps to teach music to the children, but Beth had never considered that Thomas felt anything for Hannah beyond friendship . . . until now.

Then Hannah locked eyes with Thomas and blushed, revealing yet another surprise: He wasn't the only one with a crush.

Thomas was an introvert and a bookworm. Hannah was not. Given what was said about the differences between her and Aidan during their courtship, however, Beth should have known better than to assume Thomas and Hannah were incompatible.

"Thomas and I are going to take our seats now." Lydia linked arms with her son. "I hope you have a splendid evening. You deserve it."

"It's lovely to see you again, Hannah." A shy grin accompanied Thomas's words.

Hannah flashed the bright smile Aidan always said reminded him of Beth's. "Hopefully we can catch up later."

Thomas's grin widened. "I'd like that very much."

Nicholas glared at Thomas, committed to the role of protective younger brother. "Later, Tom."

"Later, Nick." Thomas extended his hand to Aidan. "Mr. Evans, congratulations again, sir."

"Thank you." Aidan shook Thomas's hand, his expression void of knowledge of the young man's interest in Hannah. Or perhaps he was purposely ignorant.

Thomas and Lydia were soon swallowed up by the crowd, which had grown substantially in the last few minutes.

Nathan, Olivia, Constance, Matthew, and some of their children arrived shortly after. Beth and her family met them in the middle of the lobby.

"Nice of you two fellas to show up." Aidan shook hands with Matthew and then Nathan. The men shared laughs and good-natured ribbing, as they usually did whenever they were together. At times, it was as though they'd never aged beyond their twenties.

While Hannah and Nicholas greeted the McKenna and Taggart children, Olivia gave Beth a hug. She wore a forest green, sparkling dress and a black satin wrap, and her hair was styled in a classy chignon. No one could pull off trendy and sophisticated as well as Olivia. It was clear why she was in demand for every new play that hit Broadway.

Olivia clutched her hands to her chest. "The turnout tonight is incredible, Beth. You and Aidan must be ecstatic."

Beth gestured to their friends, children, and godchildren. "If it wasn't for all of you, everything wouldn't have come together so nicely."

Connie embraced Beth. She was dressed in a black, figure hugging gown, which made her permed platinum blonde hair stand out, and her stilettos accentuated her long legs. A real show stopper, as usual.

Connie won her much-deserved Oscar for Best Actress in 1981—a poignant moment in her career, given all she had gone through. As she stated in her acceptance speech, she stood at the podium representing mature actresses everywhere, proving they could be high box office draws like their younger counterparts. Her win also showcased to her critics that her talent stretched beyond the blonde bombshell image from her Starlight Studios contract days.

"The streets around the venue have been cordoned off," Connie said. "You can only get through by car if you present an invitation to the benefit."

"A police officer we spoke to earlier said that might happen." Beth smiled at her husband. "We cannot believe all this fanfare is for GWA."

Nathan kissed Beth's cheek and Matthew gave her a hug while Aidan, Connie, and Olivia conversed further about the large turnout.

Over the years, Matthew was able to reach the top of the charts with almost every album release. He also continued to play sold out shows all over the world and lent his name and money to many charitable organizations annually.

Nathan's continued success was a surprise to no one. After the six of them moved to New York, he was quick to get back on his feet and had enjoyed more triumphs and creative freedom than he ever had working for Luther Mertz. Although he was in high demand, he represented only a select number of clients in order to provide quality management. Beth, Aidan, and Connie were fortunate to still have him as their publicist.

When their friends moved on to Hannah and Nicholas, Beth and Aidan took the opportunity to say hello to their godchildren.

Charlotte McKenna, Matthew and Connie's only child, was twenty-five years old and an acclaimed actress with beauty queen good looks and a personality void of the pretentiousness people would expect someone as gorgeous as her to possess. Tonight she wore a slinky silver dress and heels higher than Connie's.

Charlotte was dating Leonard Dodd, the lead singer of a popular rock band. They'd met backstage at Matthew's concert at Madison Square Garden last year. From what Connie told Beth, they were smitten with each other and an engagement was imminent.

Leonard was in the middle of performing a three-night, sold out concert series at Wembley Stadium in London, England, so he was unable to accompany Charlotte to New York. However, he'd donated a substantial sum of money to GWA, of which Beth was notified last week. She looked forward to their first meeting so she could thank him in person.

Charlotte's success as an actress happened quickly, based on her natural talent and the camera's affinity for her. Her first film, *Stranded*, which she made when she was nineteen, displayed her abilities as a dramatic performer perfectly, and she had acted in many critically praised motion pictures since. Without the restraint of a studio contract, Charlotte was able to make her own career choices and arrive to where she was today through hard work, fortitude, and a sense of self-worth.

Connie was extremely proud of her daughter's independence and the respectable way she'd established herself in the industry. The respect wasn't one-sided. Charlotte had mentioned many times that her mother was her idol. Beth knew that meant a lot to Connie.

"I apologize for not joining you and my mother for brunch yesterday," Charlotte said. "I was jetlagged and wanted to be well rested for tonight."

"There's no need to apologize," Beth replied. "You flew in just for this event. Aidan and I are more than grateful. How do you like Spain and the shoot so far?"

Charlotte sighed, but her eyes shimmered with excitement. "The Spanish crew are very professional and a delight to work with. Do you know that we take a break every afternoon for two hours? It's written in the crew's contracts. And we start filming midmorning, none of those five o'clock call times like we have here in the States. I like the more relaxed filming pace much better, even though it means we have to work later into the evening. In fact, I hope to film more movies in Europe."

Aidan slipped his arm around Beth's waist. "When Beth and I filmed *Summer Falls* in Rome, we experienced the same thing. It takes some time to get used to it."

Beth suppressed a smile. When they filmed their first motion picture abroad, Aidan had definitely struggled with the change of pace. He wasn't used to the crew's laxer attitudes and grew impatient easily. Often, a scene that took one day to shoot in the U.S. took two or three days to film in Europe. Despite the slower pace, the quality of the work never suffered. When the crew was on the clock, they worked efficiently, and Aidan soon relaxed and came to understand and appreciate their dedication.

As Matthew, Connie, and Charlotte stepped aside to speak with a well-known film producer, Beth and Aidan greeted two of Nathan and Olivia's children, Todd and Clara. Olivia became pregnant with Aaron, the eldest, shortly after her wedding to Nathan. Two years later, Todd followed. Clara was born in 1961.

Aaron was a prominent attorney in San Francisco while Todd was a journalist for the *New York Times*. They were both married, and Nathan and Olivia were grandparents to three grandchildren, soon to be four. Todd's pregnant wife, Kimberly, was a reporter for NBC in New York.

"Thank you both for coming," Beth said to Todd and Clara.

"I'm sorry Aaron couldn't make it," Olivia said on behalf of her eldest son. "He couldn't get away from work, but he and Jody wish for me to congratulate you."

"And Kimberly wanted to be here, but with the baby coming soon, I'm afraid she wasn't feeling well this evening," Todd said about his wife of two years.

"Of course." Beth waved dismissively. "Aidan and I will visit her this week before your new arrival."

"She'd like that very much." Todd kissed her cheek, always the gentleman like his father.

When Beth greeted Clara, she caught sight of the modest diamond ring on the young woman's left hand. Clara was a petite like her mother, with a creamy, flawless complexion and jet-black hair. She also possessed Olivia's vivaciousness, while her ability to remain calm under pressure had definitely been inherited from Nathan.

Clara had opened her own dress shop on Fifth Avenue last year. Tonight she wore a bright yellow dress in a design unlike anything Beth had ever seen worn by young women these days. But that was nothing new. Clara designed all of her own outfits and was a trendsetter in the fashion industry, always pushing the limits and creating fresh, daring looks.

Clara gestured to her dashing date, who looked as if he'd stepped right out of the 1920s with his slicked back hair and three-button suit. "Beth, Aidan, this is Liam Atley, my fiancé."

Although Beth and Aidan had never met Liam previously, the buzz about him as a director had introduced them to his work months ago.

Beth offered her hand. "It's nice to meet you. And congratulations on the engagement."

"Thank you, ma'am." His reply held a distinct southern accent.

Aidan shook his hand, too. "Liam, my wife and I saw your

last film at a private screening here in Manhattan. We were extremely impressed."

Liam's eyes widened. "Thank you, Mr. Evans. It's only my second time directing in an official capacity. I still have much to learn."

"Well, you wouldn't know it," Beth said. "The film was excellent."

Clara linked arms with her fiancé. "Isn't he the greatest?"

Liam placed a kiss on her lips. "I'd be nothing without you, darling."

Olivia and Nathan exchanged smiles, reflecting their daughter's happiness.

Following a visit to the coat check, the group headed to the auditorium. As they passed the donation booth, Nathan stopped and produced a checkbook from his pocket.

Beth touched his shoulder. "Nathan, no. You've already done too much."

With a defiant grin, he removed a ballpoint pen from the fold and filled out the top check.

Nathan had achieved great financial and professional success over the years, but his greatest accomplishment was sitting on the National Mental Health Association's Board of Directors for the last sixteen years.

The public was unaware of his mother's health issues until after she died in 1967. Nathan decided to reveal the truth in hopes it would raise awareness and help to erase the stigma attached to mental illness. He had been so successful in his endeavor he'd received several humanitarian awards and was regularly invited to give talks on the subject all over the country.

After leaving the donation booth, the group entered Avery Fisher Hall. The concert hall had twenty-seven hundred seats, with prime, preferred seating on the floor, three tiers of balconies, and private boxes. It usually hosted visiting orchestras for exclusive performances. Beth was honored the Lincoln Center agreed to host their benefit in this particular venue.

An usher led the group to their seats in the front row. As Beth sat down and looked around, joy filled her heart. In October 1952, she'd moved to Los Angeles all on her own when it was uncommon and unacceptable for a young woman to do so. In less than one year, she went from working at Schwab's Pharmacy to becoming an award-winning actress and meeting lifelong friends as well as her husband. Some might say she was lucky. Yes, Nathan discovering her had been lucky, but luck had nothing to do with why she had become a success when so many others who sought the same dream had failed. Her longevity in the entertainment industry was achieved through love for her craft in addition to perseverance, hard work, and the support of her friends and family.

While writing her memoir, Beth recognized the mistakes she'd made in the past, as well as her weaknesses, but she harbored no regrets. All of her experiences made her the woman she was today. And judging from the large turnout tonight, she had fared well in life.

The lights dimmed and the projection screen at the back of the stage lifted, revealing the emcee, New York City Mayor Ed

Koch. Polite applause erupted as he walked to a podium decorated with the GWA crest.

Mr. Koch embraced the warm welcome with an appreciative smile, working the crowd like the expert politician he was.

"Welcome, ladies and gentleman." The applause subsided. "We are gathered here to honor Mr. Aidan Evans and his wife, Elizabeth, for their extraordinary work with the Golden Warriors Association, an organization that brings hope and joy into the lives of children diagnosed with cancer. Aidan and Beth have dedicated much of their time and money to GWA, and tonight we thank them. Your financial contributions this evening will help ensure that GWA continues to thrive and expand, reaching children all over the world, from our own backyards to remote parts of the globe."

The audience clapped as Mr. Koch left the stage. Next, a short film on GWA was shown on the projection screen to give tonight's guests a closer look at the organization. A video message from President Ronald Reagan and his wife Nancy followed, which shared their appreciation of Beth and Aidan's work with GWA and hailed the couple as an inspiration to all Americans.

Throughout the evening, many of Beth and Aidan's friends and colleagues took to the stage. More comfortable with public speaking than her brother, Hannah also shared a speech about her experiences teaching music at the camps and how proud she was of her parents.

Nathan was the last speaker. He approached the podium

and put on his reading glasses; though, accustomed to speaking in front of large audiences, he hadn't written anything down.

"I've known Elizabeth Evans since the spring of 1953 when she was known only as Marie Bates and worked as a counter girl at Schwab's Pharmacy in Los Angeles. Normally it wasn't my job to scout for new talent for Starlight Studios, but there was something about her I couldn't ignore. Over the years, Beth has asked what exactly I saw in her that day, why I offered her a screen test when there were thousands of girls vying for a chance to make it in Hollywood. Usually I'd reply with a teasing remark about how her uneasiness when serving actor Robert Mitchum set her apart from the typical brash and sassy young women aspiring to be film stars. Tonight, I will share the truth.

"My main reasons for approaching Beth at Schwab's are similar to those discussed by everyone on this stage tonight. Beth's outer beauty is as remarkable today as it was over thirty years ago. Anyone who has been fortunate enough to see her work is aware that her smile lights up the most prestigious theaters on Broadway and the largest movie screens. But she also possesses inner beauty—in particular, a kindness and honesty seldom seen in the entertainment industry—which makes her accessible to audiences and a role model to women all over the world.

"Back in 1953, many people—myself included—were disenchanted with the film industry. Personally, I'd thought compassionate individuals were weak and a bad fit for such a cutthroat business, so initially I questioned my instincts when I first saw Beth. In fact, it took me a good half hour to approach her at Schwab's. I'm very glad I did. Beth restored my faith in humanity. She taught me that following your heart is the best way to make decisions, and applying this philosophy over the years has never steered me wrong."

Nathan focused on the front row. "Beth, although no amount of words will ever adequately express how much your friendship means to me, I hope I have provided you with the answer you've been searching for. I also hope my speech hasn't come as a surprise, because you should already know how amazing you are."

Beth dabbed her eyes as applause broke out. Aidan leaned in and kissed her cheek while their children and friends looked on with proud smiles.

Nathan flashed a grin at her husband. "Then there's Aidan Evans. Aidan is known as a pioneer in the film industry—a talented actor and director who has inspired many notable names and fought for creative freedom. And now, this year, he has done something even greater. His organization, GWA, has reached a milestone—twenty years of providing young people stricken with cancer with the opportunity to reclaim their childhoods.

"Aidan, you are the ultimate Golden Warrior. I consider you not just my friend and client, but also my brother." Nathan placed his hand over his heart. Aidan nodded in respect and imitated the gesture. "Beth, Aidan, I think I speak for all of us here tonight when I say that you have enriched our lives and the lives of the GWA children greatly. Individually, you are incredible. As a couple, you are unstoppable. I love you both."

The audience rose to their feet and applauded. Beth and Aidan traded glances that communicated a unified thought: They were fortunate to have such dear friends.

Nathan cleared his throat. The theater quieted and people sat down again. Beth's eyebrows furrowed. According to tonight's program, the benefit ended with his speech.

"And now, ladies and gentlemen, there is a young man here who wanted to say a few words. Please welcome Theodore Timmons."

The audience burst into applause as eight-year-old Theo emerged from backstage and walked to the podium, dressed in an official Golden Warriors T-shirt, which was provided to every child associated with GWA. He had attended a camp last summer after his doctors gave him the all clear following his second round of chemotherapy. When he first arrived, he was frail and depended on a wheelchair for mobility. He was sad and withdrawn as well. By his third week at the camp, he ran and frolicked with the other children without tiring. He also performed the lead role in the end-of-season play.

Tonight, Theo looked even healthier. His hair had grown back. He had gained weight, and his complexion held a rosier hue. His parents had sent Beth and Aidan a letter two weeks ago, notifying them that he was officially in remission. They were thrilled to receive the news.

Nathan handed Theo the microphone.

"Hello." His tiny voice carried throughout the hall, emphasized by the venue's acoustics. "My name is Theo and I had leukemia, but my doctors say I'm better now. Beth and

Aidan didn't know me before the summer, but they let me come to their camp anyway. I made a lot of friends at the camp who had cancer like me. Being at the camp made me happy and I forgot I was sick. When I went back to school, I told all my classmates I'm a Golden Warrior, and they think I'm really cool. Thank you, Beth and Aidan. You're the nicest people ever."

Theo returned the microphone to Nathan and descended the steps to the main floor. Beth and Aidan stood and embraced him amongst acclamation from the crowd.

Aidan's chin quivered as he held on to the boy, struggling to keep it together. Beth couldn't hold back her emotions.

Theo grabbed their hands, pulling them toward the stage. "But wait. There's more!"

Beth and Aidan followed him to the podium. Hannah, Nicholas, Matthew, Olivia, and Connie joined them as the crowd continued to show their support.

Olivia took the microphone, her gaze twinkling with mischief. "Aidan, Beth, we have a surprise for you." She motioned to the side of the stage. "Come on out, everyone!"

Beth's hand flew to her mouth as a group of about fifty smiling children of various ages and ethnicities emerged from behind the curtain, wearing GWA T-shirts and carrying a large banner that read in multi-colored crayon, *Thank you from your Golden Warriors.*

Olivia handed the microphone to a little girl in the front, who wore a baseball hat on her bald head and a bright grin on her face.

"Hi, Beth and Aidan. We made this drawing for you because

you allowed us to go to your camp and have fun and we really appreciate it." Blushing, the girl handed back the microphone.

Matthew stepped forward. "All right, kids. This is it. One! Two! Three!" He lifted his hands like an orchestra conductor.

The children raised the banner and waved it enthusiastically, shouting, "We love you, Aidan and Beth!"

Beth retreated next to Hannah and Nicholas to give her husband space. Although she had started GWA with him, it had been his idea and she'd always consider it his success story. He deserved to be singled out for his accomplishments.

Aidan took the microphone from Olivia. His other hand remained clasped with Theo's. "I've never been very eloquent when it comes to expressing my feelings, so I ask for your patience as I attempt to tell you all how special you are to me."

Tears shimmered in his eyes as he looked at the children. Beth had never been prouder of him than in that moment. "This has been one of the greatest evenings of my life. I'm going to hang your banner in our home so I can be reminded every day of what true passion and determination to live life to the fullest is all about. You are all an inspiration and I am honored to stand amongst you tonight."

The children raced over to him, shrieking playfully and laughing. The boys and girls who weren't holding the banner circled him, their little hands reaching out for a group hug.

Aidan gathered as many of them as he could in his arms and finally allowed himself to weep openly. By this time, there wasn't a dry eye in the house.

Families often credited GWA with helping them in the fight

against cancer, but the truth was that their own resolve, love, and dedication were what got them here today. The camps merely provided a vehicle for them to tap into their inner strength.

Aidan was usually a confident man—cocky to some—but tonight he displayed the man Beth knew intimately: the vulnerable and generous Aidan he often hid from others.

On many occasions, he'd shared how alone he'd felt after his mother's death. He hadn't suffered from a physical ailment like the boys and girls on this stage, but mentally and emotionally he'd been broken.

While growing up, he had always wished he'd been given a chance to experience a normal childhood. Now, here he was, granting that same wish to other children. Without a doubt, Catherine Evans would have been proud of her son.

Flashbulbs exploded as photographers swarmed the main floor. The audience rose to their feet, whistling and clapping with enthusiasm that would never be forgotten.

Aidan waved at Beth, inviting her to join him.

Surrounded by the people they cared about most, he tucked her under his arm and brushed his lips to her ear. "I love you, little dove."

Beth replied with a kiss. She loved him more and more each day and would continue to love him even after she took her final breath. He completed her and made her a better woman. He was her friend, her husband, her lover, her soul mate. Her rebel with a compassionate, noble, and inspirational cause.

Acknowledgements

Actor Paul Newman's Association of the Hole in the Wall (now called the SeriousFun Children's Network) and The Hole in the Wall Gang Camp inspired the Golden Warriors Association and the Golden Warriors Camp. If you'd like to learn more about Mr. Newman's extraordinary organization, please visit www.seriousfunnetwork.org and www.holeinthewallgang.org.

I would like to thank Laura Smith, Chantal Lambert, and Cara Langston, author of *Battle Hymns* and *The Glassmaker's Wife*, for proofreading *Stardust* and offering valuable suggestions. I also would like to thank Tiffany for believing in the trilogy from the beginning and counting mice with me like it's 1891. To the book bloggers who have read, reviewed, and promoted *The Starlight Trilogy*, I appreciate all you've done for me. To my readers: It took six years to get to this point. Thank you for supporting *The Starlight Trilogy* and my other stories.

Finally, I'd like to thank actors James Dean and Marlon Brando, the original rebels, for their performances in *East of Eden* and *On The Waterfront*, respectively. Their groundbreaking approaches to acting introduced me to classic films, Old Hollywood, and Turner Classic Movies. From there, *The Starlight Trilogy* was born. I am forever grateful.

About the Author

Alexandra Richland spends rotating twelve-hour shifts working as a registered nurse at a Toronto hospital, indulging in her love of science and medicine and caring for patients with their own unique tales to tell. When she is not on duty, Alexandra escapes into her own imagination. Therein lies a fantasy world of thrilling adventure, gorgeous men, classic Hollywood glamour, exotic getaways, and a seductive dose of romance. Alexandra captures these stories in her popular novels, *The Starlight Trilogy* and *Frontline*, her novella, *Slip Away*, and her short story, *Gilded Cage*.

Facebook:
http://www.facebook.com/Alexandra.Richland

Twitter: http://www.twitter.com/RebelMissAlex

Official Website: http://www.AlexandraRichland.com